NEXT *of* KIN

CAROL PRESTON

rhiza press

Next of Kin

Copyright © Carol Preston 2015
Published by Rhiza Press
www.rhizapress.com.au
PO Box 1519, Capalaba Qld 4157

National Library of Australia Cataloguing-in-Publication entry
Creator: Preston, Carol, 1948- author.
Title: Next of kin / Carol Preston.
ISBN: 9781925139211 (paperback)
Subjects: Australian fiction.
Dewey Number: A823.4

In appreciation of grandmothers

CHAPTER ONE

Grafton, New South Wales, July, 1891

'Quick, get Aunty Giese!'

Fanny was startled by the distressed cry. As she turned towards the hotel door a small group of men pushed it open and stumbled in. The steaming plate of shepherd's pie she was about to put in front of a customer almost toppled into his lap. Gesturing an apology, she laid the dish on the table. The customer barely registered notice of the ruckus behind him. He was far more interested in the mound of beef and potato on his plate and began to push fork loads into his mouth.

It was not unusual in the first week of July for hotels in Grafton to be crammed with young men celebrating their winnings from the horse races or commiserating with each other over their losses. Farmers, jackaroos and stock riders from up and down the Clarence River made the trip to Grafton for the races; to watch, to bet and to ride.

However, Fanny could see that these young men who had all but fallen through the door were not celebrating. One of them was injured. As he hobbled towards an empty chair, the one beside him, who was trying to hold him up, yelled again.

'Someone get Aunty Giese! My brother's hurt.'

'Stop fussing, Jim,' the injured lad snapped, pulling his arm away and pushing himself back in the chair. He grimaced as he dragged his leg under the table.

1

Fanny headed to the kitchen where her employer was cooking. Marlena Giese had no children of her own but it seemed that most of the young men in town called her Aunty Giese. She was a large framed woman with a round, crinkly face and a deep German accent. Her husband, Hans, had built the European Hotel in the sixties, and many of the jockeys and station owners took up the hotel rooms during this week of the year. Hans provided stabling out back, where some of the bloodline horses were kept when they weren't racing. But the biggest draw card in Fanny's estimation was Marlena Giese's cooking.

When Fanny pushed through the door, Marlena had her arms in pastry to the elbows and was calling orders to the young girl who helped her in the kitchen. She looked up at Fanny, paused and smiled, her eyes twinkling.

'These two are ready, *liebling*.' She pointed at two steaming plates on the end of the bench and wiped sweat from her forehead with the back of her hand.

'There's someone hurt, Mrs Giese,' Fanny said. 'Some young men just came in and one of them is yelling for you to come.'

'Hmm.' The older woman looked down at her hands and grabbed a towel. She wiped away as much of the sticky flour as she could in the few moments it took her to stride to the door.

Fanny picked up the meals from the bench and followed, noting that the one who'd yelled for help was waving his hand and beckoning wildly. She delivered the two hot plates to a rowdy group of men at the other end of the crowded dining room. On the way back to the kitchen she slowed, curious about the men Marlena had gone to help. Both looked to be in their early twenties, a few years older than herself. They had more dirt on their faces than whiskers and their shirts were ragged and splattered with mud.

'Do you think it's broken, Aunty?' The younger-looking one was still clearly distressed.

'I told you it's not, Jim,' the other snapped. He had a mop of sandy hair and his eyes, Fanny could now see, were the colour of charred wood. When he spoke, his mouth twisted into any angry scowl.

2

'No, but I'd say it's a nasty sprain.' Marlena was pushing and probing at his lower leg. 'You'll not be getting that shoe back on, Jack, more's the pity. The stench is enough to spoil everyone's shepherd's pie.'

'All I need is to rest for a bit,' Jack snapped.

'More than a bit, I'd say.' Marlena patted him on the knee and pushed herself up from the floor where she'd been crouched. 'Jim, you go and get your brother from the front desk. Then you can both help Jack upstairs. Bob's room is big enough for the three of you for a few days. I assume you'd planned to camp by the river this week?' She screwed up her face and fixed the older boy with a disapproving look. 'I've told you both before, you're always welcome here when the races are on. Or any other time, for that matter. Why you insist on being so independent, I don't know.'

'It's Jack,' Jim said. 'He'd rather stay outside.'

'As stubborn as your grandfather, you are,' she growled at Jack. 'And before you get your feathers in a flap, I know you hate to be compared with him, but I'm telling you straight, lad. While ever you're alive, he'll not be dead.'

Jack looked like he was trying to push himself out of the chair, and from the thunderous expression on his face, Fanny was sure he'd determined to leave the hotel right then. Jim headed for the front desk.

If Bob Schmidt was brother to these boys, then Marlena Giese was really their aunt, Fanny surmised as she made her way back into the kitchen. She'd been working as a domestic at the European for nearly a year now but she hadn't seen this pair before. She knew a few of the Giese's extended family had worked here on and off; some in the kitchen, others out the back loading and carrying stock or doing repairs. Others had come in for a meal or to catch up on the family news. The German community in Grafton was close knit and Giese's hotel seemed to be a central gathering place for them.

Bob had worked on the front desk ever since Fanny had been here but he'd never mentioned that he had two brothers, which was hardly surprising. He was a quiet man who kept to himself. Fanny

3

only ever managed to evoke a smile and a nod as she passed him at the front desk on her way through to the dining room. Marlena had told her that Bob was meticulous at keeping books and a whiz at financial records, but what went on beneath the surface of her nephew was hidden from most. Marlena had intimated that she knew the how and why of his quiet nature, but any changes needed would have to be brought about by the good Lord.

Marlena was still giving orders when Fanny came back into the dining room. Bob and Jim were now hovering over Jack. Fanny could see the physical likeness between the three boys. All were tall and stocky, square of jaw and broad across the shoulders. They all had a shock of fair hair and deep brown eyes. Especially Jack. The burning darkness she'd seen in his eyes made Fanny think of volcanoes, and although she'd never seen a volcano erupt, she had a feeling that something in Jack Schmidt was close to doing just that.

'When you get him upstairs, Jim, get a bowl of hot water and some soap, and the two of you start scraping some of that dirt off,' Marlena ordered, waving her arms about. 'You both smell like wombats.'

Bob and Jim supported an agitated Jack as he got to his feet and helped him towards the stairs to the Gieses' living quarters above the hotel.

'Bob, you know where I keep that liniment. See if you can rub some into his ankle. Watch he doesn't take your head off while you're at it, though.' Their aunt's tone was playful when she said the last, clearly trying to draw Jack out of his sombre mood.

Fanny noticed that Jack's expression had become even more hostile. She wondered what could cause a young man to be so full of rage. His injury likely meant he hadn't been able to complete his horse race, or perhaps not even start. But even if he was counting on winning, surely he couldn't be so wild about his misfortune. *No, there has to be more than that behind his fury.*

'Any more of that pie, girlie?' A voice from one of the tables drew her from her thoughts.

'I'm sure there is, sir.' Fanny smiled and quickened her step.

'Mrs Giese will have more in the oven, nothing surer. She knows what big eaters you horsemen are.'

**

The following day when Fanny arrived back at the hotel before the lunch hour rush, Jim and Jack were sitting in the dining room. Jim looked more relaxed than he had the day before. Jack seemed just as grouchy. Obviously a night's sleep had not improved his mood. Both boys had a huge serving of potato soup in front of them and were scraping at the bottoms of their bowls when Fanny approached.

'Hello. I'm Fanny Franks. Can I get you some more soup?'

'I will, thanks,' the younger said. There was nothing from Jack.

'How's your foot today?' Fanny addressed him directly.

He finished the last spoonful of his soup before his eyes rose to meet hers. His forehead creased into a scowl.

'I was here when you came in yesterday. I went for Mrs Giese … your aunt.' Fanny felt she needed to explain herself.

'The foot's fine.' Jack reached for a large hunk of bread on the table.

'Actually it's not that fine.' Jim smiled up at Fanny. 'Jack likes to pretend he's all right, even if he isn't. He came off his horse yesterday and sprained his ankle real bad. He might have got a place, too, if the horse hadn't stumbled. He's a very good rider.'

'That's a shame,' Fanny commiserated, watching Jack's face. He didn't acknowledge her concern. 'What about you? Jim, isn't it? I heard your aunt call you Jim. Did you race too?'

'Yeah, but I'm not as fast as Jack. I was coming up behind. Got a shock when I saw him sprawled on the ground. I thought he'd broken something for sure. Lightning was all right though, that's the horse. That was a relief at least.'

'Yes, I'm sure it was.' Fanny grinned, her eyes flicking from one brother to the other. There was still no response from Jack. He chomped through a piece of bread, his face sour.

'Where do you live?' she continued. 'I've not seen you around here before.'

'We're usually here in July for the races,' Jim answered. 'Mostly we sleep outside. We've been working up around Murrayville, timber cutting, for the last few years.'

'Your aunt seems pleased to see you here.'

'Yeah, she likes to feed us up. In the bush we eat mainly rabbit and possum, or a bush turkey every now and then. Aunty is a great cook. It's the best part of coming into town for me.' He flashed a wide smile.

'I'll get you some more soup then, will I? And what about you, Jack?' She turned to him. He pushed his empty plate towards her and nodded.

'Jack don't say much.' Jim grinned apologetically. 'When you spend months in the bush like we do, you get out of the habit, you know.'

'You seem to manage well enough, Jim.' Fanny took the bowls and glanced again at Jack, but her intended jab at him seemed not to register. She shrugged and turned towards the kitchen.

'You don't have to be rude, Jack,' she heard as she walked away.

When she returned a few minutes later, her tray loaded with two fresh bowls of soup and another hunk of bread, they were sitting silently.

'So, Jim, if Mrs Giese is your aunt, then I suppose your parents live somewhere in town, do they? There are so many German families around Grafton and they all seem to be close.'

Fanny was immediately aware she'd said something that had aggravated Jack. *If he could be any more aggravated*. He twisted in his chair and dragged his bowl close to his mouth. He cast a dark look at his brother before his head went down and he began to push spoonfuls of soup into his mouth.

'Well, we don't … we haven't got …' Jim stumbled over his words.

'I'm sorry. I didn't mean to pry,' Fanny said.

'It's all right.' Jim recovered. 'We haven't lived at home for a few years, that's all. Ma has five young ones to care for. She's kept pretty busy.'

Jack coughed and banged his spoon on the side of his plate. Fanny could see that he didn't want his brother to continue talking, but Jim ignored him.

'What about you, Fanny? Do you come from Grafton?'

'I grew up on a farm at Brushgrove, on Woodford Island. My parents are still there, with my Pop Franks. My oldest sister, Lizzie, is married and lives here in town. I stay with her through the week and go home on my day off.'

When she paused and drew in her breath she saw a look of concern on Jim's face. 'My Nana Franks died recently,' she explained, surprised at how much losing her grandmother still affected her.

'That's sad,' Jim said.

'It's hard to believe she's gone. Because we've always lived on their property I saw a lot of her. She played cards and board games with us all when we were young. Right up till she died. She was always there for me to talk to about anything. I miss her a lot.'

'I'm so sorry.' Jim looked distressed.

'I still have my grandparents on Mum's side, though. They live on Woodford Island too. Granny's a real sweetie. Grandfather Nipperess is a good man but a serious one.' Fanny emphasized the description of her grandfather as she glanced at Jack. There was no response.

'Do you have grandparents close by?' She focussed again on Jim. 'I heard Mrs Giese refer to your grandfather.'

Before Jim could respond Jack pushed away his soup bowl and sat back in his chair. 'I reckon that soup of yours has gone stone cold, Jim.' His tone was colder than any soup might be.

'I don't mind it cold.' Jim didn't take his eyes from Fanny. 'We only have one grandparent still alive. Our mother's father is on his farm at Mororo, on the north arm of the river. That's where Jack and I were born. We go back to see Gramps whenever we're timber cutting near there. He's a wily old thing. Gran Preddice died two years ago and we miss her too. So I know how it must be for you, losing your grandmother.'

'I'm sorry to hear that.' Fanny realised she'd dropped into a chair on the other side of the table. She looked about the room, wondering if she was being remiss in her duties, but there were only a few customers and they seemed satisfied to be talking and having a drink.

'Preddice doesn't sound like a German name.' She turned back to Jim. 'Were your mother's people English?'

'Yes,' Jim answered, still ignoring his brother's obvious annoyance.

'That's unusual, isn't it? A German man marrying an English woman? It seems to me that German people most often marry one of their own.'

'They do,' Jim said. 'Our Grandfather Schmidt was pretty unhappy about Father's marriage.'

'He's passed away as well, I gather?'

Jim nodded. 'Six years ago. And we never knew our Grandmother Schmidt. She died before we were born.'

'Was your family part of the group who was brought here to work at Kirtchner's soap factory?'

Jim nodded again and took a mouthful of soup.

Fanny's grandfather had told her about a man called William Kirtchner, who'd brought a large contingent of his countrymen from Germany to Australia in the 1850s to help him establish the soap and candle factory in Villiers Street.

'Your grandfather must have had quite a story to tell about those early days?'

Fanny noticed that Jack was smirking. Not the kind of smirk that suggested he was amused, for she'd concluded that Jack was amused by very little. His expression more suggested that he found what she had said ridiculous.

'The old man didn't speak English, so how would we have heard any of his stories?' His tone was cynical.

'Oh.' Fanny was stuck for more words.

'Aunty Giese remembers it all, though.' Jim rescued her. 'She's told us lots about what it was like when they first arrived. It was tough for them. Grandfather Schmidt believed the German community should retain their own culture. He was very proud.'

'He was a bigot.' Jack's voice cut in.

'He was a hard man,' Jim conceded. 'Not the hardest man we've known, though.' He glared at his brother.

When he turned back to Fanny, his face softened. 'Grandfather Schmidt was angry when Father married Ma. Apparently he even had a German girl picked out, but Father was determined to make his own choice.' Jim's voice dropped to almost a whisper. 'Perhaps it would have been better if he'd married as Grandfather wanted.'

'Your father …?' Fanny was almost afraid to ask. She sensed Jack was about to turn on her.

'He's dead.' Jack's voice came at her angrily.

'He had a brain disease.' Jim's face dropped. 'He died when I was one and Jack was three. Neither of us can remember him.'

'I'm so sorry to hear that.' Fanny felt a lump in the back of her throat.

'Bob was five. He remembers little things but he doesn't like to talk about it,' Jim continued. 'Aunty Giese and Father were close and she says he was a good man, kind and gentle. Not much like his father, apparently, so I suppose he was a disappointment to Grandfather Schmidt all around.'

'It seems to me that you might be like your father, Jim,' Fanny said. 'Not in being a disappointment to your grandfather, of course,' she added, realising she might have been misunderstood.

Jim chuckled. 'I didn't think you meant that, and yes, Aunty Giese says I'm like Father in temperament.'

'Unlike me.' Jack's tone was almost a sneer. 'Apparently I'm my grandfather all over again.'

There was an uncomfortable silence before Fanny spoke. 'Perhaps that's more up to you than you think, Jack.'

His dark frown seemed meant to silence her, but she continued. 'Even if you have something of your grandfather's temperament, you can still choose how you behave and speak. You could be … more sociable.'

Fanny was surprised that she was being so outspoken when she hardly knew the young man opposite her, but in the past half hour she'd found herself wanting to shake him and confront him with what she considered his rudeness and thoughtlessness.

'You don't know anything about me.' His glare cut into her.

'No, I don't know much, but it's plain to see that you're not happy. Whatever's happened, you don't have to stay angry with the world. Your brothers have had the same life you've had, haven't they? They don't seem …'

Fanny realised she was out of line at the same moment as Jack reacted. He pushed his chair back and pulled himself to his feet, grimacing when he put weight on his sprained foot.

'I'm sorry,' she said. 'I shouldn't have been so forward, but I thought – '

'I don't care what you thought. You know nothing about me and I don't have to stay here and listen to you telling me how to be.' He turned fiercely to his brother. 'I'm going upstairs. And I'll thank you to keep my private business to yourself in future. I've told you before that you talk too freely. Our business is our business. You hear?'

Jim sighed and nodded. 'Hold on. I'll help you up the stairs. I'll rub some more of that liniment on your foot if you like.'

'I can do it myself.' Jack was already hobbling towards the stairs.

Jim sat back in his chair and shrugged at Fanny. 'I'm sorry about all that. He gets touchy. He's had it tough over the years, much tougher than me. I'll go and see what I can do for him.'

'I'm sorry I upset him.' Fanny felt remiss.

'It's not you. He doesn't like me talking about family stuff. I don't get to talk to many folk, so with you being so friendly, I guess I got carried away. I hope it won't put you off talking to me again.'

'Of course not. I enjoy hearing people's stories. It's the best part of this job. Your aunt and uncle don't mind me chatting to the customers, when there's time, of course. It's a bit of a shock when someone like Jack comes along. I feel sorry for him. Perhaps when his foot is better and he's able to ride … ?'

'Don't hold your breath, Fanny. He won't ever say much, and when he does it often comes across hard. But for all that, he's got a good heart. Believe me, without him I don't know where I'd be.'

CHAPTER TWO

Marlena laid her head back and dropped her knitting into her lap.

'What is it, dear?' Hans looked at her over the top of his newspaper. 'You're not going to worry yourself silly over the boys again, are you?'

'I'm concerned that Jack never seems to soften. I don't know what's going to become of him.'

'He's upset he can't race, that's all. He'll find his way. You can't be going over all this in your mind every time they come into town.' Hans leaned across to her chair and patted her knee.

'I can't help wondering if it could have been different.' She began to knit again, her fingers darting between wool and needles.

'You think too much. You'll give yourself a headache.' He winked and laid down his paper. 'I'm going to make you a cup of tea. Try and relax, eh?'

Marlena watched her husband leave the room. His gait was growing more awkward, causing him to hobble a little from side to side as he walked. Even so, he was still a strong and handsome man at fifty. His fair hair was thick and slightly waved, with hardly a grey to be seen. His eyes twinkled when he smiled and his easy-going nature and good humour were catching. He'd been a blessing to her from the first time she'd met him. She'd known right away that she wanted to spend the rest of her life with him. She laid her head back, closed her eyes, and let her mind drift back to her nineteenth year, when the family arrived in Grafton in March of 1856.

11

Hanging over the side of the steamer, she let the cool breeze play with the wisps of hair that had escaped her bonnet. Her attention was drawn to the small ducks that were dipping and splashing in the water close to the riverbank. In the reeds on the shore she could see larger birds, with long thin legs and pointed beaks.

'Storks,' she said. Letting her eyes drop back to the ducks, she noticed a line of ducklings following their mother. She smiled. 'Baby ducks … ducklings.' She mouthed the word, then fanned through the pages of her small German-English dictionary. 'Ja, ducklings,' she said with a grin.

'So this is the promised land.' The voice came from behind her.

She turned and smiled as Wilhelm approached. 'Now that we've turned into the river, it's much calmer. I'm sure we'll begin to see people on shore soon. Some farms, perhaps.'

'Don't be expecting fields of wine grapes.' He frowned. 'It won't be anything like Frankfurt.'

Marlena grinned. Wilhelm was her mother's first child. He'd only been two years old when his father died, and seven when his mother remarried to Phillip Schmidt. He'd been almost nine when Marlena was born, and as she had always been of such short stature, he liked to joke that she could only ever hope to be half his size, and that was why she was his half-sister.

'Of course I'm not expecting vineyards,' she said. 'I know it will be different here. That is why we came, after all. Our life in Frankfurt was too hard. The land had drained Papa of all hope for a future there. I will not be longing for our past home, Wilhelm.'

'It was not the land that stole our life, Lena. It was the political strife and bad decisions by our leaders.' His face hardened.

'But we'd also had harsh winters, remember. The seasons were not good to us on the land.'

'Perhaps that too.' Wilhelm sighed and shrugged his shoulders. 'I see you've been practicing your English.' He nodded at the book in her hand.

'I'm not as good as you yet.' She was glad to change the subject away from the politics of Germany. It was a topic that aroused deep anger in her father and she was weary of what seemed to her to be pointless discussions about it. 'I'm sure it will help us get settled in Grafton if we try to speak the language. It will show we're ready to fit in.'

'I'm not sure *fitting in* is what Papa has in mind.'

'We must encourage him, Wilhelm. He won't easily give up his German ways, nor his mother tongue, but he's anxious that we do well here. It's his dream to make our new life successful. We can't do that by setting ourselves apart from those who've already made their life here.'

'Perhaps.'

As Wilhelm leaned over the rail of the boat, Marlena noticed the bulge of his muscular arms below his rolled up shirt sleeves. His face was bronzed, his features angular. His eyes were deep blue and piercing, and his smile self-assured. Overly so, she often thought, and although he had every reason to be confident in his ability, she wondered if he'd be easily accepted as a foreigner in this new land. Without meaning to, he often left others with the sense that they were less than him. *Just as Papa does.* She prayed her family could find their own place in Grafton without alienating the established English community.

'I'll go and see if Mama would like to come out on deck. She may be less anxious now we are no longer being tossed to and fro in the sea.' He rolled his eyes, mimicking their mother's often voiced description of their voyage from Germany.

As he walked away, the door to the cabins below opened and Marlena's younger brother, August, appeared. He was two years her junior, and he frowned as he reached her side.

'Doesn't look like a land of milk and honey to me.' He peered over the side, squinting in the sunlight and scanning the shoreline. 'Any sign of life?'

She followed his gaze. 'The foliage along the river is thick. I haven't been able to see much else yet.'

'Are we sure there's going to be a town here at all?' His fair hair blew about his eyes and nose and he brushed it aside as he spoke. He was as tall as Wilhelm, much like him in facial features, but more slightly built.

Marlena giggled and leaned into his arm. 'Dear August, must you always think the worst?'

She turned her attention to the water as it parted for their boat, then rolled away in soft ripples towards the shore. The sunshine seemed to be playing with the tiny eruptions of water; chasing them to the line of trees and vines. Splashes of bright light danced across the river. She allowed the scene to give her hope. The river was not like Maine River in Frankfurt. There were not the familiar rows of grape vines, but this river did hold the promise of new life for her family. Surely it was a gift from God that they had been invited here to work and begin again. It didn't matter what crop they would grow. It only mattered that they could look to the future with hope and courage. It was what their father had challenged them to when he'd announced the news of their migration. Despite the misgivings of Mama and her brothers, Marlena was determined to help them be positive.

Before she could voice her thoughts to August, the door to the cabins opened and their younger brother and sister pushed through, jostling each other and laughing as they rushed to the railing and hung over the side of the boat.

'Careful Anna,' August warned. 'We don't want you falling into the river. It will be deep.'

'I won't fall. I'm good at balance.' The seven-year-old spoke without looking at August.

'You sound like Mama.' Johan waved his hand towards his older brother.

'Don't give cheek, Johan.' August said. 'And you watch out for your *schwester*.'

'Sister,' Johan corrected, screwing up his face. 'And my name is John. Wilhelm says we must use English words now. People won't know what we're talking about.'

14

'That's true, Johan,' Marlena said, 'but Mama and Papa are not ready for us to change the way we address each other. You must be respectful of them.'

'All right, but I'm still going to be John from now on.'

August sighed and turned back to Marlena. 'Papa will have to come to terms with not being able to control the young ones so much here. Especially Anna. I think Mama and Papa have spoiled our little *schwester.*'

'She's such a pretty little thing, August. With those large blue eyes, it's hard not to be taken in by her.' Marlena glanced at her sister and smiled. She was indeed a charming child, with a sweet, heart-shaped face and angelic smile. *So unlike my own features.* To be short was bearable for a woman, but to be plain of countenance with it seemed unfair. However, she had long ago stopped hoping to see a prettier face looking back at herself from her mirror. Discontentment was not one of Marlena's weaknesses, but it was clear that Anna would have no such burden to bear in regard to her looks.

'She's only seven, August,' she continued. 'Girls that age are always spoiled, especially being the youngest. She'll be growing up in a different world now. She'll adjust.'

'And Johan? He's eleven, but already headstrong, as you see. Much like Papa. They will clash as Johan gets older, you mark my words.'

'Johan doesn't clash, August. He goes his own way quietly, but he does respect Papa. He'll work out the balance. Papa will have to make concessions.'

'I have no experience of Papa making concessions.'

A squeal from Anna interrupted their conversation. 'Look, look!' She was jumping up and down at the rail and pointing wildly. 'Those people are black … and they have no clothes on.' As she swung on the rail and leaned forward, her bonnet tipped forward and if she had not grabbed the ribbons which blew around her face it would have sailed into the water.

August and Marlena were instantly at their sister's side.

Marlena rescued the bonnet and eased the young girl to the deck. 'Feet on the boards, *liebling*, and stop pointing. It's rude.'

'But they *really* have no clothes on.' Johan's mouth was hanging open. 'And they have spears.' He drew back, staring at the small group of natives who were standing on a sandbar extending from the shoreline. He turned to August. 'Are they going to attack us?'

'I believe they're fishing,' Marlena said, studying the group. 'We were warned that we'd likely see natives around the Clarence River. They've lived here since long before the white men came. Fishing is their main source of food … or one of them, I believe. They don't grow crops like white men do. They eat the native berries and plants and they fish.'

Marlena attempted to turn her small sister's head from the scene without success. She averted her own eyes and kept her mind on what they'd been told in Sydney while they were waiting to board the coastal steamer for their trip to the Clarence River.

As their boat moved past the group of barely clad natives, she noted that they seemed equally enthralled with what they could see on the deck of the steamer. No doubt her traditional German dress – full skirt, bodice, blouse and apron, complete with bonnet – would seem to them to be inappropriate and unnecessary attire for the climate here. In fact she'd been feeling the heat ever since they'd docked in Sydney but so far had had no chance to find something more suitable from their trunks.

The warm March air was so different from what they would experience at this time of the year in Germany, and while they knew the weather patterns would be different, it had seemed a detail best left to deal with after they were settled in their new home. Now Marlena felt foolishly dressed, and was surprised the natives weren't laughing at the sight before them. She looked August up and down and smiled at his knee-length leather trousers and boots, his long sleeved shirt.

'What are you grinning at?' August spluttered. 'We might have been killed.'

'Nonsense.' She could barely contain a giggle. 'I've realised how silly our clothes are. Look at Anna and Johan. Even though they've discarded waistcoats and aprons, they still look like little, overheated Germans. I can see how strange we must appear to the local people.'

August swallowed. 'So should we throw away our clothes, and dress in a few rags and wield a spear? Good Lord, Lena, I do believe the sight of naked men has caused you to lose your senses.'

Marlena laughed. 'Of course not, silly. I'm sure white people here will wear more. Still, it will be different to these traditional German clothes, and we must adjust.'

Johan wiggled away from his brother's hold and headed for the cabin doors. 'I'm going to tell Mama and Papa that we've seen naked black men,' he said as he hurried away.

'You'll do no such thing,' August called. 'Anna, you stay here,' he added as his young sister skipped after Johan. But the two were gone through the door without a glance backwards.

'Well, that should give Mama another attack of the vapours.' He shook his head and turned back to Marlena. 'She certainly won't come on deck now. Once she hears what Johan has to say she's likely to refuse to get off the boat at all. She's already afraid we'll be ostracised. To hear her, you'd think we were the only Germans arriving here.'

'That's silly, considering we left Hamburg with over two hundred passengers.' Marlena was determined not to feed into the anxiety her mother so often displayed.

'Don't forget a few died of the pox on the way.'

'Of course I won't forget that, August. It was sad, but we were fortunate it wasn't worse, as it has been on other ships before us.'

'It was bad enough, with Anna so sick. Mama was sure she was going to lose another child. She hasn't been able to think well of this venture ever since.'

'You know it's easier for Mama to think the worst than the best, August. It's her nature, and she's had some hard things to face in her life, including losing two babies after we were born. But we must help her to be positive, and you must try and be positive too. It will break Papa's heart if we aren't happy here.'

17

'Papa has promised Mama a great deal. I'm not sure Grafton will live up to his dreams.'

'It will be what we make it, August.'

'That's easy for you to say. You're a girl. You'll find a husband and settle down to have babies. It's not the same for me. Papa expects so much of me and I'm not at all sure I can live up to his expectations.'

'He simply wants us to be happy, August. He feels a terrible burden, having taken us from all we've known.'

'I don't blame him for what we've lost, but I'm not convinced that coming here was the answer to our predicament.'

Marlena pulled her bonnet from her head and breathed in deeply. 'It's good fresh air, August. They say even the winters here are warm. I won't miss the cold of Frankfurt. You always hated the cold, too. Surely the weather is something to look forward to.'

'Not if we must go about half naked,' he muttered.

They strolled to the front of the deck, taking in the changing vista. Gradually clusters of houses came into view and they could see people working in the fields and walking along the roads. The occasional horse and cart passed in the distance.

As they continued around the deck, Marlena's thoughts turned to the idea of marriage. Her father had hinted that it should be her most pressing task when they arrived in the colony, and he'd definitely given her the impression he expected she would wed a German man. She was open to the idea, of course. In fact, she hoped she would find a man to love amongst the German community, many of whom she had yet to meet. She didn't want to upset her father in any way, but she would not marry a man she didn't love and she certainly hadn't met anyone on board she would consider.

'You see, August.' She chuckled as they passed a group of people on a grassy bank. 'They all have clothes on.'

'Just as well.' He nodded as their brother and sister came towards them again. 'No Mama and Papa, I see.'

'No matter,' Marlena said. 'We must be almost there now.'

They could make out a sign at the end of a wharf. *Prince Street Wharf*. There were people milling about, some pointing at the steamer as it approached.

'Surely they're used to seeing boats arrive.' August screwed up his face. 'We can't be that much of a novelty. Those people don't look too friendly.'

'Perhaps some of the German people who arrived earlier will be here to welcome us.'

'Or to see if we have the pox.' August flicked a shock of pale hair from his forehead.

'Let's assume they know we've been in quarantine in Sydney, and that we are free of smallpox.'

As the steamer approached the wharf they could hear people bantering in English. Men jostled each other, getting ready to unload the cargo. Orders were shouted. Children chased each other in and out of small groups of women, some of whom had baskets of what looked like vegetables, bread and eggs.

Anna and Johan were again hanging over the side of the railing, straining to see what was happening on the wharf. Suddenly clods of wet sand began to land on the deck near their feet. August and Marlena jumped back and turned towards the bank where the missiles seemed to be originating. Anna squealed and brushed down her pinafore.

'My hair!' she screeched, tugging at a ringlet that had fallen forward over her blouse. 'It's all muddy now.' Tears welled in her eyes and she hurried to Marlena's side.

'It's all right, Anna. We'll clean it before we leave the boat.' Marlena kept one eye on the shore as she spoke, searching for the origin of the mud, which was still coming in small lumps.

'There,' Johan called, as he and August scanned the scrubby bush close to the water. He pointed to the side of the wharf, where two or three young boys huddled by the edge of the water. 'Those boys are throwing it.' He hung over the railing and glared at the youngsters.

'You there,' August shouted. 'Enough of that.'

Having been spotted, the boys stood up defiantly, as if not at all ashamed of their actions. They nudged each other and laughed before climbing up the bank of the river and running off.

'Little rascals.' Marlena chuckled.

'Rascals!' August said. 'They need a good hiding. If that's the welcome we can expect here, I think we're in for a bad time.'

'I'm sure they're only being cheeky boys, August. I doubt they meant any harm, and none's done.' She patted Anna on the back. 'Go back to the cabin. I'll be down in a minute and we'll get you cleaned up.'

Anna scowled after the boys, who had all but disappeared up the road, and stuck her nose in the air. 'I think they're horrid. I hope they won't be at my school.' She pranced back toward the door, still holding her ringlet as if it were irreparably damaged.

'That's likely to be the last straw for Mama.' August sighed. 'Johan, please go and make sure Anna doesn't make more of this than it was.'

Johan nodded and headed off.

August turned back to the people on the wharf. 'So much for being welcomed by Germans. Are these people going to try and sell us food?' He gaped as the boat drew alongside the wharf. 'I can hardly understand a word they're saying.'

'English does sound different without our German accent, August, but we'll get used to it. And the people will get used to us, I'm sure. We must be patient.'

'It sounds so … foreign.' August's face dropped. 'Even though we've spent so much time learning English and practicing all the way out here, I fear we'll not be understood at all.'

'Don't worry so, August. It'll be fine. Wait and see.'

'Well, some of us have been practicing.' August went on as if talking to himself. 'Not Mama, of course. And Papa keeps insisting that there will be enough Germans here that our own language will survive and we'll support each other without speaking English at all. He'll be working for a German and living with Germans, he says. So why will he need English? And as for Mama, she almost faints at the thought of speaking anything but her own tongue.'

Marlena pulled on her brother's arm and shepherded him towards the door to the cabins. 'We must get ready. They'll want

20

us to disembark soon. I believe Mr Kirchner has organised for us to be taken to a hotel.'

'I hear he's also leased allotments ready for those who have something put aside,' August said as they approached their parent's cabin. 'Papa plans to take up one of them, doesn't he?'

'Yes, he's hoping to. I'm sure he'll have a garden established in no time. He gets great satisfaction from seeing things grow.'

'I'm more interested in this timber mill Kirchner has. I'd like to get into that when our commitment to the soap factory is finished, and then perhaps into building.'

'We'll see, August. We are Australians now. Many things are possible, I'm sure.'

***

Marlena sighed and drew herself from her memories as Hans laid a cup of steaming tea on the table in front of her. *So much promise. So many hopes. Sadly, not all dreams come true, but at least I can be grateful for Hans.*

CHAPTER THREE

Fanny was wiping down tables the following day when her attention was taken by a woman entering the dining room. Her expression was agitated, eyes darting around the room. She looked wafer thin, even with a coat hanging loosely over her skirt. Her brown hair was pulled back from her face and caught at the back in a bun. She reminded Fanny of one of the small, furry rodents that scurried in the bush.

'Can I help you, Ma'am?' She approached the woman and smiled.

'I'm looking for my son.' The woman's voice was strained. She was dragging gloves from her hands.

'Children don't usually wander in here, Ma'am. Is he lost?'

'No, he's not lost and he's not a child. He's twenty-two years old.' Now the tone was sharp. 'He's staying here, so I'm told. His name is John Smith.'

'Well, there are a few guests in already for lunch. The name isn't familiar to me but if he's not here you could ask at the front desk.'

'I see him.' The woman seemed to be barely listening as she focussed on someone across the dining room.

Fanny followed her gaze and saw that she was staring at Jack and Jim, who were huddled together, their backs to the woman.

'No, that's Jack and Jim Schmidt.' Fanny thought the woman's distressed state had caused her to mistakenly identify the men.

'They're my sons,' she said harshly. 'And it's not Schmidt.

It's Smith. That's my Jim and the other is John Philip. Why he's taken to being called Jack, I don't know.' She moved tentatively towards the table.

Fanny watched, stunned into silence. She saw Jack and Jim look up as the woman approached. Predictably, Jim's expression was softer than Jack's as they acknowledged her. After a moment, Jim pulled out a chair and she sat with them. Fanny couldn't hear their conversation but she could see that Jack's expression remained sullen. After a few moments Jim reached out and patted the woman's back. Fanny suspected from the slump of her shoulders that she was weeping.

'Morning, Fanny.' The chirpy voice behind her drew her attention away from the scene in the corner.

'Mr Giese, I didn't hear you coming up behind me. I'm concerned about that woman with Jim and Jack. She seems upset.' She nodded in the direction of the threesome.

'That's Jane Clifford. She's their mother. I hope there's not going to be trouble. She'll not like them staying here and Jack's likely to get himself in a lather. I'd best see if I can smooth troubled waters.' The hotelier strode toward the table in the corner.

Fanny shook her head. She was more confused than ever. *If the woman's name is Jane Clifford she must have remarried after the boys' father died – hence the small children at home. But why did she say their name was Smith, rather than Schmidt? And why has Jack changed his first name?*

A moment later the woman rose from her chair and hurried towards the front door. Her face was stained with tears. Hans Giese was a few steps behind her.

'Jane, wait,' he called. But she was gone without a backward glance.

Fanny was still standing in the same spot when Hans came towards her. 'She's terribly upset, isn't she? I suppose a mother would want her injured boy to be with her.'

'It's more complicated than that, Fanny. The boys will do as they want, despite what Jane thinks, I'm afraid, although

I can hardly blame them for that. It's not something for you to worry yourself with, however. Best thing you can do is get them something to eat. They always enjoy Lena's cooking, if nothing else.' He winked at Fanny as he left the room.

Fanny took orders from a few other customers and headed out into the kitchen. She was still deciding how to approach Jim and Jack. She didn't want the brunt of Jack's hostility again but she was curious about them. *Something is very wrong in their lives.*

***

That evening, as Fanny was straightening the chairs around the tables after the dinner crowd had gone, she noticed ragged woollen gloves on the seat. She remembered Jane Clifford dragging them from her hands as she'd scanned the dining room for her sons that morning. *The poor woman left in such a state that she must have forgotten them.* Fanny pushed them into the large pocket of her skirt and finished cleaning up.

She didn't think about the gloves again until she had dropped into a chair in her sister's kitchen late that evening.

'You look done in,' Lizzie said. 'I'll make you a cup of tea before I head off to bed. Alf fell asleep an hour ago while he was settling Tommy down. He's been restless this evening, poor little mite. I think he's getting more teeth.' She pulled her shawl around her shoulders and rubbed her arms.

'Dear Lizzie, you have your work cut out for you with two little ones, don't you? You're looking weary. I can get myself a cup of tea.'

'I'm fine, Fanny. I'm sure I'm no wearier than you, what with serving that rowdy crowd all afternoon and evening.'

Studying her sister's face, Fanny noted that her cheeks were rosy, although she suspected that was more because of the warmth from the stove than from good health. It seemed to Fanny that marriage at seventeen, soon followed by the birth of two children, was aging her sister too quickly.

Lizzie had wheat-coloured hair, much like Fanny's, although Lizzie had hers pulled back into a severe bun, which made her look

24

older than her twenty years. People had always said the girls looked alike, with pixie faces and blue-green eyes, but the last couple of years Lizzie had become much plumper than Fanny. Marlena Giese often said there was not nearly enough meat on Fanny's bones; something she was endeavouring to change with her German cooking.

'I think being a wife and mother is more taxing than being a domestic in a hotel,' Fanny said. 'It's interesting meeting all kinds of people. Especially at this time of year when so many come to town for the horse races.'

'Some of them not so respectable, I imagine.' Lizzie pursed her lips. 'I hope you're being careful. Some of those men have been out in the wild for years. They have no idea how to behave around a lady.'

Fanny laughed. 'Lizzie, you sound like Dad. Believe me, with Mr and Mrs Giese as employers I feel more mothered than when I'm at home. I have plenty of people looking out for me.'

'You're only eighteen, Fanny. I've no doubt the men who come into that hotel find you tempting. Alf says you've put yourself in danger, and it's very foolish.'

Fanny huffed. 'Your husband sounds like Grandfather Nipperess, reminding us of *the dangers of temptations*.' Fanny mimicked her grandfather's voice and giggled. 'And Alf's more concerned with his business reputation than with my welfare, if you ask me,' she added quietly.

Lizzie handed Fanny a steaming cup of tea and sat down with one for herself, ignoring Fanny's last remark.

'I thought you were going to bed?' Fanny sipped her tea gratefully.

'I am, but it's nice to have a few moments with my sister.' Her eyes glowed with affection.

Fanny reached across and patted her sister's hand. As she did she remembered the gloves in her skirt pocket. 'I almost forgot about these.' She pulled them out and laid them on the table.

'They look nearly worn out,' Lizzie said. 'Surely you've better gloves than those.'

'They're not mine. A woman left them in the hotel today.'

25

'Then I suppose she'll come back for them, if she hasn't decided they're not worth the bother.' Lizzie turned up her nose and pinched one of the fingers of the gloves. 'They've certainly seen better days.'

'Hmm,' Fanny murmured. 'I think their owner may have seen better days as well.'

'That sounds like you're thinking of trying to help this woman in some way.'

'What would be wrong in that?' Fanny felt defensive.

'Simply that you always seem to be picking up birds with broken wings, injured animals, people whose cause you want to take up. You can't fix everything that's hurting in the world, you know, Sis.'

'Sometimes it only takes a smile or a friendly word to make a difference, and I have plenty of those to share.' Fanny flashed a bright smile.

Lizzie shook her head. 'So how do you think you might help the owner of these gloves? It looks like she's pretty poor if they're anything to go by.'

'I don't know if she's poor in terms of money, but it seems to me she's poor in regard to family. She has a couple of sons who don't want anything to do with her. Can you imagine what it would be like if Tommy and Eliza grew up and didn't want to live with you or even visit you?'

'No, I can't. Something terrible must have happened in the family. How do you know all this about the woman? Has she been in the hotel a lot?'

'No, I just met her today. But I have met three of her sons and it's clear they're estranged from her.'

'What about their father?'

'He died when they were young.'

'Perhaps that's got something to do with it, then. Sons need their father to guide them when they're growing up. You know what Mum says about Grandfather Nipperess; he grew up without his father and it took him till he was a middle-aged man before he sorted himself out.'

'That's exactly why these boys need help. Especially one of

them. He's so angry and unhappy.'

'So now it's the boys you want to help?'

'I feel sorry for all of them. It's sad.' Fanny sighed.

'You need to be careful, Fanny. You're inclined to get too involved. Mum always said she had to cook extra almost every meal because she never knew when you'd come home from school with some child you thought looked hungry.' They both giggled at the remembrance.

'Half the time we ended up with frantic parents running around the neighbourhood looking for their lost child,' Lizzie continued.

Fanny laughed, then clamped her hand over her mouth, fearful she'd wake her brother-in-law or the children. 'At least their children were well-fed when they found them.' 'Well, you're not eight years old anymore, Fanny, and these are not children you're talking about. It sounds like you might be getting involved in something serious.'

'Don't worry, I'm not going to do anything silly. But it wouldn't hurt to take this woman's gloves back to her and be a little friendly.'

'Don't you think she'll come looking for them?'

'I doubt she'll come back to the hotel at all.'

'Then how on earth are you going to find her? What's her name?'

'Jane Clifford.'

'Clifford? You mean Fred and Jane Clifford?' Lizzie's eyes flew open.

'Yes, that's the name. Do you know them?'

'No, but I've heard talk of them, from a couple of mothers I meet up with at Fisher Park. I take the children there for a walk and one of the women lives in Dobie Street. She says there's often a ruckus at her neighbour's house.'

'Yes?' Fanny leaned over the table.

'She said there's an older woman who visits. A woman who has a Spanish or Italian accent, who has emotional outbursts and yells a lot. Some of those people do, you know.'

'Lizzie, what's this got to do with Jane Clifford?' Fanny shook her head and rose to top up her cup with hot water. Her mind flashed back to the distraught expression on Jane Clifford's face that morning. It was true this was no hungry child needing a feed. This was a woman whose heart was broken. Not a problem that could be solved with a nourishing meal, but still not something Fanny could ignore. She shook her head and tuned back into what Lizzie was saying.

'My friend pointed Mrs Clifford out one day in the park with a couple of young children. That's when she told us about this older woman, who is apparently the mother-in-law ... very flamboyant. She wears colourful clothes and has a loud voice, and – '

'I get the picture,' Fanny cut in. 'So she's Fred Clifford's mother and she visits with them occasionally. That sounds pretty normal as she has five grandchildren there.'

'How do you know that?'

'Jim said his mother has five children at home.'

'It sounds complicated, Fanny. I don't see that you can possibly do any good getting involved. There can be strong feelings amongst family members, especially when it's a mixed family.'

Lizzie pushed back from the table and started gathering up their cups and saucers. She grabbed a cloth from the bench and began wiping the table, shaking her head. 'Second marriages ... as well as mixed cultures. The Spanish and Italian are different from the English, you know.'

'And perhaps from the Germans,' Fanny said, her mind going back to her conversation with Jack and Jim.

'German? Are you saying these boys you're concerned about are German?'

'Their father was born in Germany. He came here with his parents as part of the German group who immigrated to work in Grafton.'

'That makes it worse, Fanny. I think you should stay out of it. You know how worried I get about you working at The European with those Germans. They're different from us.' Lizzie slid back into her chair and leaned across the table, her face creased with disapproval.

'Please don't start with all that again, Lizzie. Mum would box your ears, old as you are, if she heard you go on like this. She taught us that people are people, regardless of the country they came from. She'd hate to hear your ideas about the Germans.'

'They're not my ideas. Lots of people say the Germans refused to speak English when they got here and they kept to themselves, and – '

'And why wouldn't they? They were trying to find their feet in a strange country. It takes time to learn a different language and new ways. You can't blame them for that.'

'From what I heard, a lot didn't even try to mix in and learn English.'

Fanny took a deep breath. She was getting annoyed with her sister. 'Lizzie, when did you get so prejudiced? You weren't like this as a child. Remember when we lived in Fiji for that year? We saw the Islanders treated badly. We felt sad for them. You as much as me. I'm sure you did.'

Lizzie fidgeted in her chair. 'That was different. We were there because Dad was sent by his company to show the Islanders how to grow sugar cane. We were teaching them. We weren't there to be their friends.'

Fanny gasped. 'How can you say that? Remember that day on the beach when we'd watched one of the ships sail out and we knew Islanders had been tricked into going aboard by dreadful men who'd bribed them and even dragged them onto the boats because they wanted cheap labourers here on the cane fields. It made me so angry, and you, too, Lizzie. We always agreed that people ought to be treated fairly and kindly, no matter what their background.'

'We were children, Fanny. Only ten and eleven. What did we understand about such things?'

'We understood enough to know they were being mistreated. And that morning when one of the Islanders came swimming back into shore after jumping ship, we didn't hesitate to help him. He'd nearly drowned, poor man. He only wanted to go back to his family. He couldn't speak a word of English, but we knew what he was telling us.'

'You always could work out what the Islanders were saying

better than me.' Lizzie chuckled, as if to lighten the conversation. 'You'd chat away to the children, you in English and they in their own tongue and you seemed able to communicate easily. You always were kind.' She patted Fanny's hand.

'You were kind, too, Lizzie.' Fanny held her serious tone. This was not something she was prepared to have brushed aside. 'We did make friends there. Our different colour and language was not a barrier. It meant nothing.'

'Perhaps.' Lizzie sighed and slumped back in her chair. 'But these things you're talking about now, people from different cultures and different beliefs living amongst us … that's an entirely different —'

'Exactly, Lizzie. It's different, not wrong. What's wrong is when people can't accept differences, when they hold prejudice against others just because they come from a different background or have different ideas. Surely you see how unfair that is.'

Fanny sensed her sister was pulling back, shutting out her words. She took hold of Lizzie's hand and squeezed it. 'Please Lizzie, you mustn't allow your mind to be so influenced by those who are intolerant and bigoted.'

'If you're referring to Alf …' Lizzie reared up, indignant. 'I'll have you know that my husband is a well-respected man in the business community.'

'Please don't be defensive, Lizzie. This is not about what Alf believes. You still have your own mind, don't you?'

'Of course I do, but I reckon Alf's right when he says you deliberately went to work at The European to make a point, to thumb your nose at those who think people should keep to their own.'

'Well, he may be right in that.' Fanny grinned. 'I was keen to work there because I believe we must do more than talk about acceptance. We must act on it. I've found the Gieses to be accepting of me and everyone who comes into their hotel. They don't put up with any kind of discrimination and I'm proud to be working with them.'

Lizzie sighed and rubbed her eyes. 'Maybe, but when push

comes to shove, people will still stick to their own kind, you mark my words. If there's going to be any push and shove going on around that German family, you'll be on the outside. That's what I think.'

'I think you're being unfair, Lizzie, but I don't want to fight with you. Anyway, Jane Clifford is not German and she's troubled. I'd like to help her. There's no harm in that, is there?'

Lizzie stood, pulled off her apron and hung it up by the stove. 'If she married a German, that's where her trouble likely started.'

Fanny was finding it hard to curb her annoyance. 'Well, it seems to me she has no less trouble now she's married to an Englishman.'

'Who obviously is part Spanish or Italian.' Lizzie pushed her clenched fists into her hips. 'You're not going to stay out of this, are you?'

Fanny didn't answer. She was getting nowhere in this conversation but was more determined about what she wanted to do. *There must be a way I can help Jane Clifford, and in doing so maybe help Jack and Jim too.*

After a few moments Lizzie shook her head. 'I see there's nothing I can do to talk you out of it. I'm going to bed.' She kissed Fanny on the top of the head before leaving the room.

Fanny sat in the fading light from the fire for a long time. By the time she left the kitchen she was resolute.

CHAPTER FOUR

'Mrs Clifford?' Fanny stood back and smiled as the front door opened.

'Yes?' The woman looked her up and down and frowned. 'Do I know you?'

'Not really. We spoke briefly at The European yesterday. You were looking for your sons. I work in the dining room at the hotel.'

Fanny waited for some sign of recognition in the woman's face. There was none. 'When you left you must have dropped these.' She held up the gloves. 'I found them on one of the chairs.'

Jane reached for the gloves. 'Thank you, but you needn't have bothered bringing them.' She looked behind her where Fanny could hear children bickering.

'I'm on my way to work,' Fanny said. 'I left home early so I would have time to drop in here. I asked down the street which was your house. I hope you don't mind?'

After a few moments hesitation, Jane shook her head and took a deep breath. 'It's cold out. Do you want to come in?' She opened the door and stepped back when Fanny nodded.

Inside with the door closed the dim light hid all but the shadowy image of two children in the middle of the floor. They stopped talking and stared at Fanny.

'This is Lance and Daisy.' Jane grabbed a couple of things from the floor and put them on a bench near the wall. 'The others are at school.'

'Hello, my name's Fanny. It looks like you're playing a board game there. I used to love to play games like that with my Gran. Do you have a grandmother who plays with you?' She looked expectantly at the children. Their faces were blank but their eyes darted to their mother.

'My mother died a couple of years ago.' Jane fiddled with the front of her apron, clearly uncomfortable.

'My Gran passed away too,' Fanny said. 'I know how sad it is for children to be without a granny. Is your husband's mother still alive?'

Jane seemed shocked at the question.

'She means Grandmother Clifford, Ma.' Lance drawled from the floor.

'I know who she means,' Jane snapped. 'Mind your business.' She waved a hand loosely at her son. He put his head down and whispered something to his sister.

Jane turned back to Fanny. 'My husband's mother is very much alive, but she doesn't play with the children.'

'That's a shame.' Fanny thought about pursuing the topic of grandfathers but decided that would be too intrusive. It was clear Jane was wishing she'd leave. 'I should be getting on then.' She was disappointed the visit had not been friendlier. As she moved back towards the door she noticed how lined and weary Jane's face was. Her heart went out to the woman and she couldn't resist another attempt to befriend her.

'When you left the hotel yesterday you seemed upset. I do hope you're feeling better.'

A soft but cynical laugh erupted from Jane's mouth. 'You're so young.' She sighed. 'You're not married, are you?'

'No, I'm not.' Fanny shook her head.

'Then take my advice and don't.' Jane's tone was brittle.

Fanny gasped. She could feel the woman's pain and disappointment. 'I'm sorry. I know your first husband died. That must have been a terrible time for you.' Fanny hurried on, realising the need to explain how she knew anything about Jane's life. 'Jim told me a little. I hope your little ones are a comfort for you now.'

'Like I said, you're young. You'd know nothing of the price a woman pays for the comforts of marriage.' Jane pulled open the front door. 'Thanks for bringing my gloves back.' She stared out at the street, a definite signal that she wanted no more conversation.

'Perhaps I'll see you again at the hotel, if you visit Jim and Jack … I mean, John Phillip. Isn't that what you called your older son?' Fanny paused on the stoop in the hope that the woman would give her a little more time.

'Everyone calls him Jack, apparently. He was christened John Phillip. It's how I know him, if I know him at all.' A tear welled in her eye. She coughed and wiped it away.

'He's likely to be at the hotel for a week or so,' Fanny said. 'Mrs Giese says his ankle is badly sprained so he won't be riding. Perhaps you'll have another chance to visit?'

Jane frowned. 'Look, you seem like a nice girl, but you couldn't understand about me and my sons.' She shook her head. 'Whatever Jim says, it's not the half of it. So if you're feeling sorry for the boys or for me, then you're wasting your time.' She began to close the door. 'Thanks again for the gloves but I'll not be back to the hotel.'

Fanny stayed on the stoop for a few moments, saddened and shocked. It was hard for her to make her legs move. The cold seeped into her and she began to shiver before she shook herself into action and headed down the front path. She had a knot in her stomach as she tried to sort out her thoughts all the way to the hotel. By the time she'd walked the three blocks she was panting.

'Whoa there, *liebling*.' Marlena took her arm as she almost fell through the kitchen door. 'What's the rush?'

'I'm sorry, Mrs Giese. I hurried to get warm and I didn't realise I was walking so fast. I've been a bit distracted.'

'Well, take a deep breath and slow down. We've plenty of time before the lunch crowd. How about you sit down here at the bench and peel these potatoes for me?'

'I went to see Jane Clifford this morning,' Fanny said after a

34

few minutes of peeling. Marlena stopped her humming and looked across the bench. 'Whatever for?'

'She left her gloves here yesterday when she rushed out so upset. I thought I'd take them back to her. My sister knew where she lives.'

'I see. How did she seem about having a visitor?'

'She was a bit disturbed, I think. I get the impression she's not used to visitors.'

'Nor does she want them, more to the point.'

'Why not? She must get lonely.'

'I'm sure she does, poor dear, especially for her sons. Nevertheless, there are reasons.'

Fanny gazed at Marlena, hoping to get more insight into the plight of the Clifford family.

'Was her husband at home?' Marlena asked.

'I didn't see him. I suppose he was at work.'

'Quite likely.' Marlena nodded and seemed relieved. 'His father has a property near Moree and he goes out there a bit. His mother lives up at Woodburn. She's remarried to an Italian man. I think Fred goes there a bit as well. There's a community of Italians who've developed vineyards and orchards. New Italy they call it.'

'I thought his mother was Spanish?'

'She was, but where on earth did you hear about her?'

'My sister has friends who live near the Cliffords.'

'No doubt anyone in the area would know about Fred Clifford's mother. She makes her presence felt, that one.'

'It seems she's another visitor Mrs Clifford doesn't like.'

'For good reason, *liebling*. You're fortunate she wasn't at the house. That might have been worse than Fred being there. Then again, I don't suppose Jane would have answered the door if he'd been at home.'

'Truly? Is he so against her having visitors?'

'I think that would depend on who they were.' Marlena huffed and wiped flour from her hands before rinsing them in the bowl of water beside her.

Fanny waited, holding her breath. *So it is Mr Clifford who is the problem, but surely his behaviour can't be so bad that Jack and Jim would refuse to visit their mother because of him.*

'That Fred Clifford has a lot to answer for,' Marlena said, as if reading her thoughts. 'I'd not like to be in his shoes when he stands before our Maker.'

'Oh?' Fanny didn't know what to ask next.

'And I'd advise you to stay away from that house.' Marlena shook a wet finger at Fanny. 'Goodness knows when he might be home. I can't imagine what possessed you. All for a pair of gloves!' She tutted as she bent to lift a pan onto the bench.

'I doubt Jim or Jack would have taken them back to her. I think it's a shame. I don't understand it at all.'

'You couldn't understand, *liebling* , so it's best to leave well enough alone. Tougher than you have tried to solve it all. Some things simply are as they are … sadly.'

This was not a satisfactory explanation for Fanny but she could see she was going to get no more from Mrs Giese, so she put her head down and got on with peeling the potatoes.

***

'How's your foot?' Fanny asked Jack when the boys came downstairs.

'It's not good,' Jim answered. 'Aunty says he'll not be able to put much weight on it for a few days yet.'

Fanny grinned at Jim. 'Do you always answer for your brother? It's not his tongue that's hurt, is it?'

She didn't want to offend Jim but she found it irritating that he made it so easy for Jack to be rude. She turned to Jack and raised her eyebrows. Something in his eyes surprised her. *Was that a hint of a smile? Does he find me amusing?* Perhaps her honesty was beginning to break down the wall he put up.

'It still hurts. Is that what you wanted to hear?' he said, his lips drawn into a thin line.

She was sure he was controlling an inclination to grin at her. 'Actually, no. That would be cruel. I was hoping you're feeling better.

I'm sure it's frustrating not to be able to get about as you'd like.'

'It is.' His expression was still hard to read.

'In fact he's mad as a fenced bull.' Jim seemed unable to hold back. 'He wants to be down at the race track and there's no walking on that foot, so he feels stuck.'

'Is that so?' Fanny kept her gaze on Jack.

'I suppose,' he admitted.

'We usually have a grand time with the other woodcutters and the stockmen,' Jim went on. 'None of us get to socialise much when we're out in the bush.'

'No, I guess not,' Fanny said. 'Maybe you could get a ride down to the track and watch for a while. You could keep your foot up there as well as here, couldn't you, Jack?'

Jack shrugged and looked away. Fanny was sure he was finding her concentration on him uncomfortable, but she persisted.

'I've no doubt your uncle would take you down in his cart. He's as thoughtful a man as you'd find.'

'Jack won't let me ask,' Jim said. 'He hates to impose.'

'Too proud to ask for help, Jack?' Fanny continued to aim her questions at the older brother. 'Or too proud to be seen at the track with an injury?'

'Now look here.' He turned on her, ice in his voice. 'I think you should mind your own business. I'm sure you've other customers to feed.'

He pushed back in his chair, grimacing with pain as he did so. His jaw flinched and Fanny could tell he was gritting his teeth.

'I don't mean to be rude,' she said. 'I'm trying to be helpful. It seems to me you're determined to be miserable. So if that's the case, I think you ought to do it alone and not keep your brother from enjoying himself.' She put one hand on her hip and stood her ground, glaring at him. *Why am I letting this man aggravate me so?*

'I've told Jim to go to the race track every day, but he insists on staying with me. I'm not preventing him from doing anything.' Jack's retort was angry. His eyes flashed darkly.

Fanny wondered why she didn't feel intimidated. No doubt

Jack frightened a lot of people off altogether.

'It's true, Fanny,' Jim said. 'He does tell me to go, but I prefer to stay with him. Those stairs are still hard for him to get up and down.'

'You're a kind brother, Jim.' She turned to him and smiled. 'But I'm not sure kindness is what Jack needs.'

'Here she goes again.' This time there was a slight chuckle from Jack. 'The girl thinks she knows what I need, as well as what I'm like and why.' He didn't look at Fanny as he spoke and his tone was sarcastic.

'She's only trying to be helpful.' Jim reached out to pat Jack's arm.

Jack pulled away. 'Well, I don't want people trying to help me.' He turned to Fanny. 'Now, I think it's time for you to get on with your work. I'm sure my aunt and uncle don't pay you to bother their customers.' Jack hauled himself up from his chair and hobbled towards the stairs, his shoulders taut, his fists clenched.

'I'm sorry, Fanny,' Jim apologised. 'He's not always so rude. He's feeling bad about not being able to get to the race track. We always have such fun this week of the year. It's special to him … to all of us.'

'You're very patient,' she said. 'I'm sure you want to do what's best for him.'

'He did it for me for long enough, Fanny. I owe him. Truly I do.'

'I see. Well, actually I don't see but I suppose it's none of my business anyway. If you want my opinion, I'd be asking your uncle to talk Jack into going down to the track. I imagine Mr Giese would have a way of making it seem a good idea.'

Jim nodded. 'I'll try that. I reckon it would help Jack if he could sit down there for a bit. Lots of the fellows would stop and chat with him. He could have a bit of a laugh like we usually do. They all like Jack. I'm sure they're missing him being around.'

'Really?' Fanny was surprised. 'Then there must be more to him than I've seen these past few days.'

'There is, Fanny. Believe me, there is.'

38

***

The following day the lunch hour came and went with no sign of Jim and Jack in the dining room.

'Your nephews haven't been down to eat yet, Mrs Giese,' Fanny said as she laid a stack of plates on the sink.

'No, they're at the race track today. I packed them a lunch. It'll do Jack good to be out in the fresh air. I'm trusting he'll sit about talking with some of the riders and the organisers. If he so much as climbs onto a horse I'll tan his hide for him, big as he is.'

Fanny smiled. 'Yesterday he seemed most reluctant to go out.'

Marlena nodded. 'Hans made up some ruse about taking the boys to the old hotel in Prince Street. Hans built it years ago, and we lived there when the boys were young. He thought the boys might be interested in seeing what the new owners have done to it. He suggested they drop in at the race track on the way back. Jim was keen. In fact, I think he cooked the whole thing up with Hans.'

'What a good idea.' Fanny grinned.

'You look like a cat that swallowed a mouse. Did you have something to do with this?'

'Not really, Mrs Giese, but I agree it was a good idea. Jack's been so miserable.'

In fact Fanny felt quite satisfied with herself. *Surely Jack's mood will be improved by his outing, and it goes to show that it doesn't take a lot to help someone along the way.*

'He can be moody,' Marlena continued, 'but he has a good heart underneath it all.'

'So I keep hearing.'

'From Jim, no doubt. He'll always defend Jack. He's a good boy, is Jim. So much like his father was.' Marlena sighed. 'It's something to give thanks for.'

'It's sad they lost their father so young but the effect on them seems to be very different. Jim is so sweet and caring. Jack is … it's difficult to say what Jack is, actually. I haven't worked him out yet.'

'It seems to me you're trying hard to do so, though, *liebling*.'

Marlena leaned on her rolling pin and searched Fanny's face.

'I hate to see someone so unhappy. Surely now that he's grown up he can find his own happiness. Jim seems to have a much more positive outlook on life.'

'Yes, they're different in nature, but just because they were brought up in the same house doesn't mean they had the same experience.'

Fanny nodded. 'I see,' she said, though in truth she still didn't see at all. 'I'll get the rest of the dirty plates.' She headed back to the dining room, her mind going over Marlena's words.

***

'Still deep in thought, *liebling*?' Marlena looked up from her cooking pot later that day and grinned at Fanny, whose face was creased with concern. 'We've almost got the soup ready for supper. Why don't you tell me what's on your mind.'

'I'm still disturbed about your nephews, Mrs Giese. They're back, but Jack doesn't look much happier. I thought some time at the track might have put a smile on his face.'

Marlena smiled. *Fanny's such a sweet girl, wanting everyone to be happy. If only it was so easy to achieve as a day at the horse races.* 'Jack's very frustrated about his foot,' she said. 'He's not himself, but he'll come good. Don't you worry.'

Fanny filled a bowl with hot water and began to wash the dirty dishes. 'It seems to me that it also has a lot to do with their mother. I feel really sorry for her and I don't understand. How come she said their name is Smith?'

'It's a complicated story.' Marlena sighed. She dragged a tea towel from the rack and moved alongside Fanny.

'Jane was married to my brother, August. Sadly, she never felt accepted by the German community. Mostly due to my father's disapproval. Papa was a good man but proud, fixed in his beliefs and not tolerant of those who were different. August met Jane up on North Arm, while he was working with my brother Wilhelm on his coffee farm. Wilhelm had married a good German girl, of

40

course, so Papa was proud of him. He grew the first coffee in the district and was doing well for himself.'

'And Jane was not a German girl?' Fanny prompted.

'No. Jane's people came from England. They have a property at Mororo. August met her in the post office there and they fell in love. She was only seventeen, a pretty young thing, but she had no idea what it would be like marrying into a German family.'

'Did your father try to stop them getting married?'

Marlena shook her head, her brother's face coming easily to her mind. A wave of sadness washed over her. 'August was twenty-six when he arrived back in Grafton, already married to Jane. He was in the process of buying his own cane farm at Iluka, and I think he'd given up trying to please Papa. It had always seemed to him that Papa preferred Wilhelm, even though Wilhelm was his step-son. Perhaps it was August's way of rebelling.'

Fanny nodded and waited. Marlena sensed her interest and let her memories flow.

'Papa wasn't pleasant to Jane, I'm afraid. He was still grieving for Mama, who'd died the year before, so he wasn't in any state to be reasonable. August and Jane headed back up north, August bought the cane farm, and the three boys were born … but we didn't see much of them at all until he got sick.'

Marlena took a deep breath and returned to the stove to stir the stew in her pot. 'Jane changed her name to Smith after August died. She married Fred Clifford a few years later and they have five children together now. It hasn't been easy for Jim and Jack, I'm afraid. They were only four and seven when Jane remarried.'

'What about Bob? He's the oldest, isn't he?'

Marlena wiped a tear from her eye as she turned back to Fanny. 'He was nine when Jane and Fred married, but he took off on a stock drive when he was fifteen and he's only been back in this area a couple of years. I know he visits his mother occasionally, but he doesn't say much. He always did keep his thoughts to himself, and believe me, if I can't get someone talking, no one can.' She grinned, pulling herself from her sadness. 'I pray he'll find a nice girl one day and be happy.'

'I'm sorry, Mrs Giese. I didn't mean to upset you. I've been concerned about your nephews, and also their mother …'

'It's all right, *liebling*. I always think about the past when the boys are here, and it helps me to talk, actually.' She sniffed as she turned to the chopping board and began to drag outside leaves from a cabbage.

'It's been a sad life for Jane,' she continued. 'Not one you'd wish on anyone. It makes me realise how fortunate I was to meet Hans not long after we settled here. We were married in less than a year. He'd come out from Germany in '53, a few years before us. He was running the brickworks when we met. Did you know he and his brother made the first bricks on the Clarence River?' It was easy to smile once her thoughts were on Hans. Her chest swelled with pride.

'I didn't know that,' Fanny said, also smiling. 'He's a clever man, isn't he?'

'He is, and a good one. He helped our family get settled here in Grafton. He gave the boys work in the brickyards when they'd completed their commitment to William Kirchner in the soap factory, then he encouraged them to seek out opportunities for buying land. I'm a lucky woman to have him.' She wrinkled her nose and gratitude for Hans filled her mind.

'Fortunately my father also thought the world of him. Hans brought some fun into our lives. He and his brother started the brass band here in town. A lot of the immigrants from Germany had musical talents and we had balls and concerts.' She sighed and began to sway, remembering how much she'd loved to dance in those early days.

'The jockey club was good for us too. It was popular amongst the German men. There was a lot of socialising, even though it was difficult for some, like Mama and Papa, to adjust to the differences here.'

As her thoughts turned to her parents, she sighed and pushed hair back from her forehead. 'Then Mama got pleurisy and died, which was a dreadful shock for us all.'

'How sad.' Fanny's smile faded and she reached for Marlena's arm.

'Those five years after August married Jane were hard ones,' Marlena said. 'My younger sister, Anna, was angry with Papa for taking the stance he had with August. She married a few years later to Richard Palmer, who was also English, so that didn't help the situation. She did make up with Papa afterwards, but he never got over August's death.' She brushed her hands down her apron as if to wipe away the memories. *Such a tragedy when reconciliation is left too long.*

'But why is Jack so hostile towards his mother?' Fanny asked, her face pleading for understanding. 'I saw him with her. He wasn't kind to her.'

'Well, that's a different story, *liebling*. Also a sad one, I'm afraid, but not my story to tell.' *Please God, don't let it be another permanently broken relationship.*

Marlena patted Fanny on the shoulder. She could see the dear girl was as keen as she was herself to see the boys resolve their issues with their mother, and from what she knew of Fanny, she wasn't a girl to back away from a challenge. *I pray she doesn't get hurt along the way.*

'Now, how about you go out and see if anyone's ready to order?' She tapped Fanny's hand. 'I reckon my nephews will be eating the chairs by now.'

CHAPTER FIVE

'So how was your day?' Fanny ventured that evening after skirting around Jack and Jim's table for a while.

'Real good.' Jim nodded, speaking with a mouth full of potato pie.

'And you, Jack? Did you enjoy yourself at the track?'

'I wouldn't say I enjoyed myself,' Jack answered after a lengthy silence in which Jim seemed too busy eating to answer. 'I'd prefer to be riding but it was better than being stuck here.'

'He worries about Lightning … his horse.' Jim swallowed a mouthful loudly before speaking. 'He misses racing too.'

'I see.' Fanny looked at Jack but he made no attempt to speak again. 'Can't someone else ride him?' Irritation niggled at her.

'Heck, no.' Jim huffed. 'No one else rides Lightning. Except Uncle Hans, of course. It's his horse, but it's a few years since he's ridden in the races. Lightning and Jack make a great pair, pretty unbeatable really.'

'He's the big black one out in the stable, isn't he?' Fanny aimed her question at Jack and her annoyance rose a notch when he continued to ignore her.

'Sure is.' Jim seemed oblivious to the growing tension. 'He's beautiful and fast as lightning too. That's why he's called … well, I guess that's obvious.' He grinned.

'I'm sure they make a great pair.' Fanny turned back to Jim. 'Lightning and thunder do mostly go together.' She scooped up

Jim's empty plate, not risking a glance back at Jack, even to see if he was finished eating. She was sure she'd have emptied any remains on his head.

Jim fidgeted in his chair. He looked from Fanny to Jack before pulling Jack's almost empty soup bowl across the table and handing it to Fanny.

'He won't admit it, but we had a fine time today,' he said.

'Why wouldn't you admit that, Jack?' Fanny couldn't resist challenging him.

After a moment's silence his eyes met hers. They were flashing almost black. 'I told you what it was like. What else needs to be said?'

'You know, if I was your mother, I'd box your ears,' she said without thinking.

He glared at her. 'Well, you're not my mother so why the hell do you keep acting like you are?' There was rage in his voice.

'All right, you two,' Jim pleaded. 'It's been a good day. Let's not spoil it, please.'

'Right,' Fanny said, more calmly. 'I'm sorry. I thought your brother might have been a little more grateful for the chance to see his friends.' She spun on her heels and walked towards the kitchen.

As she was about to push through the kitchen door there was a raucous laugh from a table close to the front door of the pub. Turning, she saw a young man standing by the table and wiping what looked like mashed potato from his face. She could see he was an Islander, likely one who'd been brought from Fiji or one of the other islands north of Queensland, to work on the cane fields. The men at the table were obviously enjoying his embarrassment, and it seemed to Fanny that they had likely caused it. The plates in front of them had the remains of meat pie and mashed potato.

'Can I help you?' Fanny said as she hurried towards the young man. She put the plates she was carrying on the table and pulled a tea towel from her shoulder. 'Here, wipe your face with this. It's clean.'

She turned to the men at the table and glared. 'If that's your idea of fun, you should be ashamed of yourselves.'

It had been some time since she'd seen one of the Islanders being harassed in the hotel. However, Fanny knew that many of these young workers still suffered at the hands of their employers as well as people in the community who considered them little more than slaves. Already incensed by Jack's attitude, she could feel her anger boiling over.

'Aw, come on, lovey.' One of the men reached for her arm. 'We was only tryin' to lighten up the fuzzy wuzzy.' He laughed loudly and slapped one of the other men on the back.

'Yeah.' The other man guffawed. 'Surely he'd prefer his skin was white … no matter how it gets that way.' There was more chortling and back slapping around the table.

Fanny gritted her teeth and turned back to the young Islander. 'I'll show you to a table, sir,' she said, as calmly as she could.

He nodded as he finished wiping his face.

'Sir,' the man closest to Fanny said sarcastically. 'She called him *sir*. Must know somethin' we don't. P'raps he's a prince in his village, eh? *Prince Kanaka*.' He threw his head back and roared with laughter.

Without thinking Fanny picked up Jack's soup bowl and tipped the remains into the man's mouth. 'Somebody should clean your mouth out with soap,' she hissed. 'But this will have to do.'

While the man spluttered and coughed and wiped soup from his face with his sleeve, Fanny moved towards the Islander and took his arm. She led him to the other side of the dining room, and indicated an empty table. 'I'm so sorry,' she said as he sat down. 'Mr Giese will throw those men out of here when he hears about this. Now, let me take your order. The food's good, I promise.' She smiled and was relieved when he smiled in return.

'Thank you. I like pie. But please … I don't want them thrown out. It will make it worse.'

Fanny patted him on the shoulder and went to the kitchen. Still seething, she dropped empty plates onto the bench.

Marlena looked up, a surprised expression on her face. 'What is it, *liebling*? You look about to explode.'

'Nothing, Mrs Giese. I'm a bit out of sorts tonight. I'll be fine.'

'It's not like you at all, Fanny. If it's women's troubles, I suggest you finish early and get a good night's sleep. Would you like a lift home in the cart? Hans would take you.'

'Goodness, no, Mrs Giese. That's not necessary. I'm fine.'

'I don't think so. You're flushed. You wait right there.' Marlena brushed her hands down her apron and headed into the dining room.

May, the young kitchen hand, was up to her elbows in suds, washing the dishes. She grinned at Fanny. 'Once she makes up her mind there's no changing it.'

Fanny shook her head. She was annoyed with herself for letting Jack upset her. *And as for those other men ...* Before she could gather her thoughts Jim came through the door, his aunt close on his heels.

'Right, Fanny. Jim will take you home. It'll only take him twenty minutes there and back in the cart. I'll not have you walking out in the night when you're not well. Now off with that apron and off you go.'

'But I need to take out some pie –'

'No buts. May will see to it.' Marlena waved her hands at the two of them as if shooing away chickens. 'I'll not hear another word.'

Jim shrugged his shoulders and waited for Fanny to remove her apron and wash her hands. Taking her hooded coat from the peg on the back door, she pulled on her gloves and let Jim shepherd her out the door.

'See you tomorrow, *liebling*,' Marlena called from the doorway. 'Now, you send a message if you're not well enough to work. May and I will manage without you if we need to.'

Fanny sighed as she pulled herself up onto the cart.

'It was because of Jack, wasn't it?' Jim said as he buckled the harness to the horse.

Fanny sat quietly, not sure how to answer.

'He can do that to a person, can Jack.' Jim climbed onto the seat beside her and clicked the reins as the horse moved off. 'You shouldn't take him so seriously.'

'I can't blame Jack for my mood,' Fanny said, her composure

restored. 'I shouldn't react so. I'm ashamed to have your aunt worry about me.'

'It's nearly your finishing time, anyway. The men will get pretty rowdy now. One of the riders had a win today and some of the others had bets on him so they'll all be celebrating. I left them with Jack. They'll probably carry on till midnight like they usually do, so they'll brighten him up.'

'I'm pleased somebody can.' Fanny was surprised at how piqued she felt at the idea. 'Don't you get fed up with trying to help him?'

'Not really. I see through all his bluff.'

'Bluff! Ungratefulness and self-pity, is what I'd call it.'

'You're very angry with him, aren't you?'

'I suppose I am, but I shouldn't let it affect my work. There are worse attitudes than Jack's.' She thought again about the young Islander and hoped he wasn't going to have any more trouble.

'Cheer up. We'll only be here a few more days. Then we'll be back to Murrayville.'

Fanny was surprised at the disappointment she felt. 'Timber cutting is hard work, I imagine,' she said, obscuring her feelings.

'It is, but we both like it. There are huge cedar trees, some of them six feet in diameter at the base. The ship builders want the forks brought down whole because they use them for the front of the boats. Being hauled up one of those giants is exciting, although getting the fork down without it crashing onto someone's head is quite a feat.'

'It sounds dangerous.'

'Sometimes.' He shrugged. 'I've seen some nasty injuries when trees fall. They don't always land where the cutters predict, and loading them is a challenge. I've seen men pinned under logs that roll when they're being lifted. A few have lost their legs that way. The bullock teams are a bit of a handful, too. Some of those animals get mighty agitated and they're giants of things.'

'You wouldn't like to do different work some day?'

'I wouldn't mind work on the river. When the creeks are flooded we can't get the logs out on the bullock teams so they have to be brought into town on the river. We roll the logs down to the water, harness sixty to a hundred together and float them down here to Grafton. I'd like to do more of that one day. I like working with wood.'

'And does Jack enjoy it as much as you?'

'I think he likes the challenge. He doesn't say much but he works hard. Some say harder than anyone they've seen.'

'Perhaps it's the way he works out his anger.'

'He's not always angry, you know.'

'You're very protective of him, aren't you?'

'Like I've said before, I owe him.'

'Please Jim, tell me what you mean by that? Everyone suggests it, even your mother implied it.'

'My mother?'

'Oh, dear. I wasn't going to say so because I thought it would upset Jack, but your mother left her gloves the day she came to the hotel and I took them back to her.'

'You went to her house?' Jim slowed the horse and turned to her. His face crumbled like that of a small child who knew he was in trouble and about to be punished.

'I was only there a few minutes. I met your half-brother and sister, Lance and Daisy.'

Jim nodded. 'Was he there?' His voice was shaky.

'You mean your stepfather?'

'Yes. Was he there?'

'No. I can see you're upset. I didn't mean any harm. I felt sad for your mother when she left the hotel in such a state.'

He flicked the reins again and the horse moved down the street. 'You shouldn't go there. It's not safe.'

'How is it not safe? What happened between you boys and your mother?'

'It's not between Ma and us. It's him! Fred Clifford's a monster. You mustn't go there and put yourself in danger.'

'What on earth did he do to you both?'

'Not to us both, Fanny. That's what I've been saying. It's what he did to Jack. He beat him. Sometimes I thought he was going to kill him. Jack wouldn't say so and he'd never show anyone, but he has scars on his back … big welts, where he was beaten to within an inch of his life.'

'Dear God. Why?' Fanny put her hand on Jim's arm. Her heart was thumping in her chest.

'For just about anything. I don't remember much about when Ma first married him. I was only four. Jack was seven and right from the start he must have tried to protect me from getting belted. Whenever Fred got mad Jack would step in front of me and take my whipping as well as his own.'

'Really?' Fanny shook her head, trying to imagine Jack as a young boy.

'Even when we got older, he always defended me,' Jim continued. 'I think he thought I'd not stand up to the beltings. Bob copped it too in the early days but he left home soon as he could get away. It was always Jack who stood up to Fred. He hated the way Ma was treated and the way Fred spoke to her. Jack took a hell of a beating but he wouldn't leave home till I was old enough to go with him. Then we went north and got onto a woodcutters' team, and we've not been home since.'

'That's terrible, Jim. But what about your mother? Does he hit her?'

'I never saw him hit her, but he yelled a lot. When his mother came to visit it was worse. I think she hated that her son married someone with German children. She's Spanish and she split up with Fred's father when Fred was young. Then she married an Italian man. He never came with her when she visited so I've never met him, but from things she said the Italians have it in for the Germans.'

'That's so sad,' Fanny said. 'I don't understand why people can't get along with each other. It's even harder to understand how a man could beat young children.' Her thoughts turned back to Jane Clifford. 'Your poor mother. Why did she put up with him?'

'She used to cry a lot when Fred belted the boys, but she couldn't stop him. She seemed to be having a new baby every year and she could barely cope with them, so she didn't know what to do for us. I think Fred only wanted Ma and his own children. He was glad to see the back of me and Jack when we left. When Jack told Ma we were going she begged us not to, but it would have been more of the same if we'd stayed. I think Jack's always been angry with her for marrying Fred in the first place.'

'I suppose she was lonely after your father died.' Fanny was trying to understand.

Jim nodded. 'I think it was hard for her with three small boys, and Grandfather Schmidt made it harder. So Jack ended up mad with all of them.'

Fanny took a deep breath and let it out with a whistle. 'That does explain a bit. I'm sorry you had to go through all that, Jim.'

'I didn't go through anything compared with Jack. In the end I knew he'd stand up for me and I'd hide behind him. I was a coward. A while back we got into a jostle with some drunken jackaroos in one of the pubs in Maclean. They started to push us around, just for the fun of it, I think. Jack took them on but I felt useless. I don't know what I'd do without Jack, but I know it's time I learned to stand on my own two feet.'

'I think it's wise not to go looking for a fight.'

'Oh, Jack's not one to look for a fight. I've seen him calm more than a few men down when they were heading for a tussle. He knows how to talk a man around when he's het up. He hates violence because he's had the brunt of it too many times. Unfortunately, some men with a few drinks in their bellies are impossible to stop any other way.'

'But why would they pick a fight with Jack?' Fanny could well imagine Jack's rudeness offending people, but according to Jim, he wasn't like that with the racing crowd. *He's such a difficult person to understand.*

'Sometimes it's because we're from German background. Jack refused to give up Pa's name for a long time, but we go by Smith now. It irks Jack to do so, but he'd rather avoid a fight if he can.'

'He's more surprising the more I hear about him, Jim. I do see now why you feel beholden to him, but you can't always excuse his behaviour. I understand he has a lot to be angry about but that

51

doesn't mean he can't be civil to someone who's trying to help him.'

'I know, Fanny. He tries to keep people at bay because he finds it hard to trust anyone, but I'm sure he respects you.'

'Respects me?' Fanny laughed. 'He has a funny way of showing it.'

'He's not used to being around women. But he likes the way you're so honest and you don't back down. I know he does.'

They were quiet for a few minutes as they approached Clarence Street where Fanny's sister lived.

'Will you go to the dance this Saturday night, Fanny?' Jim said.

'The dance?'

'There's always a dance at the end of the race week, in the community hall.'

'Yes, my parents used to take us up until the last few years. My Dad loved the races when he was younger. But Pop Franks hasn't been too good since my nana died, so Dad oversees the whole farm now. There hasn't been much time for dancing.'

'But you could go, couldn't you? Now that you live in town?'

'I like to go home on Saturday afternoon and have Sundays with the family. It's the only time I see them.'

'But you could stay over Saturday night and go home Sunday morning, couldn't you? Just this once.' Jim swallowed and his voice faded away.

'I don't think so, Jim. Thanks for asking but my parents are expecting me home. Our Sundays are precious to us. I'd miss it if I didn't go.'

'It must be wonderful to have such a happy family.' Jim's voice shook and Fanny thought he was close to crying.

'I'm sorry. I didn't mean to make you feel worse.'

'You didn't. I'm disappointed you won't be at the dance, that's all. I'll miss you when Jack and I head off.'

'I'll miss you too.' Fanny was surprised to feel the truth of her words. In spite of her annoyance with Jack and the sadness she felt about the life the boys had endured, she would miss her conversations with Jim.

'Please don't feel sorry for us, Fanny.' Jim touched her arm lightly. 'Especially for Jack. He'd be angry if he knew I'd told you all that. He doesn't like people to know and he hates to think people feel sorry for him.'

'I won't say anything, but I'm not good at keeping secrets. I've always been taught that honesty is the best policy.'

'When you've had a family like mine, you learn that keeping your thoughts to yourself is the best way to survive.'

'I see that, Jim. I understand more about Jack now, so I'll be careful what I say. Thank you for telling me. And thanks for bringing me home. This is Lizzie's house on the left.'

'I was glad to have some time with you without you and Jack getting into an argument. Don't be too careful with him, though. Jack will guess that I've told you things if he thinks you're tiptoeing around him.'

'It's a bit hard to win with someone like Jack, isn't it?'

'I've never thought about winning anything from him. Every time I've needed anything he's given it to me.'

***

'Are you sure Alf doesn't mind giving Mum and Dad a message?' Fanny asked her sister as she prepared to go to the hotel on Saturday morning.

Lizzie nodded. 'He has to ride to Brushgrove to pick up some building supplies from the steamer. It's only a few more minutes to the farm. I'm sure he'll be happy to have a catch up with Mum and Dad.'

'I appreciate it, Lizzie. If I get the early paddle boat in the morning I'll still be home for church.' Fanny adjusted her bonnet.

'So what made you decide to go to the dance tonight?'

'It's the two brothers I met at the hotel. The younger one is sweet and he's asked me three or four times in the last couple of days. They'll be going back to Murrayville on Monday so I thought it wouldn't hurt to stay over just this once.'

'You don't mean the German boys you were talking about

earlier, do you?' Lizzie looked distressed.

'Yes, I do, and please don't let's have this discussion again. I don't want to hear any of your prejudice.'

Lizzie drew in her breath. 'You said your visit with their mother didn't go well. How do you know you won't be causing more trouble by seeing more of those boys?'

'This has nothing to do with their mother. She'll not even know the boys are going to the dance. Now, enough. I won't discuss it further.' Fanny slapped her hands on the table and turned to leave the room.

'I'm sorry, Fanny. Let's not fight. You may as well go to the dance before you get married and have little ones to look after. There's little dancing then, except around the parlour floor, rocking them to sleep.' Lizzie's face softened into a smile.

'I know you wouldn't swap a dance for your beautiful children.' Fanny kissed her sister on the cheek. 'You're very fortunate. Although I'm well aware a good marriage doesn't happen by accident.'

'You don't have feelings for this German boy, do you?' A worried frown spread across Lizzie's face.

'Not those kind of feelings. I was thinking about his mother, actually. She seems to have made an unfortunate choice and it's caused a lot of unhappiness.'

Lizzie held up her hands. 'Like I said, Fanny. You be careful what you get involved in. You could end up with your fingers burned. Now I won't say another word.'

Fanny blew a kiss as she headed for the door. 'I must get off to work or I won't be finished in time for the dance.'

'Do that coat up, won't you? It's bitterly cold out there.'

'Yes, *Mother.*' Fanny laughed at Lizzie's tone. 'You have enough to mother of your own. I can take care of myself.'

CHAPTER SIX

Jack looked up as Fanny approached the table. He sighed and put his head down. He wasn't in the mood for defending himself, which he seemed to do every time Fanny was around. What it was about her that got him going he hadn't worked out. He hadn't felt like himself at all these past few days, which was most likely because of his foot, but there was something about Fanny that disturbed him. He looked across at Jim's face as it broke into a beaming smile.

'Did you hear that, Jack? Fanny just said she'll come to the dance with us. Isn't that great? You will save some dances for me, Fanny, won't you?' Jim went on without waiting for Jack to reply.

'Of course. I wouldn't be going if you hadn't asked me.' Fanny chuckled.

'Jack, you did hear me, didn't you?' Jim nudged his arm. 'Fanny's coming to the dance with us.'

'With *you,* Jim. She's going with you. I won't be going to the dance.' Jack continued eating his pie.

'He's kidding,' Jim said, his eyes still on Fanny. 'Of course he'll go. We always go to the dance.'

'There's no point in being at a dance if you can't dance. I'll be fine right here.' Jack looked across at his brother but couldn't catch his attention, which had been riveted to Fanny's face each time she'd been in the dining room with them. Jack had never seen his brother so infatuated.

'You don't have to dance to enjoy yourself, Jack,' Fanny

chided. 'You could enjoy watching others dance. You'll have plenty of company. There are never enough girls for all the men to be dancing at once from my recollection.'

'Maybe so,' Jack murmured without looking at her.

She dropped down into the seat beside him. The faint smell of her soap, mixed with kitchen odours, wafted across in front of him. He turned slightly towards her, trying not to be affected by the closeness of her. A few strands of wheat-coloured hair played around her ear. Her face was childlike, her expression inviting. There was no hint of the usual confrontation in her manner. He wasn't sure how to respond.

'Come on,' she said when he remained silent. 'Jim and I won't leave you sitting alone. We won't dance unless you have someone to talk to.'

Jack looked fully into her eyes for a moment and sensed a knot forming in his stomach. 'I don't need you to look after me.' He knew his voice sounded steely. He sensed the familiar wall go up around his feelings, but was helpless to change it.

'You'd prefer to be looking after someone else, wouldn't you?' Her eyebrows rose and she grinned.

'You think you know me, don't you? But you know nothing.' The last word was like a blast from his mouth. He sighed and looked down, wishing she wasn't so close to him. *I'm overreacting and I don't know why.*

'Now, that's enough, you two,' Jim interjected. 'It's silly to argue over going to the dance.' He tapped Fanny on the shoulder. 'If Jack doesn't want to go, then I'm sure there'll be men here having a drink. It's the last chance for some who'll be out in the bush for months.'

'So you don't want me to go then?' Jack frowned at his brother.

'Of course I want you to go, but I don't want you fighting with Fanny over it. It's not like you to be so argumentative.'

'Is that so? So now you're an expert on me, too. Seems you two have had your heads together.' Jack was surprised at how much the idea gnawed at him.

'Not at all, Jack. I've been at the track with you these past couple of days, haven't I? I gave up trying to figure out what goes on in your head a long time ago.' Jim laughed and began to rearrange the cutlery on the table.

'I wouldn't have thought I was that hard to figure,' Jack said. 'Not for my brother, anyhow.'

'You're right, Jack. Most of the time I understand you well enough. It's when we're around women that I get confused.'

'Women!' Jack scoffed. 'I wouldn't call this skinny girl a woman. She looks like she'd break in two if you twirled her around the dance floor more than once.'

Jim gasped and seemed lost for words.

Fanny stood up and planted both hands on her hips. 'You're so rude.' She swallowed before she went on, as if her words were choking her. 'I suppose you prefer your women well-rounded and buxom? Like German girls?' She almost spat the last.

He was shocked at her words and sensed his lips twitching as he searched for an answer. 'No, not like German girls.'

His shock was replaced by a deep sense of sadness. He wanted to look away from her, having no inclination to continue this line of talk. But their eyes remained locked on each other.

Fanny didn't move. Her eyes were green and glowing. He watched them soften as a crinkle formed around the corners of her mouth. She seemed to be holding back a grin. 'So are you coming to the dance or not?' There was a dare in her tone.

'I'll see,' he answered, dragging his eyes from hers and turning back to his plate.

'Can we have some more pie, Fanny?' Jim broke into the tension between them, his voice boyish.

'Certainly, Jim,' Fanny answered. 'I'm sure your aunt has saved some for you. She knows how you love her apple pie. You, Jack? Do you want pie too?'

'I think I will, yes,' he said, realising a smile was spreading across his face, a smile he was no more in control of than any of his other reactions around this frustrating girl.

Jack hobbled to the corner of the community hall, insisting that Jim not hold his arm as if he was a cripple. It still hurt to put his foot to the floor, but it wasn't so bad that he had to be carried. He dropped onto the bench and waved away Jim's attempts to put a chair under his foot. He hated people fussing over him.

His aunt had tried to give him a walking stick when he'd left the hotel that evening. She said it belonged to a customer who'd left it behind, but he knew better. It had been his grandfather's stick. He remembered seeing the old man hobbling around with it. *Aunty Giese knows I'd never use something of Grandfather Schmidt's.*

She was right in that, too. Jack wanted no reminders of his grandfather. Not that he ever forgot. His mind was often invaded by an image of his father and grandfather having an argument when he was three years old. He couldn't recall any of the words, because they were in the German language that he'd always found harsh and intimidating. Even now he could hear their shouting in his head. He could see the angry expressions on their faces. Sometimes he still had nightmares about that day.

Of course there had been many occasions after his father died, when he'd seen that same scowl and heard words of disapproval from his grandfather. Philip Schmidt had never spoken English in his home but the meaning behind his words was plain when he was angry. It was always about maintaining the German culture, about loyalty to one's roots, about keeping the bloodline pure. *But that wasn't possible for me. My blood was already contaminated.*

Aunty Giese had tried to explain Grandfather's passion for the German community. She'd also protected Jack and his brothers when Grandfather Schmidt had stood over them, trying to instill his ideas into their young heads. She'd shown nothing but love and care for Jack and his brothers, especially after their run-ins with Fred Clifford. Even now he shuddered as he remembered the many times he'd dragged Jim through the streets and banged on Aunty's door, desperate to save his brother from a beating like the one he'd taken himself from Fred.

Jack often wondered if his mother had only married Fred Clifford for his English name. Perhaps Fred hadn't shown his true colours before they'd married, but it didn't take long for him to reveal himself. Even as a young boy Jack had refused to take his stepfather's name, which no doubt increased Fred's disdain of him. He'd wanted to use his father's name in honour of him, rather than through any desire to be associated with his German roots, but the thought of succumbing to his grandfather's demands caused a deep conflict in him.

Sadly, he'd soon discovered that it wasn't only his stepfather who was riled by a German name, so he'd reverted to Smith to avoid unnecessary hostility. It had always been confusing and even now Jack struggled to know if there was anywhere he truly belonged.

There was little that Jack wanted to remember about his past and he grimaced at the thought that even the mention of his grandfather's walking stick could arouse all this feeling in him. Shaking his head, he focussed on the brass band that had begun playing. Uncle Hans was right in the middle of it. He had a beaming smile and was using his deep, melodic singing voice to get the gathering crowd into a party mood.

'What do you reckon, Jack? Glad you came?' Jim pushed a cake into his mouth and nudged Jack with his elbow.

'Probably.' Jack was grateful for his brother's loyalty and concern. He knew he should show it more.

He grinned as he watched couples dancing, kicking up their heels and spinning around the floor. Truth was, he didn't mind having an excuse not to get up. The dance was not his favourite part of race week. He loved riding Lightning, the feel of the horse under him, and the wind in his hair as they raced around the track. Of course it was great to win, but win or lose, he still enjoyed riding fast, joining his skill with that of the horse, becoming one with such a beautiful animal.

He also looked forward to being with other men who shared his love of racing and of horses. Men who, like himself, had been out in the bush for weeks or months and had wrestled with massive trees, pitted themselves against bullock teams, strong river currents, floods, snakes, freezing temperatures, blazing heat and bushfires. Jack loved the challenge of all that, too. Perhaps it was the only place he belonged. He knew his time in the bush had helped him grow into a man who was hard to rattle; a man who could work out how to solve most problems, and who could find a way to get along with most men. *Women, on the other hand, are a complete mystery.*

'Have you seen Fanny yet?' Jim sat forward and looked about the hall.

Jack bit into a cake and shook his head. 'Nope.'

He could see that Jim could hardly wait for Fanny to arrive. The two of them seemed to hit if off so well, and Jack wondered again why he was so easily rattled by the girl. He knew he hadn't been on his best behaviour this past week, but he was sure it was because of his disappointment at having Lightning stumble on the first day, putting an end to his planned enjoyment. It had been a relief when Uncle Hans said the horse would not have to be put down. He should have been more grateful that his own injury hadn't been worse. It was his pride as much as anything that had been hurt. He'd already decided he'd come back into town for the spring races in September. *Lightning and I will both be in good condition by then, and perhaps we'll have a better week.*

Jack realised Jim was no longer beside him and looked up to see his brother returning with a drink for him. He also had a plate of cakes, made by the local women, and much acclaimed as a highlight of the race week.

'Thanks for that,' he said, winking at Jim and moving along so he could sit back on the bench. 'Don't worry. I'm sure Fanny will be here soon.'

At that moment there was some jostling and laughter near the entrance. Jim rose and peered at the group for a moment before he sat back down. 'I hope she doesn't change her mind.'

'You really like her, don't you?'

'Sure, she's nice.' Jim's face coloured a little.

Jack could see that his brother had taken care in getting ready

60

for the dance. His hair was slicked back and his face scrubbed. He was wearing clean pants and a shirt he'd saved all week. Even his boots looked shinier than Jack had seen in years.

'So, how keen are you?' Jack asked.

'I don't know,' Jim answered, shuffling his feet. 'When you hardly see a girl for months, it's hard not to be taken by one as sweet as Fanny.'

'I suppose.'

'Don't you think she's pretty?' Jim chuckled. 'Or was she right and you prefer your women a little plumper?'

'Plumper wasn't the term she used.' Jack sensed his tone hardening.

'She was only joking. She didn't mean anything by mentioning the German thing.'

'How do you know what she meant?'

'I don't think it's in her to be mean. You get her going, is all. You've been pretty rude to her most nights at the hotel.'

'Have I?' Jack felt a little remorseful.

'I know you're making sure she doesn't get too close. You do that.'

'Do what?'

'You push people away.'

'Do I?'

Jack felt he'd been analysed this week a whole lot more than he was comfortable with. While he liked to reflect on himself he wasn't so keen on someone else doing it. Before this week Jim had always accepted him without question and trusted his judgment. It was Fanny who'd got under his skin the most, though. Always asking him questions, looking at him like she knew what was in his mind, and standing on her dig as if she was determined he was going to admit she'd guessed him correctly. It was unnerving.

'Come on, Jack. Let up for tonight will you?' Jim nudged him again. 'Let's enjoy ourselves. We've missed out on a lot this week already.'

'You got to race this past two days, didn't you?'

'Yeah, and that was great, but it's not the same without you racing along with me.'

'In front of you, you mean?' Jack smirked and bumped Jim's arm.

Jim laughed. 'Do you think you're ready to get back to Murrayville yet? I mean, is your foot going to be all right?'

'By the time we get up there on the river boat, I reckon I'll be walking fine. Have to be, won't I? We can't live on fresh air.'

'We haven't spent much this week, have we?'

'No. It saves a bit of money when you fall and sprain your ankle.'

Jim sniggered. 'You know what I mean. Anyway, I'm sure Bob will be glad to see us go. He'll get his room back to himself. It's been good to catch up with him though, hasn't it?'

'Yeah, that's been good.'

'He hasn't changed. Still doesn't say much. Like you.'

'Like me, eh? There's been a bit too much speculation this week about me, I think.'

He pushed his hand through his hair. He felt annoyed with Jim for blabbing about their family, and mad at himself for losing control. It wasn't new for Jim to talk so much, but Fanny seemed able to draw all kinds of personal things from Jim that other people refrained from asking about.

What's more, it was clear that Jim was completely smitten with the girl. Jack had a strange sensation about that as well, one he hadn't figured out yet. He didn't want Jim to get so tangled up with a girl that he'd give up woodcutting and stay in Grafton. Not that Jack wanted to control his brother's decisions, but he'd worry about his safety if he was in town. Jim would likely try to make up with their mother, and that would give Fred an opportunity to get to him again. Jack couldn't stomach that.

A shiver ran up his spine at the mere thought of Fred Clifford. He could hardly think about the man without the fear that one day he'd meet Fred again and not be able to hold back his rage. It was a good thing he and Jim would be gone from Grafton after this weekend. He'd have a good talk to his brother once they got away and remind him that he could still cause a cart load of trouble if he got talking about family like he'd been doing this past week.

'There she is.'

Jim's voice jolted Jack from his thoughts. When he looked up Jim was on his feet and waving at Fanny who was crossing the hall.

'Wow, she sure looks pretty.' Jim ran his fingers down the front of his shirt as if checking his buttons were straight.

'Yeah, well, how about you dance with her and don't let your mouth do all the work?' Jack was still trying to deal with his annoyance.

'What?'

'You know what I mean. Keep quiet about our family and concentrate on dancing.'

'Right,' Jim said, although he was clearly distracted. He waved again in Fanny's direction and watched her face light up with a smile as she headed towards them.

Jack sensed that Jim was holding his breath and he felt perhaps he was doing the same. He shook his head and took a swig of his drink.

'Hello there, Jim, Jack,' Fanny said. 'How are you both? All spruced up, I see.'

'It's the last night,' Jim said. 'We have to make it special. I was getting worried you weren't going to make it.'

'I was helping my sister get her little ones settled.'

'I imagine you're great with little ones.' Jim's face was beaming.

'It's one thing to be an aunty. It's quite another to be a mother. Much harder I think.' As soon as she'd said the last Fanny glanced at Jack and looked back to Jim with an apologetic expression. Jack sensed that the pair of them had some private exchange going on, like they'd made a pact of some kind. The notion disturbed him but he pushed it away.

'Aren't you two going to dance?' he said.

'How about it, Fanny?' Jim held out his hand.

Fanny laughed and Jack thought it sounded like a tinkling bell. 'Of course.'

Jack watched as Jim took her hand and led her into the middle of the floor where they were swallowed by a sea of other couples. He realised he had a knot in his stomach and rubbed it. *I must have eaten something that didn't agree with me.*

*****

It was well into the night when some of the men began to get rowdy. More than a few had left the dance for a time and visited one of the hotels. A small group not far from where Jack and Jim were sitting started to jostle each other. They became louder in their ribaldry; making fun of dancers and urging each other to break in and steal away a partner.

One of the group swayed towards where Fanny was dancing with a local boy. Jack watched as the man pulled at her shoulder and started jigging up and down. His crude invitation for her to dance with him was shrugged off by Fanny, who turned back to her partner. However, the man was not put off and a moment later Jack saw him shoving Fanny's dance partner away and grabbing at her arms. He rose and went to move forward, flinching with the pain in his foot as he did so.

'What's wrong?' Jim asked.

Jack pointed towards Fanny, who was now struggling to free herself from the man's clutches.

Jim jumped up from the bench. 'I'll get her,' he said, running towards the middle of the dance floor. Some of the couples had moved back to avoid what was clearly turning into a fight.

The young man Fanny had been dancing with recovered his footing and was now behind the intruder, pulling him away from Fanny. Jim reached for Fanny's hand and began to shepherd her to the edge of the ring of dancers.

'Come on, love,' the drunken man called after her. 'Share yerself around, eh? Yer don't know what yer missin', sure yer don't.'

He flung off the man who was trying to restrain him and launched himself again at Fanny. She gasped as her skirt was grabbed and she almost toppled to the floor. For a moment she leaned into Jim, then spun around, facing her attacker.

'Look here, mister. I'm not interested in dancing with you. You're drunk. Now, leave me alone.' She stood her ground, staring the man down.

'Sure, isn't it the luck of the Irish that I get a wild one.' He whooped, apparently excited by her courage. Again he came at her, regardless of the man behind him attempting to hold him back.

Jim put his arm protectively around Fanny's shoulder and turned to the intruder. 'Go away, you fool. Leave her alone. She said she's not interested in dancing with you.'

At that point Jack's patience ran out and he pulled himself to his feet.

'He's not to be reasoned with,' he said, coming up behind the wiry Irish man. He pulled the man around until they were face to face. 'All right, fella, it's time you were put out.'

With that he punched the man hard in the jaw, spinning his head sideways and sending him sprawling to the floor.

'You knocked him out.' Fanny's dance partner knelt beside the unconscious man.

'That's the idea,' Jack said. 'Somebody needs to drag him out into the fresh air where he can sober up. I can't manage that with this foot.'

He limped back towards his bench seat, leaving a ring of men and women staring at him with their mouths open.

Jim and Fanny waited until a couple of the Irish man's friends dragged him towards the door. As they headed back to Jack the musicians began to play again, having gradually stopped as the drama had unfolded.

'I suppose you want me to thank you for that,' Fanny said as she reached Jack, who was lowering himself to the bench.

'No need.' Jack let out a sigh and readjusted his foot.

'I wasn't going to, actually. Firstly, I don't believe hitting someone achieves much good, and I thought you, of all people, would hate the idea.'

Jack turned to her, surprised at her words. Before he could

think what to say, she continued, though her voice was softer. 'Besides, you might have done damage to your foot. It wasn't sensible to come rushing into the middle of the floor to rescue me.'

'I didn't rush to rescue you,' Jack snapped. 'I'm sure Jim would have done that. The fellow was spoiling the dance for everyone. His friends needed to know what happens to fools who get out of hand. There would have been another four or five trying the same thing if he got away with it, then there'd have been a lot more hitting. If you don't agree with the way I handle things, I'm sorry.' He held Fanny's eyes with his glare.

'He wasn't going to get away with it. I'd have sent him on his way myself,' Fanny said. She turned to Jim. 'Not that I'm not grateful to you both for caring.'

'He might have roughed you up, Fanny.' Jim was obviously shaken by the incident.

'I'm not unused to young men getting a little out of hand in the hotel, you know.' She aimed her words at Jack.

'I see.' Jack shrugged his shoulders. 'Next time I'll let you handle things yourself. I'm sorry I intervened.'

'Anyway, you should have been more mindful of your foot. You ought to still be resting it. It'll do you no good if it's not healed enough for you to go back to work.'

'You're a hard girl to please.' Jack shook his head. 'Just as well you don't need to worry about us for much longer.' He was aware that he was being defensive. *Blasted girl! Here she is again, bringing the worst out in me.*

'You're taking me the wrong way, Jack. I'm merely trying to express my concern.' Fanny's eyes flashed at him.

Jack thought how pretty she was when she stood her ground. *Damn, where did that come from?* He leaned back against the wall, relieved that in a day or two he'd be back in the bush where he felt in control.

'Do you want to stay on at the dance?' Jim patted Fanny's shoulder. 'I could walk you home if you like.'

'Thank you, Jim. I'd appreciate that. I am feeling tired.'

66

'You're not sorry you came, are you?'

'No, of course not. I've had a lovely time. The last few minutes can't take away from the fun I've had. I'm glad I came.'

'Good.' Jim let out a relieved sigh. 'I'd hate to think you regretted me talking you into coming.'

'You didn't talk me into coming, Jim. I made my own decision and I've no regrets.' As she said the last she looked at Jack and her eyes pierced his. His breath caught in his throat.

'Good night, Jack. I imagine you'll be gone by the time I get to work on Monday morning, so I hope you have a good trip up river and all goes well with the recovery of your foot.'

'I'm sure it will. Thanks for your concern.'

He smiled as warmly as he could, given that his throat felt constricted. He reached out to shake her hand in farewell and was horrified to see that his fingers were shaking.

'See, you've strained yourself,' she said, also noticing.

'Perhaps I have,' he admitted, preferring she think he was suffering from punching her aggressor rather than from the strange feelings that were churning in his stomach.

'Jim said the two of you are thinking of coming back for the spring race in September.'

'Maybe.' He was almost afraid of the depth of desire he suddenly felt to return. 'Perhaps I'll see you then.' She smiled and her eyes glistened.

'Here's your coat, Fanny.' Jim held her coat open so she could slip her arms into it.

'Thank you, Jim.'

'Will you be warm enough outside? It's pretty brisk.' Jim patted the shoulders of the coat as she straightened it and did up the top button.

'I'll be fine.'

'Right then.' Jim turned to Jack. 'Will you be all right here? I guess Uncle Hans will be packing up soon and I'll help him get everything into the cart when I get back. I won't be long.'

'I'll be fine, Jim. Stop fussing.' Jack waved him off.

'Goodbye, Jack,' Fanny said again. She looked about to say something else but Jim was already shepherding her towards the door.

Jack watched her walk away with his brother. She didn't look back. The disappointment that had been rising in him as they'd said goodbye now sat like a rock in his chest. He folded his arms across his ribcage and held tight. He felt foolish and confused by the emotions swirling around in him. *Jim is thoroughly smitten, any fool can see that, and if he is then I should just be happy for him.*

What Fanny felt, Jack couldn't tell. Perhaps she wouldn't give either of them another thought once they were gone. She saw so many come and go, especially at this time of the year, and there'd be plenty of young men who would find her attractive. If they could manage her strength of character, for she wasn't one to be dominated. *It's one of the things I like about her.*

There, he'd admitted it to himself. He did like her. None of it mattered, though, for he'd be back in the woods in a day or two and all this would be behind him. If he hadn't fallen from the horse he and Jim would have been sleeping under a fig tree by the river and racing every day. They might not have met Fanny at all. Or she'd simply have been the girl in the hotel who dropped his meals in front of him. He'd have been too busy talking with the other fellows about the races to notice her. *Wouldn't I?*

He wasn't sure. He wasn't sure how he felt about Fanny, about his brother's infatuation with her, about coming back into Grafton and seeing her again. He wasn't sure, and he hated being unsure. He caught the eye of one of the men from the race track and beckoned him over.

'Could I bother you for a drink? I'm still having a bit of trouble with this foot.'

'Sure thing, Jack. I'll get you one. I saw you earlier, rescuing the damsel in distress.' He laughed heartily. 'Probably messed up that ankle a bit, eh? But she looked worth it.' The young man was still chuckling as he headed for the supper table.

Jack dragged his fingers through his hair. 'Blasted girl!' he muttered.

CHAPTER SEVEN

Marlena breathed in the freshness of the dough as she kneaded. There were loaves of bread almost ready in the oven and the tantalising smell took her back to her first months in Grafton thirty-five years earlier. She shook her head. *Why had even bread been an issue for Papa?*

She cringed as she remembered him barking at the baker in German. '*Wie viel?*'

She'd leaned over the counter and quietly explained. 'My father wants to know how much for the bread?'

'Why didn't 'e say so?' The baker had scowled.

'Please be patient with us, Mr Broadbent. It's difficult for some to make the change.'

'Well, 'e best make more of an effort if 'e wants to fit in 'ere. The King's English is what's understood in these parts. You're not in Italy now.'

'We're from Germany, Mr Broadbent. I'm Marlena and this is my father, Phillip Schmidt. We've moved onto an allotment in Mary Street.' She'd nudged her father's elbow and nodded towards the baker. 'Papa, this is Mr Broadbent.'

The two had faced each other with blank stares.

'*Ich versteke nicht.*' Papa had continued in his own tongue, his steely blue eyes not leaving the other man's face. He'd stood almost head and shoulders above the young man behind the counter and looked down on him defiantly.

'Papa, please,' Marlena had implored.

'What'd 'e say.' The baker's scowl had deepened, his chest had expanded and he'd clamped his fists onto his waist. He was a stocky man and Marlena had been afraid he was about to challenge her father to a fight.

'He said he doesn't understand,' she'd explained. 'He's trying, Mr Broadbent, truly he is.'

'Tryin' is right,' Broadbent had sneered. 'Tryin' our patience is what. You continentals come 'ere an' think yer can live as yer did over there. Well not in my store, yer won't. I suggest yer find yer bread elsewhere.'

Marlena had pulled at her father's sleeve and guided him out of the bakery.

'Come, Papa, I'll make bread at home. But you must try harder. You can't expect people here to converse with you in German. What are you thinking?'

'I don't understand them. They don't speak English.' He'd spat out the words in German.

'Of course they speak English. They have their own accent, and their grammar is not always correct, but we must get used to it, Papa. Otherwise we won't be accepted here at all. You see those who refuse to try. They are ignored at best. There have been some awful rows. In future I will shop alone. We could starve to death before anyone serves us if you keep this up.' She'd grinned half-heartedly and patted his arm.

'I don't like their bread, anyway. It's soft and tasteless.'

'Yes, it's different. I will cook as you like it when we get home.'

His shoulders had slumped then and he'd slowed his pace. Turning to her he'd taken both her hands in his. She could still remember looking up into his handsome face, his features square and tanned, his jaw strong. Though his fair hair was graying, it had still been thick and always neatly brushed. He'd been an imposing figure, and although he could appear to be harsh and unbending, she knew that he'd have protected his family with his life.

'I'm sorry you are left with the cooking, my dear,' he'd said.

70

'It is not as I'd hoped.'

'I don't mind cooking, Papa. I like it, in fact. I was disappointed at home when Mama insisted I stay out of the kitchen. We will not have maids here, Papa. We must get used to a new way of living. I'm happy to cook.'

Papa had shaken his head and continued to walk. 'It should not be like this.'

Marlena had wrapped her arm around his and leaned into him. 'We can make a good life here, Papa. I know we can. We have one of the best allotments, with a cottage already built. Many have started in tents. We should consider ourselves fortunate.'

She'd gone on when her father made no objection. 'Look how your garden's coming along. Johan and August are working hard and some plants are growing already. We can grow vegetables, just as we did in Germany.'

His stride had made it difficult for Marlena to keep up.

'The vegetables are different here,' he'd said. 'The seasons are all wrong. Such heat in April. It's unheard of.' He'd waved his arm at the sky as if to reprimand it. 'And such animals. Kangaroos and wombats smashing the plants. I didn't know such animals existed.'

'Papa, you make problems where there are none. It's different, that's all. The land is fertile, as you promised. We've had good rain already in the months we've been here, as well as beautiful sunshine. What more could you ask for the beginning of a garden? We have seeds for carrots and onions and spinach. Soon you'll see a harvest for your work.'

'If the magpies and – what do they call them … galahs – don't steal all the seedlings.' He'd huffed and flung his arm about again. 'Anyway I have long hours at the factory. So little time for gardening.' His brow had furrowed. 'What do I know about soap? What do I care? Anyone can do this work. I am nothing but a labourer. I am ashamed.'

'No, Papa, you have nothing to be ashamed of. Soon your time at the factory will be past and you will concentrate on your garden. We have enough room for you to grow vegetables for others. You can teach others to garden. It will all be good, you'll see.'

'Wilhelm will not stay here. He talks already of his own farm, of growing coffee or sugar cane.' His voice had been full of disappointment. 'I had such hopes. I was a fool to believe I could succeed here.'

'No, you were not. This has been a good decision for our family. Give it time. Please don't be despondent.' She'd put her arm around his waist and squeezed.

'You're a good daughter, Marlena.' He'd paused in his stride. 'I want your mother to be proud of you. She worries that you'll not find a good husband, that you'll end up ...'

'An old maid? Is that what she thinks? I'm no beauty, Papa, but I doubt my time has passed yet. I'm not twenty. There's plenty of time for me to find a husband.'

'Of course you are a beauty, my dear.' He'd touched her cheek. 'Such a kind face and beautiful skin. Your mother worries about you being outside in this climate. She thinks the sun here is harsh.'

'I can't sit inside and embroider cushion covers as she does, Papa. Goodness, Mama has the house looking like our parlour in Frankfurt. I can't believe she brought so many of those things: bed covers, doilies, table centres. All those ornaments and trinkets. Who does she think is going to dust and polish them? She must adjust to life here, Papa. She can't lock herself away and pretend she's still in Germany.' Marlena's voice had risen uncharacteristically. 'Forgive me, Papa. I don't mean to be disrespectful.'

'You must be understanding with your mother.' His tone had held a deep sadness. 'She's used to the life of a lady. This is difficult for her. You can't expect her to change overnight.'

'Of course not, but I want to help her accept the changes that are inevitable.'

When they'd reached the gate of their allotment Marlena had paused and looked into her father's eyes. 'We must speak English, Papa. We must try and fit in. You need to help Mama to do this. Please.' She'd stretched up and kissed his cheek.

'I'll try, dear,' he'd said in English, shaking his head. 'Anna and

72

Johan barely say anything in German already. We can't understand our own children in our own home. How can that be right?'

'They've been at school for a couple of months now, Papa. All the German children are learning English, and they learn quickly. They don't want to be different. It is right.'

'I don't want them to lose the language of their birth. Surely they can retain that as well.'

'I'm sure they will, Papa. Some of the local children are interested to hear them speak in their own tongue. They're amused by it.'

He'd frowned and his voice had risen angrily. 'It is not for entertaining the locals that my children will remember who they are and from where they have come. In our home I will see to it that they respect their heritage.'

With this he had turned on his heels and marched up the dirt path to the front door of their cottage. Marlena had followed him, shaking her head, and wondering if she was expecting too much of him in a short time. She had prayed for strength and wisdom, then headed to the kitchen to make bread, just as he liked it.

***

'My bread,' Marlena shrieked as she came back into the present and saw smoke coming from the stove.

She grabbed her mitts and pulled open the oven door.

'Papa, even now you cause me grief,' she mumbled.

'What's that smell?' Hans came through the back door. 'It's not like you to burn things, love.' He eyed her suspiciously as she rose and dumped a tray of blackened bread on the bench.

'Don't start, Hans.' She wrinkled her nose at him.

'Mind somewhere else?' he asked. 'Didn't I say you're to stop worrying about those boys? They are not children anymore. Jack is almost back on his feet. It did him good to go to the dance last night, I'm sure.'

'Is that so?' Marlena stood tall and put her hands on her hips. *What do men know about these things?* 'He didn't seem in any better a mood this morning to me. He reminds me of Papa. He's so stubborn and fractious on the outside, but I know he's hurting on the inside.'

'And you want to fix everything.' Hans rubbed her shoulders. 'It can't be done, love. You should have learned that a long time ago. Haven't you tried to make everyone happy for long enough?'

She shrugged and turned into his chest. 'I was thinking of Papa, actually. For all his harshness, he only wanted the best for his family. Australia was to be the promised land for us. I'd like to think he could rest in peace, knowing his grandchildren all had a secure future.'

'Most of them have. And if Jim and Jack are a little slow in settling, then you'll have to trust it will happen in God's time.'

Her eyes filled with tears and they rolled down her cheeks for a moment before Hans brushed them away.

'If only August had lived to see his boys grow up. Things would have been so different.' She sniffed back more tears.

'They might have, love. But it wasn't to be. Only God knows why these things happen.'

'I suppose if they'd had their father, they might not have needed me so much, eh? I can't say I regret the love they gave me when they were young.'

'There, you see? There's always a brighter side to even the worst of situations. What would have happened if they hadn't had you to care for them through those bad years?'

'I only did what any aunt would do. Those dear little boys, so frightened and confused. I loved them so much.' She looked up into his eyes, then snuggled into his chest again. 'I still love them as if they were my own, Hans, but it wasn't the same for you as having your own sons.'

'We've been through all this before, Lena. It's something I accepted many years ago.'

'I know, and I love you for it, but sometimes I still wonder. There's my brother, Wilhelm, God rest his soul. He and Magda had eleven beautiful children. Anna and Richard have nine, John and Mary three … and me not able to carry a single one past a few months.' She wiped her eyes. 'God must have His reasons.'

He pulled her close and patted her back, then held her shoulders

74

as he looked into her eyes. 'We have much to be grateful for, Lena. We've done our sorrowing over not being blessed with children, but we must keep focussed on the good things we do have. Isn't that how we've managed all these years?'

She nodded. 'Sometimes I forget that I decided a long time ago to be grateful for what I have, rather than miserable about what I don't have. And that hasn't been so hard, not with you by my side.' She hugged him. 'I'm a silly old woman sometimes.'

'You're not a silly old woman at all,' he chided. He took her face in his hands and kissed her on the nose. 'My beautiful Marlena, that's what you are. Now, dry those eyes. I think you'll need to make more bread for your nephews and the rest of the hungry hoards who'll be here for lunch. Can't let your reputation down.' He grinned and patted her backside.

'Right you are, my love.' She returned his kiss as May walked through the door.

The young girl's cheeks flushed rosy and she looked away. 'I'm sorry, Mrs Giese. Am I too early?'

'Not at all, love.' Hans grinned. 'Just in time.' He turned and left by the back door.

'I've burned a batch of bread, is all,' Marlena said, chuckling. 'How about you help me get another batch ready?'

***

All through that morning Marlena's memories of her nephews as children kept coming into her mind. She wondered what she might have done differently from the start. She'd tried to befriend Jane while August was sick, despite Papa's disapproval. But when August died, Jane had been so devastated that she'd left the boys with her and gone back to her parents at Mororo. It seemed only natural that she would need her mother and father, but to leave the boys seemed to Marlena to be most unnatural.

Even when she returned months later, Jane was clearly not coping and on three or four occasions over the next two years she'd left them again. That had convinced Papa that she was an unfit mother. The boys were better off with Marlena as far as he was concerned, and he'd taken every opportunity to influence them towards their German heritage. It had all been a disaster, and Marlena had felt caught in the middle; wanting to do the best thing by the boys, but conscious they were Jane's responsibility and wanting to help her be a mother to them.

When Jane took up with Fred Clifford, everything became so much worse. He took over Jane's life, made all her decisions, and once they were married, made it clear that he would enforce his will by whatever means necessary. Jane was quickly pregnant, and gave birth to Fred's children almost yearly for the next six years.

Marlena's blood ran cold whenever she remembered the wide-eyed terror on the faces of the boys as they pushed their way through her back door; Jim shaking from head to toe and jabbering about his stepfather having thrashed Jack. Jack would insist his brother be quiet and would refuse to show Marlena where he'd been beaten. Bob would pace about, looking as if he was about to explode. Jim was the only one who'd allow her to hold him until he calmed down. The other two would sit in a corner and whisper in growling tones, as if planning some dreadful revenge. Sometimes freshly baked bread or scones with lashings of jam eventually brought pained smiles to their faces.

Sending them home always broke Marlena's heart. Hans had confronted Fred on one occasion, mostly to prevent Marlena from barging into their home and giving him a piece of her mind. But that had ended badly. Fred had merely smirked at Hans's warning and said he was head of his home and would discipline the boys as he thought necessary. Marlena had spoken to the local constable but he'd said that domestic disputes were not in his brief, and he'd be in trouble with his superiors if he interfered, especially as Fred was well known in the town and had connections with many of the businessmen.

Speaking to Jane had never been successful. She was obviously terrified of her husband and insisted it would be better if Jack didn't stand up to him so much. Fred was a man who demanded a great deal of respect, she'd said, and it was hard for him to have young boys around who were not his own children and clearly didn't like him. Jane would dissolve into tears at the end of any conversation and eventually refused to see Marlena at all.

In hindsight, Marlena could see that Jane felt helpless and even jealous that her boys found comfort and solace in their aunt's home. As each of them left home she clearly resented Marlena for her continued connection with them.

What else could I have done but take them in, love them, and try to help them? Hans was right. Like a mother hen, she still wanted to gather them into her arms and make them happy, even though she knew in her heart it would take a power greater than hers to accomplish that.

CHAPTER EIGHT

Brushgrove, Woodford Island, September, 1891

'Good morning, all.' Fanny smiled as she entered her parents' kitchen.

She glanced around the table where her five younger sisters and her young brother were sharing out a pile of fried eggs and toast. A couple of them mumbled a greeting with their mouths full. The rest nodded and went on with their chatter and eating.

'Aren't you chipper this morning?' Her father glanced up from his newspaper and winked at her.

'Aren't I always chipper?' Fanny laughed as she helped herself to toast and jam.

'Not always,' her mother said. She turned from the stove and grinned at Fanny. 'Although you have been getting excited about the spring race day this last week.'

Fanny gave her mother a pleading look. 'Mum, you promised.'

'What did you promise her, Betsy?' her father asked, his fork balanced in front of his mouth, laden with egg.

'Nothing,' Betsy answered. 'Nothing for you to worry about, Francis. Just girl talk.'

'Oh, that.' Francis said with a chuckle. 'I guess I'll know when I need to, then?'

'Mum, you told him.' Fanny scowled.

Betsy looked remorseful. 'I might have let it slip that you're looking forward to seeing a young man who might be coming to the spring race, that's all.'

'That's all! That's what I asked you to keep between you and me.' Fanny aimed a mock frown at her mother. 'They might not even come, Dad. So don't ask me about them, all right?'

'Them? How many young men are you planning to see?'

'It's the one you've been getting letters from, isn't it?' Betsy said.

'I've had two letters from Jim, that's all. He's out in the bush, woodcutting. I'm surprised he's been able to send any letters at all. He asked if he could write to me the last night of race week in July and I said I didn't mind.' Fanny tried not to look flustered.

'You've written back, haven't you?' her mother asked.

She nodded. 'I've written a couple of times. Jim told me to send letters to the general store in Murrayville. They handle the post there, but it's a tiny village, so I don't know how often the mail would get through.'

'It sounds to me like he's keen, love.' Francis smirked.

'I only met them during race week in July, Dad. I barely know them, but I think they get pretty lonely out in the bush. They're with a team of woodcutters but they don't get much news from the outside world.'

'You keep saying *they*. Is there more than this Jim?' her father persisted.

'Jim works with his older brother, Jack. They were both here in July and I imagine they'll both come back for the spring races.' Fanny felt as though she was colouring up in the face and she moved from the table to pour herself a cup of tea.

She noticed a look pass between her mother and father and wished she'd not mentioned meeting the boys, but it would have been most uncharacteristic of her not to talk to her mother about anything that was on her mind. And Jack and Jim had definitely been on her mind this past two months. Jim's two letters had said little about Jack except that his foot was completely healed and he was working hard, as he always did.

Jim's other news was about funny incidents that happened while he was sawing or rolling logs, about the small animals they were trapping and eating and how he was looking forward to his aunt's cooking come September. He'd asked lots of questions about how she was getting on, what she was doing on her Sundays off, and whether she would come to the spring race the first Saturday in September and watch him ride. He was sure his aunt would give her some time off.

Fanny had mixed feelings. She was excited at the thought of seeing Jim again but she was aware that her feelings were affected by her hope that Jack would be there, too. She was troubled by the effect that thoughts of Jack had on her and wondered if her feelings about him would also trouble Jim.

She hadn't said much to her mother about Jack, mostly because she didn't know what to say. She could hardly describe her feelings to herself. Jack had been rude to her. He'd been offhand and dismissive. She couldn't understand what kept drawing her thoughts to him. She'd woken on many a morning conscious of an image of his face, his smouldering eyes and that hint of a smile around his mouth. There was something about him that intrigued her. It all sounded so silly, even to herself.

Fanny's thoughts were interrupted as her brother, Thomas, came into the kitchen, pushing hair back from his face and yawning. He was a welcome distraction. He had the wiry build of her father, but still a boyish face, and this morning he looked like a child still half asleep.

'Hello, Thomas. I went to bed before you arrived last night. I was exhausted by the time I got home, but I'm so glad to see you.' She moved across the room and threw her arms around his neck. He shook his head as if to fully wake himself and hugged her.

Pushing back, she looked him up and down. 'It's been an age since I've seen you. You've grown up. I think you're taller.'

'I turned seventeen since I was here last, Sis. Had a growth spurt. It must be the cane cutting. It's jolly hard work.'

'How are Aunt Matilda and Uncle Bernie?'

'They're fine … and all seven kids. Uncle Bernie reckons Aunt Matilda will have another one early next year. She gets a certain look, he says. Not that I'd notice.'

'I don't suppose you would, Thomas,' Betsy said. 'And speaking of another one, I think our Alice is calling from the bedroom. She must have just woken, poor pet. She didn't have a great sleep last night. More teeth on the way, I think.'

'That's like Lizzie's little Eliza,' Fanny said. 'There's your eldest daughter with a teething infant and you with the same, Mum. I think it's time you stopped getting that look about you, don't you?'

'I'll get Alice, love.' Francis patted his wife's arm and rose from the table. 'I don't think I want to hear the rest of this conversation.' He sniggered and kissed her on the cheek. 'You'd best lead your oldest son to the food before he collapses. He has that hungry look.' He was still chuckling when he disappeared into the next room.

'I am hungry, Mum.' Thomas headed for the table. 'Those eggs look good.'

'They'll be cold, love.' Betsy shook her head. 'I'll do some fresh ones for you. We've plenty of eggs.'

'And plenty of kids,' Fanny said, looking along the table. Four of her younger sisters were giggling with their heads together at the far end. They were aged between nine and sixteen and seemed to be always twittering about some boy or other from school. Fanny had never been as interested in romance as they seemed to be. They had chided and teased her for not having a beau ever since Lizzie married three years earlier.

I wonder what they'd think of Jim? The thought surprised her for she had not for a moment seriously considered Jim as a prospective husband. It had occurred to her often over this past two months, however, that Jim might consider her a prospective wife. She turned her attention back to her brother.

'Sit here with Frankie and Ivy.' She shepherded Thomas towards the two youngest children at the table. 'Move along you two. Your big brother hasn't seen you for an age. I'm sure you've missed him, Frankie, what with all these girls and their silly talk.'

Fanny chuckled as she and Thomas wriggled onto the bench beside the six-year-old. Frankie beamed up at his older brother. Four-year-old Ivy put her arm through Fanny's and snuggled close to her.

'Are you coming to church with us, Fanny?'

'Of course I am, sweetie. I love our Sundays together.'

'Goodie,' Ivy said with a toothy smile.

'Now, Thomas.' Fanny turned again to her brother. 'Tell me, do you like living with Aunt Matilda and Uncle Bernie at Palmers Channel?'

'It's fine,' Thomas said, his mouth already crammed with toast. He swallowed awkwardly before he went on. 'Aunt Matilda is a bit of a worry wart, but Mum warned me she would be. Uncle Bernie's pretty easy going but he works like a trouper.'

'It was good of him to give you a few days off to come home.'

'Yeah, he said he'd be in the bad books with Mum if he didn't make sure I kept up with the family. Plus, he knew that I wanted to come back for the September races since I didn't get home in July. There'd been heavy rain and he wanted us all on hand in case we had to sure up the levy banks around the river. Last year a few of his fields were flooded and it ruined a lot of the cane.'

'Dad said he's been getting Bodington ready for you to ride.'

'Yep, I'll take him out after breakfast so he gets used to me before Saturday.'

'Are you going to win the race on Saturday, Thomas?' Ivy beamed.

'I'd like to think so,' Thomas said. 'We'll see. As long as I finish and Bodington does his best I'll be happy. Racing's meant to be fun, so we won't be too worried about coming first. I'm sure there'll be lots of competition.'

'What will you win?'

'A ribbon.' Thomas was distracted by the plate of hot fried eggs his mother laid in front of him. 'Maybe a few shillings if someone bets on me.' He plunged his knife and fork into the centre of one of the eggs and watched the yolk run across his toast. 'Are you going to come and see me ride, Fanny?' he asked when he'd devoured his first mouthful.

'Perhaps,' Fanny answered. 'I'll see if I can get some time off on Saturday. There'll be a few extras at the hotel. Most of the racers who bring in horses from out west stable them at The European and have rooms there themselves. There'll be a lot of meals to serve.'

'Not in the middle of the day when the race is on. They'll all be at the track.'

'I guess so. I know there's always food stalls at the track. I think Mrs Giese wants to set one up herself. She'll sell a cart load of her pies if she does.'

'Maybe you could sell them for her. That way you'd get to watch the races and work.'

'I'll ask, Thomas. It would be fun to be there.' As Fanny spoke she could feel her heart quicken. An image of dark eyes flashed into her mind. *Would he be as cold and angry as he had been in July? Perhaps if he's able to ride he'll be happier.* She felt a warm rush of pleasure.

'Are you all right, Fanny?' Her mother leaned over her. 'You look flushed.'

'I'm fine, Mum. I'm going to get dressed for church. Will you be able to go, with Alice so restless?' Fanny glanced across the table at her youngest sister who was now fidgeting on their father's lap.

'Alice will be so busy watching everyone else she'll forget about her teeth. You know what a social butterfly she is.'

'She's only eighteen months old, Mum.' Fanny shook her head as she pushed back from the table and headed for the bedroom.

She found it hard not to think about Jack as she readied herself for church. *Will he stay at The European? If he's focused on getting his uncle's horse ready for the race, will he even speak to me?* She looked at herself in the small mirror in the bedroom she shared with three of her sisters. She would be turning nineteen at the end of the month. Suddenly she felt old.

So many girls her age were married and already having families. She'd never been bothered about it before. She'd always felt marriage would happen naturally, with someone she'd meet at church, who would make a wonderful impression on her mother and father. Someone who would be charming and respectable and good-mannered. None of this sounded a bit like Jack, although why she was thinking about marriage and Jack at the same time was beyond her understanding. *It's so improbable as to be ridiculous*. She shook her head, chasing away her silly thoughts, and drew her hair back into a sensible bun.

***

'Are you sure you can handle this lot, Fanny?' Hans turned to her as he finished setting up a barrow loaded with pork pies, apple pies and griddled biscuits.

'Of course I can, Mr Giese. I'll be fine. I've got this apron with a pocket for the change, and a tin to transfer the money to. I'll put it under the barrow where I can keep an eye on it. I have this pile of papers to wrap the pies. I'm all organised and I reckon I'll sell this lot in no time at all.'

'Lena has another batch in the oven. She'll want me to bring them up a bit later. Some of these young men can be larrikins when they get riled up, though. I'm not comfortable leaving you here alone.'

'I'm not alone, Mr Giese. There's a crowd gathering.' Fanny glanced around at the people milling in groups at the edge of the race track. On the outskirts she could see a large group of blacks, who were always well represented at the races. Their chatter and laughter could be heard in the crisp morning air. 'My brother, Thomas, is here somewhere and he'll be looking out for me.'

'Jack and Jim were in the stables earlier getting the horses rubbed down. They'll be here somewhere too. They've done nothing but ride for the past two days and they're fixed on winning a couple of these races. I'll be surprised if they stop for long to eat, but maybe they'll check on you. Otherwise they'll be starving come nightfall and they'll eat enough to feed a dozen horses.' Hans laughed and slapped his thigh.

'It's good that Jack's able to race this time, Mr Giese. He seems more relaxed than he was in July. He was almost sociable last night in the hotel.'

'Yeah, he's a different boy, all right. He was mighty frustrated in July. I think he's gone in every race today, trying to make up for

84

it. There's a lot betting on him as well. He's quite a rider, you know.'

'So Jim says. Jack doesn't say much about himself.'

'No, he doesn't, but Jim makes up for him, doesn't he?' Hans eyed Fanny curiously. 'He seems quite taken with you. Have you noticed that?'

'Jim? Yes, he's been very friendly.' Fanny tried to control the flush that crept up from the collar of her blouse. 'He's written to me a couple of times since July. I don't think he sees enough people with that wood cutting. He needs to be in a more civilised job, I reckon.' She felt awkward and laughed lightly, hoping Mr Giese wouldn't see her discomfort.

'I'd be surprised if it wasn't more than that, love, but you need to remember that those boys are gone for the best part of the year. They're not likely to come back into town to live, so anyone who gets involved with them ought to know the situation. I wouldn't want you to get hurt.' There was genuine concern in his expression.

'You don't need to worry about me, Mr Giese.' Fanny kept her voice even but she was aware of butterflies in her chest.

'Right, if you're sure about staying to sell these pies, then I'll get back. I'll come with the next lot in a while. I think your first customers are on their way.'

Fanny raised her eyes and saw a group of young men approaching. They were laughing and nudging each other.

'You sellin' pies, love?' one said, a broad grin on his face.

'I am.' Fanny looked about the group. 'These are the best pies you'll find in town. They're made by Mrs Giese of The European.' She beamed at the young man at the front of the group. Four others were pushing and jostling behind him.

'Ask her if she sells kisses as well,' one called. His remark was followed by an outburst of guffaws.

Hans, still only about twelve paces from Fanny, turned and strode back to the barrow. 'Right, lads. I'm happy to see you drool over my wife's pies, but you say one word out of line to Miss Franks and I'll have your hides. Do you understand?'

Hans stood at his full height, which was taller than any of

the boys. His shirt strained over his well-built chest. His sleeves were rolled up, showing muscled, tanned arms. He looked much younger than his sixty years, and well able to handle himself in a fight. All of the boys shrank away at his words, backing into each other. Their faces dropped.

'We meant no harm,' one stuttered. 'Just a bit of fun.'

'Then have your pies here and fun elsewhere,' Hans responded, his voice hard.

'Yes, sir,' another of the boys answered. 'I'd like a pie, Miss.' He held a hand out with some money in the palm.

Fanny could see that it was sweaty and shaking. She smiled to herself as she picked out a pie and wrapped it in a small piece of paper.

'Sixpence,' she said. 'Thank you.'

The others followed suit in turn and in a few moments all were on their way biting into their pork pies.

'I think I could have managed, Mr Giese.' Fanny looked to her employer, who'd watched, stony-faced while the boys purchased their pies.

'Perhaps, love, but I thought it wouldn't hurt to let them know that you've help at hand.'

'Thank you.' She smiled. It warmed her heart to know that she had such caring employers. 'Look, here comes my brother, Thomas. I'll definitely be able to deal with him.' Her laugh tinkled across the grass.

Thomas's face lit up as he walked toward her. He was digging into his pocket by the time he reached the barrow.

'This is Thomas, Mr Giese. Thomas, this is my employer.' She watched as the two men shook hands.

'These look mighty good.' Thomas licked his lips. 'I'll have a pork one and an apple as well. I'll be riding soon, Sis. Watch out for me, won't you?'

'I'll try, Thomas. I can't leave the pies but I'll certainly see you start and finish. I can see the starting line from here.'

'Good luck with the race, Thomas.' Hans smiled and turned

86

to leave. 'I must get back now. Lena will have my hide if I'm not there when the next lot of pies are cooked. Nice to meet you, Thomas. Look after your sister, eh?'

Thomas nodded as Hans walked away. He was biting into one of the pies. 'Do you need looking after, Sis?'

'Of course not. Mr Giese is being protective.'

'I'll be off then. See you later.'

'Ride carefully, Thomas. No falling off Bodington. Dad will be upset if you hurt his horse.' She chortled. 'He'd like to be here riding himself, you know.'

'I'll be careful.' Thomas waved as he walked away.

CHAPTER NINE

Lightning's muscles rippled against Jack's knees. The white fencing around the track slipped past his vision in a blur. He leaned into the horse's neck and gripped the reins, the sound of thundering hooves loud in his ears.

'Good boy,' he whispered, sensing that winning the race was as exciting for Lightning as it was for him.

From the corner of his eye Jack could see there was another horse not too far behind him. He couldn't tell if it was Jim or one of the other riders. It didn't matter. They were almost home. There would be no looking back. It was one of the things he loved about racing. He made it a policy never to look back. There was far too much of that in his life without bringing it onto the race track.

If only I could always focus on what's ahead instead of what's behind all the time. As the thought flitted across his mind he crossed the finish line to hoorays and shouts, and let Lightning pull up in his own time. Turning, he grinned at Jim, who was one of three almost crossing the line together.

'I'll get Lightning rubbed down and watered, and then I'll get us a pie,' he called.

Jim nodded and waved. He looked like he'd be a few minutes catching his breath. Jack could see the same excitement surging through his brother as he felt himself.

Half an hour later he headed towards the pie cart, where Fanny was pushing her remaining pies to the front of the barrow.

She gasped as she looked up into his eyes. 'Jack! You scared me. I didn't see you coming.'

'Sorry. I didn't mean to frighten you.' He smiled and was glad when she responded with a grin. 'The pies look good.'

'They're Mrs Giese's – your aunt's – but of course, you know that.' She seemed a little flustered.

He pushed back his hat and wiped sweat from his forehead. 'I've been looking forward to having one,' he said, pulling his money pouch from his pocket.

'You seem much happier than the last time you were here.' She reached for a paper bag.

'I'm not invalided anymore, so it's hardly surprising is it?' He tried to keep his tone light, but sensed they were heading for one of their sparring matches. *Why do we always do this? I don't know why I can't talk calmly to this girl.*

'No, it's not.' She took a deep breath and stared at him with brazen eyes, her shoulders going back in a defensive stance. 'It's obvious what makes you happy, then.'

The three times he'd been in the hotel for a meal in the last few days had been the same. She'd been friendly, shown an interest in Jim's description of their trip down river on the log raft. She'd enquired about their campsite on the river bank. Were they comfortable? Did they need anything? Were they hoping to win at the races? He'd tried to join in the conversations pleasantly, but inevitably it had ended with him feeling like they were in some kind of duel which could turn into an argument at any moment.

He certainly hadn't been morose, as he knew he'd been in July, but still he felt she was trying to draw him out, testing his mood. He'd worked hard at curtailing the temptation to respond with some smart retort, although one had often come to mind. Obviously his humour didn't go down well with her, which left him at a loss as to how to get along with her.

Even now she was staring as if daring him to smile. 'So do you want a pie or not?' 'Sure do, and one for Jim as well.' He gave her his best smile.

'Are you racing again soon?'

'Pretty soon. Jim's hoping you'll be watching.'

'I'll watch as much as I can from here.'

'Jim will be on the piebald gelding. Do you know what that looks like?'

'Of course I do. My father has horses, you know. And what will you be riding?'

'Lightning, of course.' *She knows which horse I ride, so why is she asking?*

'Of course, the black stallion.' She took the money he was holding out in his palm. As she did their fingers brushed together and a burning sensation raced up his arm. She pulled back as if also shocked and began to fiddle with the change in her pocket.

'I gave you the right money. No change needed,' he said.

She looked up and glared at him. 'Then you'd best be on your way. You don't want to miss your race.'

'I certainly don't. I'll send Jim over for a sweet pie later. To celebrate my win.' He grinned and tipped his hat. *That sounded cocky. It's sure to annoy her. What's wrong with me?*

'You do that.' Fanny shook her head as she transferred money from her apron pocket into the tin under the barrow and began rearranging the few remaining pies so that they were in a line at the front of the barrow.

He wanted to say something else, something that would relieve the tension between them but before he could think of anything another voice broke into the awkward quiet.

'You've done well, Fanny.'

They both jumped and turned to see his uncle a few feet away, carrying a large box.

'Mr Giese, you startled me,' Fanny said.

'I noticed. You haven't been bothered by more young larrikins, have you?'

'Not at all. The men are all much more interested in the pies and their races than they are in bothering me.'

'Good. Here's another lot. This will be enough, Lena says.

90

She's started cooking for dinner now. She wants to do a stew and she's cutting up vegetables.'

He turned to Jack and grinned. 'Enjoying your share, I see. How's Lightning going?'

'Great, Uncle Hans,' Jack said, finding his voice.

'Does Mrs Giese have enough help?' Fanny asked his uncle, as if Jack was no longer there.

'Yes, she has two girls with her. They're going nineteen to the dozen with their knives. It's a good place to be out of.'

He chuckled as he emptied the box of pies until the barrow was again covered with a mixture of the deep browned pork pies and the lighter golden apple ones.

'They look wonderful,' Fanny said. 'I'm sure the riders will be back for more soon. Quite a few of the races are over already.'

'I'll be back in an hour to get you and take the barrow back to the hotel. See you then. You're doing a great job. See you later, Jack.' His uncle patted Fanny on the shoulder and hurried off.

Jack nodded at Fanny and turned to go, deciding it was better to say nothing more, than to risk making things more strained between them. He could feel her eyes following him but had no idea what she was thinking.

***

A little while later Fanny looked up to see Jim beaming at her as he approached.

'Did you win?' she asked, returning the smile.

'Came second, of course. Jack was in the race.' He shrugged. 'Can't beat that brother of mine.' He huffed. 'He always wins.'

'Does he just?' Fanny still felt annoyed, though she couldn't work out why. A tear welled in her eye. Conversations with Jack never went the way she would have liked. It was so much easier to talk with Jim. There was no sense of competition, no discomfort. She felt cared for and special when Jim spoke to her. *So why on earth am I so bothered by Jack? They'll both be gone again in a day or two anyway, so it's foolish to be so affected.*

'Why don't you go in a race that he's not entered in, then?' she said, as calmly as she could.

'I don't mind him beating me, Fanny.' Jim grinned. 'He's the better man. That's the truth of it.'

'Maybe in some ways, Jim, but there's a lot about you that makes you the better man.'

'I'm glad you think so, Fanny.'

Jim looked at her with such adoration in his eyes that she wished she'd not encouraged him. She didn't want him to get the wrong idea. Not that she had a clear idea of what she felt anyway.

'I've only a few apple pies left now,' she said. 'Have you come for one?'

'Yes, and for Jack. He said we should have apple pies to celebrate.'

'Yes, he said he'd be celebrating his win. He's confident, isn't he?'

'He knows he's a good horseman if that's what you mean. Everyone does. The other riders all respect him a lot. He doesn't boast about it, though.'

'It sounded like he was boasting to me.' Fanny knew her voice had an edge.

'He likes to bait you. He enjoys a bit of banter.'

'Is that so? Well, he can be annoying.'

'I told you before. He's not used to women. Doesn't bother with them at all most of the time.'

'Oh?' Fanny's stomach twisted.

'I think it's to do with Ma. But I don't say that to him. He'd not admit it but I reckon he finds it hard to trust women.'

'Surely he can't blame your mother for what your stepfather did to him.'

'Doesn't seem reasonable, does it? Maybe I'm wrong but I think he expected Ma to do more to stop the beatings. Maybe he thought she'd leave Fred when it was clear he was going to be so violent. I'm not sure, but it seems to me that's where Jack's problem with women comes from.' Jim took the pies from Fanny and gave her money.

She fiddled with the change, pausing to think. 'You don't blame your mother, do you?'

'No, I always felt sorry for Ma. She wasn't strong enough to stand up to that man.'

'Then why don't you try and make up with her? She must be suffering badly with you three boys all staying away from her. It hardly seems fair to me.'

'I guess it's not fair, Fanny, but I wouldn't do it without Jack. I wouldn't want to hurt his feelings.'

'What about her feelings?' Fanny's chest tightened. 'She's your mother, Jim. Surely that counts for something?'

'Of course it does. I don't know what I could do, though, without Jack. I wouldn't leave him and go back and live with her. I couldn't.'

'You could visit. You could let her know you care for her. You could help her out a bit. She has her hands full with those little ones and no family to help that I can see.'

'She has a couple of sisters in Maclean. I think they visit sometimes, but they don't like to be around Fred either, and they made it clear they wouldn't have him around their children. It's sad, but we figure she made her bed and now she has to lie in it, Fanny. She made her choice.'

'We figure!' She snorted. 'No, Jack figures. You don't seem to have any mind of your own at all. Don't you think it's time you stood up for what you think? You're not a little boy any more, Jim.'

Fanny stopped short when Jim's face dropped. He looked as if someone had smacked him across the cheek. 'I'm sorry, Jim. I didn't mean to get so het up. I feel sorry for your mother, that's all.'

Jim stared at her for a few moments, looking crestfallen.

Fanny felt remorseful and annoyed with herself. She knew it was a failing of hers that she always had to speak her mind, and Jim obviously found the truth hard to hear. Perhaps she was being audacious to come to the conclusions that she had.

However, one thing was now clear to her. *I could never feel safe with Jim.* He did not have the kind of courage that would give her confidence in him as a man. He was soft and caring but he didn't have the strength of character that she saw in her father and in Pop Franks. He didn't have the conviction about wrong and right that she'd always feared a little and yet admired in her Grandfather Nipperess. *No, he's not a man I could become seriously interested in.*

'I'd best get back to Jack,' Jim said. 'He'll be waiting for his apple pie.'

'Yes, I'm sure he will,' Fanny said.

'Perhaps we'll see you at the hotel tonight?' His expression was pleading, childlike. 'I'll be there, Jim. Enjoy your pies.'

***

By late that evening Fanny could feel the effects of the long day. She hoped the crowd in the hotel would thin soon. They'd been particularly loud; men huddled in groups whooping and laughing, sorting out bets and trying to outdo each other with boasts about their horses.

'Is that mob of Brits out there still ordering food?' Marlena asked when Fanny entered the kitchen.

'I think they're done with eating. Certainly not with drinking, though.'

Marlena nodded. 'If they weren't staying here at the hotel Hans would have thrown them out by now. They're acting like they own the place. I'm glad they'll be going tomorrow.'

'I've not seen them here before,' Fanny said. 'Where are they from?'

'Not long from England, I'd say. Hans said they're up from some big property north-west of Sydney. They were particular about their horses. They acted like Hans and the boys had no idea how to stable them.'

'Did they win at the races?'

'From the noise they're making it sounds like they might have. All I've heard all night is the British accents. Seems they're doing a lot of boasting to me.'

'You look worn out, Mrs Giese. It's been a long day what with all those pies you cooked for the stall at the track.'

94

'You must be tired too, *liebling*. You were standing there all day in the heat.' Marlena pushed hair from her forehead and wiped her face with her apron. 'I am going to call it a night as soon as there are no more food orders. My feet are killing me. Hans and Bob will keep the bar open till midnight, no doubt. Hans likes to let the racers celebrate and spend their winnings.'

'I think you can rest easy,' Fanny said. 'I've been around the tables and got nothing but empty plates. They all look full as ticks. You go upstairs when you're ready. I'll finish up here in the kitchen.'

'You're a good girl, Fanny. I'll go and say goodbye to those nephews of mine. Likely I won't see them again until next July now. Then I'll leave the kitchen to you. You make sure May helps, though.'

'I will.' Fanny grinned at May who was in her usual position at the bench with dirty plates on one side of her bowl of suds and clean ones on the other.

May rolled her eyes and winked at Fanny as Marlena pulled off her apron and disappeared through the door into the dining room. 'She thinks the sun shines from you, Fanny. I feel invisible when you're around.'

'Don't be daft, May.' Fanny chuckled, stacking the dirty dishes she'd retrieved from the dining room.

'I wouldn't be surprised if she's not eyeing you off for one of her nephews. Bob's a good man, even if it's hard to get more than two words at once out of him. That might be a blessing in a husband. Better than one who yells at you all the time.'

'You're not married, are you, May?'

'No, and not likely to be any time soon. I keep my distance from men. I don't trust them. My father drank like a fish and when he'd had a few he was all too free with his fists. He took off when I was hardly more than a girl and it was good riddance to bad rubbish in my opinion. I only have to poke my head out that door to be reminded what happens to men when they get a few drinks in them.'

'That lot aren't too bad. They're only celebrating.'

'I'm glad it's you has to go out amongst them. I'm happier in here.'

'You do a wonderful job on the dishes, May. I'm sure it's part of why The European has such a good reputation. Everything's as clean as a whistle.'

'I doubt they'd care if there was a little left over pie on their plates, Fanny. Not as long as you're setting it before them.'

'I'm sure you're exaggerating. I'll get the rest of the dirty dishes. Then I'll leave them to their drinks. We'll wipe down the tables in the morning before the lunch rush, eh?'

'Sounds good to me. I'd like to be away before too long. I don't like walking home when it's too late.'

Fanny had her arms loaded with plates when a young man blocked her path back to the kitchen. He stood grinning at her for a moment before he spoke.

'Can I help you with those plates, love?' His voice was a little slurred.

'You could move aside so I can get to the kitchen,' Fanny said. 'That would be a great help.'

'Come on, let me carry them. I'm sure they're too heavy for a sweet girl like you.'

'They're not heavy and I'll not be so sweet if you don't move aside.' Fanny raised her voice a little.

He threw back his head and chuckled. 'Ooh, a fiery lass, eh?' He reached out and pinched Fanny's cheek.

Fanny was about to speak again when another man stepped up behind her, pushed some chairs aside and planted himself in front of Fanny's assailant. 'Look here, Archie, old chap, you're making a nuisance of yourself. Now move away and let the girl do her job.'

'Mind your own business, Clarence. I'm only trying to be helpful.'

'I doubt it.' Clarence elbowed the other man out of the way, glaring at him. When Archie was backed up against a chair Clarence gave him a shove, causing him to drop onto the seat. 'Now you stay put.'

'Spoilsport.' Archie huffed and turned to a man who was sitting close by. 'What do you reckon, Gerald? Don't you think

Clarence is being a spoilsport?'

'I think he intends to spoil your sport. That's what I think.'

'Please excuse my friend, Miss.' Clarence took Fanny's elbow and guided her past the pair at the table. 'Now, let me open the door for you. You've got quite a load there.'

'Thank you.' Fanny moved into the kitchen and laid the pile of plates on the bench. 'These are the last of them, May.' She saw a shocked expression on May's face and turned to see that Clarence had followed her into the kitchen.

'Fanny?' May looked the man up and down.

Fanny noticed in the better light in the kitchen that his face was pale and rounded. He had a small moustache and his black hair was slicked back neatly.

'I wanted to apologise for Archie's behaviour,' he said. 'I thought I'd best make sure he didn't come after you. He can be persistent when he gets an idea in his head.'

'I'm sure we'll be fine, now.' Fanny nodded. 'We've only these dishes to clean up and we'll be off for the night.'

'You live close by, do you, Fanny?'

'Quite close, yes,' she answered cautiously. 'You don't come from around here, do you?'

'No, I came up from the Hawkesbury River for the races. With that lot out there, I'm afraid.' He grinned. 'Archie is part of our crew. He and a few of the others in the dining room work on our property. My father sent us up here with his best horses. He wanted us to trial them before we take them to the Sydney races.'

'I see,' Fanny said. 'I hope you did well, then.'

'Quite well, yes.' He flashed a broad smile at her. 'Now, I'll let you ladies get on with your work. It was nice to meet you, Fanny.' He bowed slightly before leaving the kitchen.

'Ooh, I think he took a fancy to you. He looks like aristocracy, that one, he does.' May whistled as she plunged her arms into the suds again.

'He certainly had more manners than some out there.' Fanny laid the dishes on the sink. 'It's the British accent that makes him sound toffy. It'll wear off when he's been here a while. He must be one of the group Mrs Giese was talking about. They have their horses stabled out back. Now, let's get on with this lot. I'm ready for a good night's sleep.'

When Fanny did a final check of the dining room tables a half hour later the British group had gone. Jack and Jim were still sitting in the corner, their heads together. Their brother Bob was at the table with them. He tipped his hat as Fanny approached.

'Still counting your winnings, Jack?' she said.

'We've spent most of it.' Jim grinned up at her. 'Can't resist Aunty's cooking.'

'Plus a few drinks to celebrate, I'm guessing.' Fanny kept her eyes on Jack.

He didn't look up at her and she was about to walk away when he spoke. 'We didn't think you'd be here tonight.'

'What made you think that?'

'Jim said you usually go home to Brushgrove on Saturday afternoons.' Jack shrugged his shoulders as he spoke.

'Well, today I'm staying over because of the race. We knew it would be busy and Mrs Giese needed me to work late. I'll be going to Brushgrove on the first boat in the morning.'

'I guess it will be a while before we see you again, then?'

'I suppose it will.' She studied Jack's expression but he was giving little away. *I wonder if he'll think of me once he's gone.* 'Will you be going back to Murrayville tomorrow?'

'Likely. Or perhaps the next day,' he answered.

'We could get the early boat up river as well, eh, Jack?' Jim's eyes lit up. 'We could go as far as Brushgrove with Fanny and then on to Murrayville.' He turned to Fanny. 'We could meet you at the wharf first thing.'

His expression was boyish and pleading. Fanny could see how smitten he was with her and she didn't want to encourage him. 'I'll be with my brother, Thomas. He's staying at my sister's house with me tonight. He's been racing all day. He'll want to tell me all about it, I'm sure.'

'Oh.' Jim's face dropped.

'I'm sure Thomas would be glad to meet you both, though, if you happen to be on the early boat.' She smiled and tapped Jim on the shoulder, not sure if she was giving him mixed messages, but trying not to disappoint him. 'He probably saw you race today. Likely he's been wondering who the winner on the big black stallion was.'

She tried to sound jovial but her voice almost caught in her throat and she felt annoyed with herself for continuing this kind of bantering with Jack.

'We'll see then,' Jack drawled.

CHAPTER TEN

Fanny pulled on her bonnet and coat and left The European by the back door. She was deep in thought, and still annoyed with herself for sparring with Jack. A voice coming from the shadows near the stables surprised her.

'Hello, Fanny. I've come to walk you home.'

She couldn't make out the man's face. His voice was slurred.

'Thank you, but I'm used to walking home alone and it's not far.' Fanny's heart began thumping in her chest and she turned away from the shadowy figure and began to walk in the opposite direction.

'It's not a good idea for a young lady to be walking the streets without an escort.' The voice was now closer behind her and she could hear his footsteps scraping on the gravel path.

'It's not necessary.' She made her tone as firm as she could.

'But I insist. A gentleman wouldn't dream of leaving a lady alone late at night.' He was right behind her now and took hold of her arm.

'Please don't.' She pulled away. 'If you persist, I'll go back into the hotel and get my brother. He'll be coming along soon.' She took a few quick steps forward.

'Now, don't be so skittish.' His voice softened. 'You remind me of our young fillies when we're trying to tend to them.' He moved in close to her again. 'We have to give them something to calm them down, so they won't go hurting their fine legs prancing about.' He reached around Fanny and waved something in front of her face.

Fanny saw a white cloth and ducked her head away. She smelled a strong odour, one she thought she recognised but couldn't name. A fog filled her head and she sensed that her legs were crumbling under her. She heard a voice as if it were a long way away.

'That's it, darling girl.'

Then everything went black.

When she came to she was lying on a mound of hay beside the stables. She could smell hay and horse manure. Someone was calling her name. She looked about and hunched up, trying to hide herself close to the stable wall. As she pulled up her knees she felt a sharp pain between her legs. She grabbed at her skirt and realised that her clothes were in disarray. She tried to think but her mind was hazy.

What am I doing here? Did I fall? Someone called her name again. She felt afraid but couldn't think why. The next time the voice called she recognised it.

'Thomas?' she tried to respond but her voice was thin and breathy. 'Thomas. I'm here.' She heard the sound of someone running across the yard in front of the stables.

'Fanny? Fanny, where are you?'

'I'm here.' She was trying to get to her feet and had to balance herself against the wall of the stable.

'Fanny!' Thomas reached her and held her up. 'Where on earth have you been? I went to Lizzie's and when you weren't there I came back. I thought you left ages ago. What happened? Are you ill?'

'I don't know.' She leaned into him and tried to push down her skirt. 'I was on my way home. There was a man.' Her words came slowly as she struggled to think.

'A man? Who? Did he hurt you?' Thomas was searching her face in the darkness, pushing hair back from her face, brushing straw from her back. Fanny began to shake all over.

'Dear God in heaven,' Thomas said. 'He didn't … attack you, did he?'

'I can't remember anything, Thomas. Only a strange smell. I must have fallen. I came to a moment ago, here by the stables.' She couldn't say any more. Her throat seized up. Her mind was reeling.

'Are you hurt? Can you walk?'

'I think so,' she said, but as she took a step she doubled up with pain and cried out.

'I'll carry you. I'll get you home to Lizzie.' Thomas lifted her into his arms.

'No, Thomas, you can't carry me all that way. I can walk.' Tears welled in her eyes and began to roll down her face. Her emotions were raging, but she still couldn't think clearly.

'I've brought the cart.' He carried her out onto the road where the horse and cart stood. 'Now, rest against me while I lift you in. I'll have you home in no time.'

Fanny wondered if she'd passed out again as they drove home. It seemed no time at all before she was being laid on the sofa in Lizzie's parlour. Her sister was hovering over her.

'Fanny, what's happened?' Lizzie brushed hair from her forehead and rubbed her cheeks. 'My poor darling.'

'I'm all right, Lizzie. I'm not hurt.' She wanted to reassure her sister, who looked distraught. 'Please don't wake everyone up. I'll be fine.' When she tried to sit up she felt the searing pain again between her legs.

'I'll make a cup of tea,' Thomas said, and headed for the kitchen.

'Poor Thomas,' Fanny whispered.

'Poor Thomas?' Lizzie exclaimed. 'Fanny, I was frantic when he came home without you. I thought you must already be asleep. I didn't know what to think when your bed was empty.'

'I'm sorry. I didn't mean to worry you. I left to come home. There was a man out by the stables. One of the jockeys, I think. It was dark. I should have left by the front door and walked around the road. It was silly of me.'

'Who was the man? Did he hurt you? Oh, Fanny, I can't bear it.'

'I don't remember anything, Lizzie. It was so dark.'

'Here's Thomas with tea. Can you sit up?'

Fanny tried not to grimace as she sat up and took the steaming cup from her brother.

'I must have fallen,' she said after taking a sip. 'He frightened me and I must have run off and fallen over in the hay near the stable.'

Her hands were shaking as she gripped the cup and tried to calm her thoughts. She tried to remember but there was nothing past the white cloth and the strange odour. She sipped her tea and searched her mind. She'd smelled that odour somewhere before. But it was no good, she couldn't focus.

'I'd like to go to bed, Lizzie. I'm sure I'll be fine in the morning. I must have hit my head and knocked myself out when I fell against the stable. I feel hazy.'

'Help me get her into bed, Thomas.' Lizzie took the cup from Fanny's hands. 'We'll see if we need to get a doctor in the morning.'

'I won't need a doctor. I'll be right after a good sleep.'

***

The next morning Fanny woke with a start. Her mind was full of blurry images. *Was it a nightmare? Why was there pain?* She pulled back the covers and saw that she was still in her petticoats. She knew before she looked that she'd been bleeding. Easing herself from the bed, she felt a cramping ache, as if she'd been bruised. She washed her face and hands, then bathed her body, soothing the tender, reddened flesh on her inner thighs.

Once she'd changed into clean clothes, she bundled the soiled ones into a tight ball and pressed them into the bag she brought with her each week from Brushgrove. When she had brushed her hair she gazed at her face in the mirror. Her eyes were red and swollen, her cheeks flushed. She looked as if she'd been thrashing about in the bed all night. Suddenly she was on her knees beside the bed, sobbing.

'Please, dear God, help me. Please don't let this be true.'

***

'She's not here, Jim.' Jack watched his brother scanning the crowded boat as it began to move away from the wharf. He leaned over the side railing and watched the boat's wake surge. 'Maybe she's on one of the other boats. There's enough of them.'

103

'Sundays are gala days on the river.' Jim frowned and continued to look around the crowded water way. 'Those boats with all the flags flying will be full of day trippers to Yamba. I'm sure Fanny would catch the regular boat. She'll want to be home as quick as she can to go to church with her family. That's what she always does.'

'I didn't see Fanny on the wharf so maybe she changed her mind. Maybe she's staying with her sister for the day.' Jack kept his head down, not wanting his brother to notice that he was also disappointed. He didn't even want to admit that to himself.

'She said she'd be here,' Jim persisted. 'It's not like her to say she was coming and then not show up. I'm worried about her.'

'You didn't see her again last night then?'

'You mean after we left the hotel?'

'Yes, you didn't come to bed for ages. I thought you might have gone back to walk her home or something.'

'No, I went and sat down by the river. I couldn't sleep.' Jim shuffled his feet on the deck.

'Are you worried about something?'

Jim shook his head. 'I needed to think. I was a bit under the weather. I needed time to get my head straight.'

'About Fanny?'

Jim nodded. 'About Ma too.'

'What about Ma?'

'Some things Fanny said. She thinks it's unfair of us to blame Ma for what happened with Fred.'

'You told Fanny about that?' Jack's heart missed a beat and he glared at his brother.

'A bit. She wondered why Ma was upset that day she came to the hotel to see us.'

'You talk too much, Jim. That's nobody's business but ours. I've told you before you'll cause trouble if you go talking about all that.'

'For who? Fred can't get to us now. We haven't seen him in years.'

Jack took a deep breath and tried to keep his voice even. 'Ma sees him though, you idiot. She's got to put up with him whether

104

we're there or not. I reckon he'd lay into her if he thought people were talking about him? Best he thinks we're out of her life for good. She'll be safer that way.'

'I thought you were mad at her. I thought you wouldn't visit her because you hated that she'd married Fred.'

'I did hate that she married Fred, once I found out what he was like. But it was her choice, and if that's what she wants then she'll have to put up with him. I'm certainly not giving him another go at me. And I don't want to give him any reason to turn his rage on her. That's why you've got to keep quiet about it all, Jim. I thought you were smart enough to work that out for yourself.'

'Well, I'm not smart, am I? Neither is Ma, I reckon. I'm sure she thinks you hate her. That's what upsets her the most.'

'Perhaps it's best she does think that. She won't be looking for us too often if that's the case, will she? She'll not put herself in danger.'

'Sometimes I don't understand you, Jack.'

'You understand what I just said, don't you?'

'Yes, I do.' Jim nodded sullenly.

'Then that'll do for now.'

'What about Fanny?' Jim's eyes flicked around the boats again. 'Now she's got the wrong idea too.'

'She's not likely to have anything to do with our mother, is she? So what does it matter?'

'I'd like to put her straight, is all.' Jim bit at his bottom lip for a moment, then hung over the side of the boat again, scanning the diminishing wharf.

'Not much you can do about that now,' Jack said.

'Not that you'd worry, would you? You don't care if you never see Fanny again either.' Jim's tone was irritable.

'What do you mean?'

'You had a go at her again last night.'

'I didn't have a go at her.'

'Well, you didn't sound like you'd care if you saw her again or not.' Jim was still straining to look around the boats. Some people were hanging over the side. Others were waving and yelling to passengers as vessels passed each other on the water. A group of people were sitting inside the covered area, their heads down as they talked together over the drone of the engine.

'It's you who's so keen to see her,' Jack said.

'You still could have been more sociable. I'm sure she's got the idea that you don't like her. Why would she want to be in our company if she feels like that?'

Jack sighed. He wasn't going to let on to Jim that he had mixed feelings about Fanny. She had definitely aroused something in him that he'd not felt before. He'd found himself seeking her out these past few days, wanting to be near her, and yet feeling annoyed with himself about it.

He didn't want to have any feelings for a woman at all. It was certainly not in his mind to consider getting involved and he was not one for having quick flings with girls the way many of the woodcutters did. They often boasted of their conquests when they'd been in town for a few days. It seemed to keep them happy for the weeks or months that they spent in the bush. Jack thought that kind of behaviour was shallow and dangerous.

He'd always thought that one day he'd find a woman to marry and he'd settle down, perhaps get a job in one of the towns along the river, or at one of the sawmills. But that was a long way off. He wouldn't entertain that idea for years yet. *Certainly, I couldn't consider Fanny as that woman.*

Besides, it had been clear since they'd first met her that Jim was smitten. He was like a man possessed, although it didn't seem to Jack that Fanny returned Jim's feelings. If anything she'd paid more attention to him when the three of them were together. At times she even seemed to enjoy his teasing and gave as good as she got.

Jack had to admit that he liked her spunk and her honesty. There was something about the way she looked at him sometimes that caused his heart to lurch and certainly his manhood to stir. However, he was determined to keep all that at bay. If Jim wanted to pursue her, that was his decision, and Jack could only hope his brother wasn't going to get hurt.

'I don't see the point of encouraging the girl when you'll be out in the bush again for months.' He turned to Jim and tried to focus on how his brother was feeling. 'She'll likely have herself a town boy by the time we get back to Grafton. You'll make yourself miserable if you're going to mope about her till next July.'

'I might come back to town before that.' Jim stuck out his chin. 'I don't always have to do what you do.'

As soon as he'd spoken Jim's face dropped. 'I'm sorry, Jack. I didn't mean that. Of course I want to be with you. We're a team, eh?' He chuckled. 'I'm concerned about Fanny, that's all. I know I won't see her for a while, but she did write a couple of times last time we were away. She might again. You never know what the future holds, do you? When the time comes, she's the kind of girl I'd like to settle down with.'

He looked at Jack plaintively. 'You do like her a bit, don't you?'

Jack pushed his hat back from his eyes. 'She's nice enough. I just don't want you to be hurt.'

'She's not the kind of girl who'd hurt a fellow. I'm sure about that.'

'No, I don't think she'd intentionally hurt you, Jim. Let's wait and see if she writes. She might explain why she's not on the boat this morning. That's all you can do.'

CHAPTER ELEVEN

November, 1891

'Right, *liebling*, are you going to tell me what's going on?' Marlena rubbed Fanny's back and drew strands of hair away from her face.

From her doubled over position Fanny shook her head and gagged as if she was about to throw up again.

Marlena's heart sank. 'You haven't been yourself for weeks, and I'll not be moving from this spot until you tell me what's happened. I've notion enough now, after seeing you out here these past few mornings. Just because I've no children of my own doesn't mean I don't know the signs of one on the way.'

Fanny stood upright and gripped Marlena's arms. Her face was flushed with the strain of throwing up. As her eyes flew open tears flowed down her cheeks.

'Please don't say that, Mrs Giese. Please don't.'

'Whether it's said or not, *liebling*, it's true, isn't it? I wondered if all this moping about was because of Jim leaving, though it seemed most unlike you. Now, what am I to think? Is my nephew less of a man than I thought he was?' Marlena could feel her chest heaving with rising anger.

'No, Mrs Giese. You mustn't blame Jim for this. It wasn't him.'

'Well, who then? You're not a girl to get into this situation without a lot of pressure. If I'd thought so, I'd never have hired you.' She looked squarely into Fanny's eyes and saw fear and horror but not guilt. *Someone has forced himself onto this poor darling girl.*

Fanny's attempt to speak gave way to sobs and she leaned into Marlena's chest and buried her face.

'Have you told anyone about this?' Marlena said, trying to keep her voice soft, although she wanted to scream her outrage.

Fanny shook her head without looking up.

'You have to tell me who did this to you, Fanny,' Marlena persisted. 'Whoever it was now has a duty to you and I'll be making sure he fulfills it. If it's my nephew then I'll be sending for him right away and what's more he'll be finding out exactly what I think of him.'

Fanny pushed back and looked up into her face. 'No, you mustn't send for Jim, Mrs Giese. He had nothing to do with this. But I'm afraid I can't tell you who it was because I don't know.' Fanny's words came out between sobs and deep breaths. 'It was dark. I came out to go home and he was here in the shadows. He put a cloth over my face. It had chloroform in it. I realised later what the smell was. I passed out and when I came to he was gone.'

'Chloroform? What they use on the horses? Someone knocked you out and took advantage of you? Dear God in heaven, that's outrageous.'

'He was drunk. His voice was slurred and he was speaking quietly. I was sure I could put him off at first. I started to hurry away and that's when he reached around from behind me and put the rag over my face.'

Marlena pulled Fanny back into her chest and patted her back. 'Dear God, I don't know where to start. We'll find him, I promise. We'll make him take responsibility. Hans will know what to do.'

'Please don't tell Mr Giese. Please, I couldn't bear it,' Fanny pleaded.

'You can't bear the brunt of this alone. If I'm right there's going to be a little one now. You have to think about the baby.'

Fanny pushed back and shook her head. 'Whatever happens now, I never want to see that man again. I want nothing to do with him.'

Marlena gasped. 'So you do know who it was? You're not

trying to protect my nephew, are you? Because if I find out this was his doing I'll have his hide, whether you have anything to do with him or not.'

'No, the voice I heard was not Jim's. Please let me work this out. I need time to think. I need to go home to my parents. They'll be broken-hearted, but they'll help me, I'm sure.'

'Of course they will. But they'll want to find whoever did this and have him take responsibility. Any parent would. You can't bear the shame of this alone. The man ought to be horsewhipped, and as it happened behind my hotel with you in my employ, I need to take some responsibility too.'

'Lena?' A voice came from the back door of the hotel.

'I'm here, Hans,' Marlena answered. 'I'm having a chat with Fanny. I'll be in soon.'

'Is everything all right? May thought she heard crying.'

Fanny gasped and began to wipe her eyes. 'Please, Mrs Giese,' she begged.

'Everything's fine, Hans,' Marlena called over Fanny's shoulder.

'Thank you,' Fanny whispered when Hans had disappeared back into the hotel.

'I'm not at all sure about this, *liebling*.'

'Tell people I'm not well, if they need to know. I'll go home to Brushgrove right away. I can't stay with Lizzie. She's not long told me she's having a baby herself. I've managed to hide my sickness from her because she's so unwell, but I can't imagine how she'll deal with this. Not well, I expect.'

'You haven't told anyone?'

'Only that I was frightened by someone and tripped when I ran off. I didn't want to worry them.'

'Dear Lord, *liebling*. You can't shoulder this alone. You will tell your sister, won't you?'

'Not yet. I can't risk upsetting her and I need to talk to Mum and Dad first.'

'You'll send word, then? You'll let me know what you decide?'

110

'Yes, I will.'

Fanny smoothed down her blouse and wiped her face. She straightened her shoulders and raised her chin. 'I'll work this out, Mrs Giese. I thank you for your concern. You've been a wonderful employer. You mustn't feel this is your responsibility.'

Marlena's shoulders slumped into her chest. *Another little one, abused and hurting, right under my nose, and I can do so little.* Tears ran down her cheeks. 'That's easier said than done,' she said. 'I need to know how you get on, and if there's anything at all that I can do, you've only to ask. Do you understand?'

Fanny kissed her on the cheek and nodded. She was clearly determined to work this out for herself.

Marlena put her arm around Fanny's shoulder and led her back into the kitchen. *So like my nephew. Jack and this one make a good pair.*

***

'What do you mean, you're going home?' Lizzie paced around the room as Fanny packed her bag. 'You never go home at this time of the week. And you never take all your things with you. What's going on?'

'Please, Lizzie, don't go on. I don't feel well and I need to go home for a while, that's all.'

'You haven't been yourself since you were knocked down at the hotel that night. Has that man been after you again?'

Fanny shook her head. 'No. The jockeys have all gone. I'm sure it was one of them. Please don't upset yourself.'

'Have you lost your job then? You know I've never been comfortable with you working for those Germans. They stick to their own, you know. Have they fired you?'

'Of course not. Mrs Giese wouldn't do that. She's been nothing but kind to me.'

Lizzie grabbed at Fanny's shoulders and spun her around. 'You stop shoving those clothes in that bag and talk to me. Something's wrong and you're keeping it from me. I can tell you're frightened. You must tell me what's going on.'

'For goodness' sake, Lizzie, leave off. There's nothing more to say. I need to go home for a bit, that's all.'

'It's those German boys you were hanging around with, isn't it? One of them tried to attack you, didn't he? Or perhaps the two of them?'

'No, Lizzie, you have it all wrong. It was not one of them.'

'You said you heard an accent. You told us that when Thomas brought you home.' Lizzie kept standing in front of Fanny and trying to keep her attention from her packing.

'It wasn't a German accent, and anyway, Jim and Jack don't have German accents. They were born here. For goodness' sake, Lizzie, why do you always come back to blaming them for everything?'

'Because you always try to protect them, and you haven't been yourself since this happened and they left. It's as if you're pining for them even though they hurt you.'

'They didn't hurt me.' Fanny slammed her bag closed. 'Why won't you believe me?'

'Because you've hardly told me anything. What else am I to believe? I told you those boys can't be relied on. They're here one week and gone the next. They're only interested in the horse races … and maybe having a bit of fun with a girl.' Lizzie dropped into a chair and rubbed her eyes. She looked exasperated and about to start talking again.

'You must stop going on about the Germans, Lizzie.' Fanny cut her off. 'It wasn't one of those boys and if you continue to talk about them like that, I'll leave here without speaking to you again. The man who … frightened me … had more of a British accent, quite proper.' Fanny took a deep breath and went on with her packing as calmly as she could.

'Anyone can put on an accent like that if they want to disguise themselves,' Lizzie huffed.

Fanny ignored the comment and put the last of her things in her bag. 'That's it, then. I'll catch the afternoon ferry if I hurry. I can be home well before dark.' She took her sister's hands and drew her to her feet. 'I'll be in touch, I promise.' She put her arms

112

around Lizzie and gave her a hug. 'Please don't worry, and thank you for everything.'

'You make it sound like I'll never see you again.' Lizzie's voice cracked.

'Of course you'll see me again.'

'I know there's something you're not telling me, but I'll not go on any longer. I'd walk you to the river, but the children are asleep.'

'I'm fine to walk to the river on my own. I've done it hundreds of times. Please say goodbye to Alf and the children for me.'

Fanny was glad to be away, not sure how much longer she could contain her angst about the future. She had no idea how to tell her parents what had happened. They'd be devastated. And the thought of having a baby almost caused her to faint.

When she reached the ferry stop, she slumped onto a bench seat by the river and let her tears flow. She tried to think about what was ahead for her but her mind kept going blank. She couldn't imagine how she was going to get through it. Until today she'd pushed all thoughts of a baby away, telling herself she was feeling ill because of the attack, that it was the rising heat as summer approached, that she hadn't had enough sleep. Now she could avoid it no longer. *But I can't accept it either.*

The sun glistened down on the still waters in front of her. Birds twittered in the nearby trees. It was a lovely spring day, her favourite time of the year. A couple of months ago she'd been so happy. How could her world be turned upside down so quickly? The chatter of children playing a little way along the bank broke into her thoughts. She loved children. *Surely having a child of my own would not be so bad? But like this? With no husband, no father for the little one?* The utter shame of her situation overwhelmed her. *How could God let this happen? What have I done to deserve this?*

The sound of the ferry approaching interrupted her agony, and just as well, for she was near to contemplating throwing herself into the river. Not that she would do so. She knew deep down that whatever was ahead for her, she would face it with as much courage as she could muster. She knew God would not condemn her for her predicament, for even if she'd been foolish in heading out into the night unaccompanied, she'd done everything she could to escape the fate that had befallen her.

Didn't I? Surely I did nothing to lead any man on. Or did I? Is this because I'm too outspoken, too ready to speak my mind? She pushed away the doubts and clung to her belief that God would help her face whatever was ahead for her. *Though I'm not sure anyone else will face it with me.*

***

Over the next few weeks Fanny's confidence in her strength to face the future waned. Each time she thought about talking to her mother about what had happened and what was going to happen, she lost her nerve. There was hardly a time when her mother wasn't busy with one child or another of her own, or with the never ending tasks around the home.

Everyone in the family was obviously worried about her. They hadn't had her home for this long in over a year, and it was clear they all knew that something was wrong. She'd evaded every question with vague answers about needing a break, about missing home, about having a head-cold. No one seemed convinced. Especially her mother.

From her seat on the back porch she looked out over the field of sugar cane beyond the house. The air was so still that the voices of her father, brother and two of her uncles could be heard as they worked somewhere between the rows of eight-feet-high plants. The sky was soft blue with puffs of white clouds. The same sky that had hung over her when she'd grown up here; safe and happy, loved, protected from harm.

I should never have left home. I've ruined everything. Tears rolled down her face. Her sense of aloneness was overwhelming. *How could my life have come to this?* When she heard the back door open and soft footsteps coming towards her she knew she could hide her misery no longer.

'Right, my darling girl, I'll not leave your side until you tell me what this is all about.' Her mother sat down on the wicker chair beside her and took her hand. 'You asked me to give you some time to work out whatever is troubling you. You've been home more than a month now and I've hardly seen a smile on your face. I think it's been long enough, don't you?'

'I'm sorry, Mum. I know I've been avoiding it. But with the preparations for Christmas and everyone so happy, I wanted us to enjoy this time with the family.' Fanny turned to her mother and dropped her head into her hands. Her tears flowed unchecked.

'Now you're frightening me, love.' Betsy moved closer and put an arm around her shoulder. 'You must tell me what's going on.'

'I don't know where to start.'

'Do you think I've haven't been watching you all through the Christmas celebrations? I can see your heart is breaking.' Betsy stroked Fanny's arm. 'Is it something to do with those two young men you met during race week?'

Fanny wiped her eyes and shook her head. 'No, Mum. It has nothing to do with Jack or Jim. You must believe that.'

'I'll believe whatever you tell me, if you'll come out with it. I'm tired of trying to guess.'

'It's so awful I don't know how to say it and I don't know what to do about it. I can't bear to hurt you.' Fanny's words caught in her throat and she dropped her head into her hands again. A deep sense of shame overcame her.

'Darling, you know whatever it is, I'm here to help you. I can't imagine what you could think would be so awful.'

Fanny sniffed and pushed hair away from her eyes. 'I didn't tell you the whole truth when I said I'd fallen behind the hotel after a man frightened me in September.' She paused and looked into her mother's eyes.

'I see.' Betsy reached for Fanny's hand and waited.

'The man put a cloth over my face, with chloroform on it,' Fanny continued. 'I didn't have time to run. I passed out and when I woke up Thomas was calling me. He took me back to Lizzie's and I went to bed. I was confused and I was hurting, but it wasn't until the morning that I fully realised what had happened.'

'Dear God, Fanny, you're not saying that you'd been ... interfered with?'

'I could tell I had, but I still couldn't remember any of it. I tried to put it out of my mind. I didn't want anyone to know because I knew how upset you'd all be and there was nothing to be done. I didn't know who the man was and within a couple of days all the jockeys were gone. I wanted to forget about it.'

The colour had drained from her mother's face. 'Forget about it! Darling, that's not something you forget about. You should have been taken to a doctor. Goodness knows what harm might have been done. If I'd had any idea I'd have had you home long ago.' Betsy drew Fanny close and kissed her cheek, brushing fresh tears from her cheek. 'My poor darling.'

'You're not angry?'

'Of course I'm angry.' Betsy's chest was heaving and her eyes filled. 'With this man! We need to find out who he was and have him charged. I wish you'd confided in us earlier. We would have done all we could to see you were safe and well.'

'I didn't want to worry you, and I was afraid you'd want to blame Jack or Jim. Everyone else seems to.'

'What would make anyone think they'd do such a dreadful thing?'

'I think it was clear that Jim was taken with me, and people saw us together. But I know it wasn't Jim. I hate to hear people say bad things about the Germans. They've been so good to me.'

'All right then. I trust your judgement. So who do you think it was?' Betsy took a deep breath and sat back.

'I don't want to know who it was, Mum. I never want to see him again. I've been so afraid that if you and Dad knew, you'd go chasing after him. I couldn't bear it.'

Betsy's lips pursed and she shook her head, clearly having trouble controlling her emotions. 'I can understand that you wouldn't want this known abroad, love. We wouldn't want to cause you any more hurt. But we should try and see that he's held accountable.'

'What if it was even worse?'

'What do you mean? What could be worse? It's a truly horrible thing you've endured, reprehensible. I don't care if the man was dead drunk and can't even remember himself what he did, he still needs to – ' Betsy stopped. Realisation of what Fanny was saying spread across her face. 'Oh, no, Fanny, you're not saying that you're …?'

Fanny nodded. 'I was sick for weeks, in the mornings. Mrs Giese found me throwing up and she knew what it was. I'd been trying to deny it but … I think I'm going to have a baby.' She leaned into her mother's chest and sobbed.

'Dear God in heaven,' Betsy gasped. 'Lord have mercy.' She wrapped her arms around Fanny's shoulders and rocked her.

***

Fanny couldn't help but overhear her parents talking the following morning. She'd been restless all night. She knew she'd caused her sisters to have broken sleep as well. It was early in the morning, well before light, when she gave up and crept from the bedroom, hopeful that the other girls would be more comfortable with her gone from the bed. She curled up on a large chair in the parlour and hugged her knees close to her body. Her heart was calling out to God, seeking answers and some sense of direction. But it was not God's voice she heard, at least not directly.

As the sound of hushed whispering reached her ears, Fanny sat up, tuning her ear to the snippets of words coming from her parents' bedroom. She knew her mother would talk to her father about the situation. They never kept secrets from one another. Fanny was desperately sad that what she was going through would hurt all of her family. She had to know what they were thinking, how they were coping with her news. She tiptoed to the door of their room and pressed her ear against the wood.

'What can we do, Francis?' came Betsy's anguished plea. 'I'll not have her suffering the prejudice of people who'll know nothing of the circumstances and who'll make all kinds of assumptions about her.'

117

Her father's voice sounded strained. 'I'm not sure we can prevent her suffering some of that, love.'

'It only takes one or two to be cruel to leave a dreadful mark on a young girl's life. I know it too well.'

'You're thinking of your father, aren't you? I know he was harsh with you when you were young, but he's softened over the years. I doubt he'll have anything but concern for Fanny.'

'I'm sure that's true, but still, knowing this is what happened to Mum when she was young … it will bring it all back to them both. It will break their hearts.' There was a deep sob. 'Dad still struggles with why God lets bad things happen to good people.'

'Don't we all,' Francis said. 'But we must deal with it the best we can and trust God will bring good out of it … eventually.'

'That may be a long way down the track. We have to trust in the face of incomprehensible things sometimes, don't we?'

'We do, love, and we will. And so will Fanny, I'm sure.'

There was a long silence before there were any more sounds. Fanny realised she was holding her breath. She could barely take in what she was hearing. *This happened to Granny Nipperess!* She was wondering if her parents had drifted back to sleep when the sound of sobbing resumed. Fanny gripped her nightdress, her heart almost breaking for her parents.

'It seems to me Fanny's more concerned with the reputation of those German boys than she is of her own,' Francis murmured.

'That might make it worse,' Betsy said. 'Some people thought it unwise of us to allow her to work for Mrs Giese. They might assume that Fanny's been involved with a German boy, willingly or not. If Fanny starts defending them it will make it worse.'

'We need to think about how we can make things easier for her, rather than worrying about what other people will say.'

'That's precisely what I'm thinking about, Francis. We know she'll be safe here, and the baby will be loved as one of our own. But we can't keep her locked up, and she's not one to shrink back. If she feels people are being judgemental of her or of her German friends, she'll speak out for sure, and goodness knows where that will lead.'

'A lot of people will assume she's best to give up her baby and let the church adopt it out.'

'I don't think Fanny will agree to that, Francis, and I don't know that I could bear it either. It's our grandchild we're talking about.'

'I understand how you feel, love. It would be hard to bear, but we have to think of the child, too. What's going to be best for a child born under these circumstances? There may be a lot of pressure on Fanny to give the baby up. If she's fighting against that it's not going to be good for the child or her.'

'We'll have to protect her from that, Francis. The child will be one of ours. In fact it could be ours. Alice is not yet two. It'd be no surprise to see us with eleven children instead of ten. It's the way many families handle these situations. Maybe if we're careful people needn't know that Fanny's having a child at all.'

'How would Fanny feel about that?'

'We didn't get that far in our discussions. What she needs for herself right now is what's uppermost on my mind.'

'What she needs is to feel safe and cared for, Betsy, and while I know we could do that best, I do wonder if … all things considered, she mightn't be safer somewhere else. I've heard that home in Grafton is good. The nuns would –'

There was a loud gasp. 'Francis no, you can't be serious. Fanny would be broken-hearted if we suggested such a thing.'

'Of course she would at first, but when she thinks about the consequences of staying here, not only what might be said to her, but what about the other children? Fanny's a sensitive girl for all her outspokenness. She'll feel the response of her sisters and brothers keenly. We have to explain this to them somehow. And we risk them receiving the brunt of others' cruelty too.'

'We've raised them to be loving and loyal to each other. We'll have to trust they'll live up to that.'

'I'm sure they'll try, Betsy. But Thomas will be furious. He's probably guessed there was more to what happened to her that night than what she said. He's likely to go after her attacker. He'll want a reckoning, I'm sure.'

'Wouldn't we all, but since we have no idea who it was, what point is there in thinking that way? Anyhow, Fanny doesn't want to find the father.'

'I doubt that will stop Thomas from wanting to take the man to task.'

'We'll deal with Thomas's reaction when it happens. Right now, we must focus on what's best for Fanny.'

'I agree, and that's why I wonder about somewhere safe and discreet. Lizzie's in Grafton so she wouldn't be so far from family ... and we could visit. People around here would assume she's still working away.'

'I worry how Lizzie will deal with this, Francis. She's having a baby herself and you know she can be a little fragile. She's likely to feel responsible since Fanny was staying at her house. She's never been happy about Fanny working at that hotel. She's sure to blame the Germans, one way or another. I don't know if it would be good for her to know yet.'

'Yes, she's a worrier by nature, unfortunately. I think she's been too influenced by her husband's attitudes in regard to the German community. I'm sure his father had some unpleasant dealings in business with a German family.'

'That means nothing, Francis. There are difficult people in any nationality.'

'I know that, dear. I'm only saying ...'

Fanny couldn't listen any longer. She was shivering all over. She made her way back to the parlour chair and curled herself up in a ball. Her mind was racing with thoughts. The ache in her heart was unbearable. Her understanding of right and wrong, good and bad – an understanding which had once seemed so clear and indisputable – now seemed blurry and ungraspable.

How can I make the decisions that need to be made? How presumptuous I've been to think I know what's best for others – thinking I can help others resolve their issues – when I don't know what to do for myself. What did seem clear was that she had to think beyond herself. She had to protect her parents from all this pain. She couldn't watch them go through this with her as well as worrying about how all the other members of the family would deal with it.

Her stomach churned and she rubbed her belly through the light nightdress. She had to think about her child, too. She couldn't bear to have a baby coming into the world with all this angst about. And the idea that she would let her baby be adopted out to someone else was incomprehensible to her.

Slowly things became clearer and she could see what she needed to do. Her parents had unwittingly painted a picture of what was ahead if she stayed at home, not only for her, but for the baby and for all the members of her family: siblings, parents, grandparents, aunts and uncles and cousins; all of them trying to protect her and her child from cruelty and prejudice, trying to work out who to blame, and perhaps pressuring her to have her baby adopted. No, she would not allow that to happen

CHAPTER TWELVE

Three weeks later Fanny awakened to find her sisters gone from the bed. It was the first time for months that she hadn't woken early with her stomach growling.

'Is everyone gone?' she said when she found her mother clearing up in the kitchen.

'They are, love. Your father's been out working for ages. The girls left for school an hour ago. They were excited about starting back for the new year, though I suspect it was more about seeing the friends they've missed over the holidays, than the school work.'

'And the little ones?' Fanny slid into a chair at the end of the table.

'Frankie and Ivy are next door with Pop. I'm waiting for Alice to wake up, then I'm going to take them to my Mum's. It's a beautiful day out. Would you like to come? You look much better this morning. You've obviously had a good sleep for a change.' Betsy wiped her hands on her apron and ran her fingers through Fanny's hair.

Fanny nodded. 'The nausea has eased.'

'That's good, love, but you know it won't be long till you're showing. You're such a slight girl and you'd be over four months along now.'

'I've been careful what I've been wearing.'

'That won't make any difference soon. We have to decide what to tell the girls. They've been concerned about you being ill, but a baby's the last thing that will be on their minds. Then there's Mum and Dad. I'll have to say something to them. I even noticed Pop looking at you strangely the other day. He's no fool, and he sees you almost every day. I know it's hard but you'll have to make some decisions soon.'

'I know we're running out of time, Mum, but I've been too ill and tired to think straight lately.'

'I'm sure you'll feel better over the next few months. That's how it was with me. Sick as a dog for four months, then blooming with health for the rest. My sister, Rose, hasn't fared so well with childbearing though. Her baby's six months now, and from her last letter it doesn't sound like she's picked up at all. This was her seventh child, so maybe she's reached her limit.'

Betsy continued to chat about her sisters and their children as she refreshed the tea pot and set hot toast and jam on the table. But Fanny had stopped listening. A plan was forming in her head.

'So will you come to Mum's with me?' Betsy sat down beside Fanny. 'Your grandparents would love to see you. We don't need to say anything about the future, if you're not ready.'

'Thanks Mum, I'd like to see Granny and Grandfather soon, but I'd rather enjoy the quiet here at home this morning.'

Betsy nodded as she pulled her apron from her waist. 'All right. I can hear Alice stirring in the bedroom so I'll get her ready and we'll be off. You have some breakfast and rest. Perhaps you could sit in the sunshine for a bit. It'll put the roses back in your cheeks.' She kissed Fanny's forehead and headed for the bedroom.

'Give Granny and Grandfather my love, won't you?' Fanny said as her mother walked away. 'And Mum … thank you … for everything.'

Betsy nodded and smiled. A quizzical look crossed her face as she left the room, but she didn't say any more.

By the time Fanny had finished her cup of tea and toast, the house was completely quiet. She ran through her plan in her mind and then hurried to the bedroom. Within the hour she'd dressed, packed all she thought she'd need in her small carry bag and written a note to her parents, which she left on their bedside table.

'Fanny?' Rose Hitchens opened the door and stood staring at Fanny for a moment before she spoke again. 'Goodness, is it your mother? Is something wrong with Betsy?'

Fanny remembered her mum saying that Aunt Rose always anticipated trouble. Doubt about her decision crept into her mind, leaving her speechless for a moment.

'No, Aunt Rose. Mum's fine, and so are all the rest of the family.'

Rose visibly relaxed. She was fine-featured, with mousy-coloured hair and the same blue-green eyes that most of the women in the Nipperess family had. Her body showed the accumulative sagging of bearing children, much like Betsy's did, although Fanny thought in her mother the result was a softly rounded woman, whereas in Aunt Rose there was more of a weary, dragging demeanor.

'Then do come in, girl.' Rose jolted Fanny from her assessment. 'If you've not brought bad news then I'm glad to have a visit.' She stood aside and ushered Fanny into the hall.

As she walked towards the kitchen of the house a small boy's head appeared in the opening. His forehead creased at the sight of a stranger and he looked to his mother.

'Freddie, this is your cousin, Fanny. She's come to visit.'

Freddie's eyes roamed over Fanny and settled on her carry bag.

'That's quite a load you have there,' Rose said, following her son's gaze. 'Are you on your way to somewhere else? Did you come by ferry?'

'Yes, I came on the ferry, Aunt Rose, and no, I'm not on my way to anywhere else. In fact, I was wondering if I could stay with you for a while?'

Fanny reached down and fondled Freddie's hair. He looked up and squinted at her for a moment before his expression softened and a grin crept across his face.

'He wouldn't remember you, Fanny. He's just turned five

and it's a while since you've been here.' Rose tickled the little boy under the chin. 'Why don't you go and collect the eggs, love, while I make a cup of tea for Fanny.'

He nodded and headed for the back door.

'Looks like he enjoys that job.' Fanny smiled as she watched him go. She put her bag against the wall in the hall and followed her aunt into the kitchen.

'He likes to be helpful, thank goodness. With the others at school I need him to do a bit around here through the day. Henry's got his hands full with the animals and the yards and such. Not to mention the veggie garden. Proud of it all, he is.'

'That's great, Aunt Rose. And the baby? Is she asleep?'

'She is, thank the Lord.' Rose sighed. 'She's not been a good sleeper, and she wears me out. I lost two between Freddie and her, so I wasn't good to start with. I've not been at all well lately.'

'Yes, Mum said.' Fanny sat when Rose gestured towards a chair. 'That's one of the reasons I decided to visit. I thought I might be able to help you with the children, or whatever else you need.'

'Not the only reason, though, I gather.' Rose raised her eyebrows into a question mark as she laid two cups and saucers and a jug of milk on the table.

Fanny waited until the kettle came back to boil on the stove and her aunt had poured fresh water into the teapot. 'You'd best sit while I tell you about it, Aunt Rose.'

'I'm sensing trouble.' Rose frowned as she sat down and began to twist the teapot in circles. 'Give me a minute while this tea brews and I'll check on Vera. She's not long gone off so hopefully she'll sleep a while. Freddie will take his time getting the eggs. He's a fiddler, that one. So we should have a bit of time without interruption. I can tell by the look on your face that you've got bad news after all.'

While they drank their tea Fanny explained her situation as calmly as she could, assuring her aunt that she had accepted the idea of having a baby and was ready to raise the child herself. Her decision to leave home was because she wanted to save her family the worry of watching her go through the next few months and trying to protect her from gossip and condemnation.

Rose's face drained of colour as she listened. After moments of silence Fanny wondered if it had all been too much for her aunt, who seemed to have gone into shock. Fanny noticed streaks of grey in her hair that she'd not noticed earlier, and it seemed the worry lines around her eyes had deepened even in the last few minutes.

'So you've left without telling your parents your plan?' Rose eventually said. Her voice was tight and strained. 'Don't you think that will be more of a worry for them?'

Fanny sensed her aunt's disapproval and her heart sank. 'I've left a note for them and assured them I'll be safe and in good hands.' She reached for her aunt's clenched fist on the table and tried to cradle it. 'I want them to tell the rest of the family that I've taken a domestic position for a while.'

'But you didn't say where you'd be?' Rose's fist was cold and hard against Fanny's fingers.

'No. I wasn't sure you'd have me, and I don't want them to come after me. I'm sure they'd try and talk me out of this, but I believe it's best for everyone.'

'I'm not sure you're old enough to know what's best for everyone, Fanny. I don't think you know what you're asking.' Rose's eyes flicked around the room as if she was looking for an escape.

'I've thought about this so much, Aunt Rose. I don't want to hurt anyone else. I certainly don't want to make anything difficult for you. I'll go, if you'd rather.'

'You're asking me to keep something important from my sister. Betsy doesn't take kindly to deceit. She's a stickler for the truth.'

'I know that, and I won't keep my whereabouts from them for too long. They're used to me being away working this past year, so it won't be so different, and the other children won't question it. Nor will my grandparents, which will make it easier for Mum and Dad. As long as they know I'm safe, I'm sure they'll be all right with it. I'll keep in touch with them by letter, I promise.'

Rose sighed. 'Well, I'm not about to throw you out, if that's

126

what you're afraid of. I could certainly use some help around here at the moment. Mind, as you get further along you'll likely need help yourself.'

'I'm sure I'll be healthy up to the end, like Mum always is,' Fanny said. 'I've had a bit of morning sickness, but it's gone now and I feel fine.'

'I suppose there's no point in talking about the father?' Rose frowned.

'No, Aunt Rose, there's not. There's no use in speculating about who it was. There were so many men at the hotel that night.'

Fanny held her breath, praying her aunt would not start talking about the issue of her working for German people. Thoughts of Jim and Jack came unbidden into her mind. *What will they think of me now? Will they care what's happening to me? Jim would, I'm sure, but what conclusion will he come to about what happened? And Jack?* Her mind went blank. What Jack thought about anything was a mystery.

'Disgusting is what it is.' Rose's lips pursed. 'A man like that ought to be horsewhipped.'

Fanny shook her head and brought herself back to the present. 'I'd rather not think about that, Aunt Rose. I want to concentrate on being healthy and happy for the baby's sake.' She took a deep breath to calm her mind.

'Well, that's to your credit, I suppose. And have you considered giving the child up for adoption?'

Fanny's breath caught in her chest. 'I couldn't. I know it's what some people expect, but I couldn't.'

'Well, you might change your mind when you see how people feel about a young woman with a baby out of wedlock. Some are not likely to be kind, you know, especially in the church. You do know that we go to the Catholic church, don't you?'

'Yes, I know that,' Fanny said. 'I'll stay away from there if you like. I'm used to going to an Anglican church, so your friends at church needn't know.'

'I'm not sure hiding from people is the best thing.'

'As long as you're all right with me being here, that's the main thing. I don't mind if we don't say I'm your niece. No one around here knows me. Would it be easier if I wasn't related to you?'

'I can't pretend that, Fanny, not to the children, and at school they're sure to talk about having a cousin here. I can't have them telling untruths.'

'Of course.' Fanny shrank back in her seat. 'I'm trying to make things as easy as possible. I don't want people thinking badly of you. What will your neighbours think?'

'I imagine they'll think I'm trying to help my niece, which is exactly what I'll be doing, so they can hardly criticise me for that, can they?' Rose's eyes glazed over and she stared at the wall of the small kitchen.

'What about Uncle Henry?' Fanny asked after a few moments of silence.

Rose shook her head. 'Apart from threatening to hang the man from the rafters if he ever gets hold of him, Henry will be nothing but concerned for your welfare. It's not in his nature to be anything else.'

'That's how I remember him,' Fanny said. 'You're not wishing I'd gone somewhere else, are you? Because I could –'

'Don't be daft.' Rose flapped her arm in the air. 'You can't be wandering all over the countryside looking for someone to take you in. You're family and this is what we do for each other. You've come here first and there's no good reason not to stay.'

'What about when I'm showing?'

'Let's worry about that when the time comes.' Withdrawing her hand from Fanny's, Rose slapped her palms together. She seemed to have come to terms with her decision.

Fanny relaxed into her chair and wrapped her hands around her teacup.

'Now,' Rose said, as if her mind had gone into overdrive, 'if you don't mind a small room, you can have one to yourself. Henry's been saying he wanted to clean out the storeroom he originally built onto this place. He's built a shed down the back and he's got most of his tools out there now. He'd been thinking we could give the two older boys the storeroom for themselves, but they can wait a bit longer for that.'

'I'm happy to bed down anywhere, Aunt Rose. I'm not used to my own room.'

'I'll get Henry onto it, but until then you'll have to bunk in with the girls.'

'Of course.' Relief flooded Fanny's mind and she took a long drink of tea.

'How about you freshen that teapot and get another cup,' Rose suggested. 'You need to keep up your fluids. I'll check on Freddie. He's likely got distracted from collecting the eggs.'

'Thank you, Aunt Rose. I can't tell you how grateful I am.'

Rose nodded as she pushed herself out of her chair. 'You'll need all the help you can get. I'll do what I can, but I'd be asking the good Lord for an extra measure of guidance if I were you. It's not going to be an easy road ahead.'

'I know that, I'm only thinking a little ahead for now. I'm sure God will guide me a step at a time.'

'Good. Then let's take one step at a time.'

***

The next day Fanny sent a letter to her parents, assuring them that she was safe in Maclean with Aunt Rose and helping to look after the children. She pleaded with them not to come after her, and not to tell anyone about the baby. There was no point in anyone else being worried for now. She would let them know regularly how she was going and when the time was right, she'd come home.

She also sent a letter to Marlena Giese, letting her know that she was doing fine, but not saying where she was staying. She didn't want to risk anyone else finding out.

'Do you think you'll have put your parents' minds at rest?' Aunt Rose asked as they made the beds one morning the following week.

'I hope so,' Fanny said. 'I know Mum will worry until I'm home, but I think she'll rest easier now. I'm not so far away that

129

they couldn't reach me if it was necessary.'

'I'm not sure Betsy will thank me for doing this.' Rose tucked in the bottom edge of the sheet and patted it down.

Fanny bit her bottom lip. She wondered every day if she was doing the right thing, but always concluded it was better than any alternative she could think of. 'I can only pray in time I'll be proven to have done the best thing, Aunt Rose.'

'I pray so too. The children have told their friends that they have a cousin who's come to be their nanny. They came up with that explanation themselves, which will suffice for now, but once you're showing I'm not sure I can control what they say. One of the other mothers is likely to work things out and be snooping around.'

'I'm sorry this is hard for you.' Fanny's stomach turned over.

Rose shrugged. 'I'll manage, but you'll have to prepare yourself. A couple of the women at church asked why you didn't attend services with me. They find it hard to believe that some of our family is Catholic and others are Protestant. It makes it sound like there's been a rift in the family.'

'Well, there was for a while, wasn't there?'

'Years ago, when your mother first married, but that's all healed now. We've come to accept that Betsy and Francis have their own religion.'

'If people worry about which church we attend, then what on earth are they going to say about –'

'Exactly, Fanny. This is what you need to think about seriously. It raised a few eyebrows when I said you were going to the Anglican church.'

'I would have gone to church with you, but I thought it would be more of an issue when your friends see that I'm carrying a child.'

'That's likely to be the case anyway, I'm afraid. There's no escaping that.'

Fanny shook her head, not sure what to think. Her aunt seemed to be withdrawing from her emotionally, as if she was protecting herself from an inevitable disaster.

***

It came as no surprise to Fanny when late in March she overheard one of her aunt's neighbours in the parlour.

'It won't be ignored, Rose. I can't imagine what Father O'Rourke will say. There are places for girls in this kind of trouble, you know. She'd be looked after and out of – '

'Out of sight?' Rose finished.

'Wouldn't that be better for everyone? I mean to say, you have your children to consider. Whatever will they make of this?'

'They'll make of it what they hear from others, I imagine,' Rose said curtly.

From her position in the hall Fanny heard a gasp of air as if the woman was shocked by Aunt Rose's reply.

'I'd best be going,' Fanny heard a moment later. 'I only meant to warn you that this is likely to cause trouble for your family, Rose. People are talking. Surely the girl's going to give up the baby, so why would she parade her problems around here? Will her own family not have her?'

Fanny couldn't hear Aunt Rose's answer. There was a shuffle of feet and the clatter of cups being picked up. Then the voices faded towards the front of the house. The sound of the door being closed was sharp and Fanny drew in her breath as she moved into the parlor.

'I'm guessing you heard some of that,' Rose said as she came back into the room. 'It'll be all over town now. Mary Quigley is not one to keep a secret, even when it's of a positive nature, let alone something that will have the ears of her listeners burning.'

Fanny dropped into a chair and rubbed her swollen belly. She'd started to feel the small movements of her unborn child recently. The wonder of it was something she'd have liked to share with someone, but she was afraid it might seem she was gloating over her situation if she showed any enjoyment in her confinement.

'I don't see why these women are so interested in me,' she said. 'It's hardly going to affect their lives if I have a child. It's got nothing to do with them.'

131

'This kind of thing shakes their understanding of the world, Fanny. Women like Mary have daughters of their own and they'd faint at the thought of one of theirs coming home carrying a child out of wedlock. It's many a family's worst nightmare.'

'And you, Aunt Rose? Bertha and Rosie are nine and eight years old, and no doubt hearing things at school now. Are you worried I'll be a bad example to them?'

'It's not something I'd planned on them having to deal with yet, but you're here and this is happening, so we'll have to help them work through it. I was their age when I was told that my oldest sister, Lotte, was born out of wedlock. In fact, it was your mother who told me, and what's more, she had a hard time explaining it to me. She worked out that Mum and Dad were married after Lotte was born, but it didn't change how we felt about Mum. She was a saint; still is.'

Rose stared at the wall behind Fanny for a moment. 'I'm sorry,' she said. 'I didn't mean to shock you. It's long past now but I assumed Betsy told you about Lotte, being the stickler for truth that she is.'

Fanny didn't want to say how she'd found out about Granny and she'd not thought too much about what happened after the birth of Granny's baby.

'Did Granny ever say how she felt about having a child out of wedlock? I can't imagine what it would have been like for her.'

'About the same as it's going to be for you, I imagine. I doubt much has changed, but we didn't talk about it. I don't know how Mum managed, but Dad eventually married her, so it never affected Lotte.'

'So you assume that Grandfather Nipperess is Aunt Lotte's real father?'

'Of course,' Rose said, but then her eyes strayed again. 'Well, we did assume that. Perhaps it wasn't the case. Goodness, I don't know. Dad always treated Lotte as if she was one of his own. I don't think she's ever questioned that.'

Fanny sat back and wondered about Granny; a woman she'd only ever seen as a loving mother and grandmother. *Perhaps I should have*

132

gone to Granny for support. But the fact that Granny Nipperess had been a young unmarried girl with a baby was still a shock to her.

***

Over the following weeks Fanny often lay awake at night trying to imagine how her Granny would have protected her child, and herself, from the gossip and prejudice she likely faced. *How supportive was her family? Who helped her?*

Then her thoughts would stray to Jim and Jack. They were only children when they'd had to cope with prejudice against them because of their German heritage and also brutality from within their family, as well as the terrible loss of their father, and in a sense the loss of their mother, too. Fanny's heart sank at the thought.

I was so quick to judge Jack for his hostility towards the world, his mistrust of people. How naïve I was. From her safe, controlled world everything had seemed so clear. She had wronged Jack with her attitude. *Will I ever have the chance to remedy that?*

Many nights she wrestled with herself, wracked with compassion for the boys, guilt over her insensitivity, and fear about her own future. Eventually self-pity would creep into her heart, chased away only by prayer and concern for her unborn child, until she descended into restless sleep.

CHAPTER THIRTEEN

By late April Fanny could not walk down the street without feeling every eye was on her, and there seemed to be not an ounce of compassion in any of them. Women turned to each other and hurried past as if they might catch some awful disease from her. Their *'tsk tsk'* could be heard as they bustled off, no doubt whispering their disgust. The man serving in the general store often ignored her until he'd served everyone else, whether they'd come in before her or not.

More than once she'd had children following her as she walked home from church on a Sunday. They'd giggle and hiss, repeating words they'd no doubt heard from their parents and hopefully didn't understand. Fanny had given up attempting to talk to people on the streets. They were either determined to punish her with their disdain, or too afraid that someone might see them talking to the *'hussy from Hitchens' house'*, to even pause in their stride and acknowledge her presence.

At home with Aunt Rose and Uncle Henry there was barely a reference to her condition. Henry was kind to her and she often caught him looking at her compassionately across the dinner table, but he didn't ask how she was or mention the coming baby.

It seemed to Fanny that Uncle Henry preferred to think about his garden and his animals, rather than people. No doubt they were less complicated. He'd intimated early in her stay that he couldn't understand the fuss over one more baby coming into the world. As long as it was going to have a warm place to sleep and a mother to feed it, then nature would take its course, as happened with the farm animals.

Fanny had been relieved at the time, because she'd felt no condemnation from her uncle. But she knew that life for people was not as simple as it was for animals, no matter how much farmers like Henry wanted to pretend. People had much deeper expectations of each other, and whether because of their prejudices or their fears, they did not easily accept those who stood outside the norms, even through no fault of their own. She'd seen this often enough in others' lives and abhorred such discrimination. But she'd never expected to face it herself.

Aunt Rose seemed to have put Fanny's situation in a corner of her mind and made clear that it was separate from the family's everyday life. Each evening when the meal was over, she set the children chores to do, after which she focused on getting the smaller ones into bed while Fanny cleared the table and washed up the dishes. She checked that Fanny was keeping physically well, and assured her if she felt the need of a doctor that she'd accompany her to town to see the local practitioner. But it was clear that making sure Fanny was kept busy was Aunt Rose's way of leaving little time for ruminating about what was to come.

'Suffice to say,' she said, 'the baby will let us know when it's ready to come and I've had enough of them to know how to help you through. Until then it's best to keep your mind occupied and with the work my little ones make, there's no shortage of things to do.'

Billy, Rose's eldest boy, was nearly fourteen and most evenings tried to talk his father into letting him finish school and help on the farm. The next two boys, George, twelve, and Percy, ten, often had schoolwork they needed to finish after the evening meal and Fanny was happy to help them with it. George sometimes eyed her suspiciously as he scribbled into his workbook, but Percy was meticulous with his writing and numbers and looked to Fanny for encouragement and guidance.

'One of the boys in my class called you a bad name, Fanny,' he said one evening as they were finishing his spelling list.

135

'Did he?' Fanny was surprised at his statement, being now used to the family avoiding any talk of her condition. 'It's probably best to ignore things like that, Percy. I'm sure everyone will forget about me when I'm gone and I'd hate to think you'd lost a friend over me.'

'He's not my friend.' Percy's large brown eyes fluttered up at her. 'He's a mean boy, and I told him he should have his mouth washed out with soap.'

'I see.' Fanny hid a smile with her hand. 'You didn't get into a fight, did you?'

'No. I'm bigger than him so I could have beaten him, but he walked off with his friends. They were all laughing, but I didn't think it was at all funny.'

'You're a nice boy.' Fanny ruffled his hair.

She didn't want to know the word that had been used and hoped that Percy didn't know the meaning of it. As she looked into his innocent face; the rounded cheeks, full mouth and neat eyebrows, she wondered what her baby would look like.

Will it be a boy or a girl? Will he or she have fine, dark hair like Percy or fair hair like mine? Will my child be sweet natured and generous with other people? Or will I have to deal with less lovable traits? Will he be like his father – the thought was there before she could block it – *and if so, will he be careless with other people's feelings? Hopefully I'll have a girl so I won't be reminded of that man again.*

She roused herself from her thoughts as Percy continued to gaze up at her. She felt moved to have this small boy so willing to come to her defense. A tear welled in her eye and she wiped it away. 'I think you've done a grand job on your spelling list, Percy, but I suspect it's your bedtime now.'

'Would you come and say my prayers with me when I get into bed?' he said, closing his book and packing up his pencils.

'I'd love to do that,' she said, trying to control a tremor in her voice.

She wondered if her heightened emotion was because she was getting closer to delivering her child or because she was missing the love and affection she was used to from mother and father. She'd had a letter from her mother recently, begging her to come home. Her father was almost beside himself, and they both wanted Fanny safely with them when the child came.

***

Fanny made her decision in late May, with only a month to go before the birth. She woke early one morning with such frenetic movements in her womb that she wondered if the baby was going to come early, but then the kicking and rolling settled and she drifted back to sleep. She was not hungry when she woke, so spent some time sewing the set of clothes she'd almost finished for the baby. When she made her way down the hall, she heard voices in the parlour.

'The girl's had enough time to decide what she's going to do, if you ask me, Mrs Hitchens. I told you weeks ago that these things are best dealt with early in the piece. There's too much inclination for second thoughts when a girl's in this situation. She has your children about her and she may begin to like the idea of being a mother. She should have been packed off to the convent long ago. She'd be in good hands and all the talk could have been avoided. It's set tongues wagging all through the parish. I've more to do than to try to quell gossip over this sort of thing.'

'I know, Father O'Rourke, and I'm sorry. I thought Fanny would have come to the decision herself by now. I've not tried to sway her. It hardly seems my business to do that.'

'What about her parents? Surely that's their responsibility? Or has she avoided their counsel by hiding away here? They must have read reports of what happens to girls in this predicament. And what happens to the babes is more than a decent person can stomach.'

'I'm not sure what you mean, Father.' Aunt Rose sounded mystified.

'It's reported in the papers often enough, Mrs Hitchens. Babies murdered, is what I mean. Abandoned, dead babies. Some starved, others drowned, found in privies, parks, mine shafts. Girls have babies they can't care for, and once they realise it they get rid of them any way they can.'

There was a sharp gasp from Aunt Rose. Fanny found she wasn't breathing at all and her head began to swim. She could hardly believe what she was hearing.

'I know it's shocking,' the priest went on, 'but you must realise that no decent man will want to marry a girl who has someone else's baby. Once that reality sets in, girls soon look for a way out of their dilemma. Why, there was a prosecution reported a month ago. A baby found mutilated by a young woman who was sentenced to hang. What's more, there was a legal penalty for her mother, who was found to have assisted her in the heinous crime.'

'Please, Father ...' Rose's voice sounded choked.

'I'm simply trying to press home the seriousness of this situation, Mrs Hitchens. Your niece could end up as desperate as one of those girls. Who knows what she might feel driven to? And what about these babies ... left in limbo for eternity because they've never been christened, most of them. It doesn't bear thinking about.'

There was a long silence. If Fanny had been able to collect herself she'd have marched into the parlour and ordered the priest out of the house. *The audacity of him!* She was still trying to bring her breathing back to normal when he started to speak again, this time more quietly, as if he was satisfied he'd shocked Aunt Rose enough.

'You've taken on more than a good woman ought to have. You've put your own reputation in jeopardy.'

'I'm not worried about my reputation.' Rose spoke now with some surety. 'It will all blow over for me soon enough. It's Fanny who has to bear the brunt of it. The father's taking no responsibility at all, not that she wants him to. She doesn't even know who it was –'

'That's absurd, and you know it. The girl might want to protect the man, or he's already said he'll take no responsibility ... or he's married, or worse. But there's no way a girl wouldn't know who she's had relations with.'

'I assure you, Father, she's adamant –'

'Of course she's adamant. I've not even had a conversation with her but I'm well aware she's adamant. She's obviously a willful and determined girl. But that will do her little good in dealing with this. The community will not turn a blind eye to this sort of thing. She'll be discriminated against and so will the child.'

'If she does decide to keep the child, I've no doubt she'll go home to her parents. They're worried about her, and I know they'll help her care for the baby. They'd not allow anything to happen to it. I've been writing to my sister to assure her that I'm taking good care of Fanny. I didn't want to deceive her. I've said that I wouldn't be able to have Fanny here after the baby's born.'

'Well, this is all most unsatisfactory,' the priest insisted. 'If she'd come to church with you and come to confession, I might have been able to get her to see reason. As it is, she's apparently been going off to the Anglican church on her own, as if that's not scandal enough, and Reverend Sloan is a weak man. He'll have ignored the problem as much as possible and likely told his parishioners to mind their own business.'

'Perhaps that's as it should be,' Rose said.

'You don't seem to be grasping the gravity of the situation, Mrs Hitchens. We've a standard to uphold in this community and it's the responsibility of all of us to do our part.'

'Yes, Father, I do see your point, but I'm not sure what I can do about it. I can't throw my own niece out of my home. She needed my help and I'm bound to give it. She's a good girl, basically. This has been most unfortunate for her, and regardless of whether she knows who the child's father is, she was attacked and badly used and that's not her fault.' Rose sounded irate.

'Be that as it may, she still had the choice of what to do about it, and the right choice should have been put to her more strongly.'

'I have suggested it, and I agree it seems best for the baby to be adopted out, but I imagine from a man's point of view that's an easier decision.'

'Only because a man is likely to think more clearly about it, Mrs Hitchens. A woman's mind is not to be trusted at a time like this … if ever. '

His last words were barely audible and followed by another

long silence during which Fanny wondered if the priest had left. Her fists had clenched as she'd been listening and her heart was hammering in her chest. She was still restraining herself from marching into the room and giving the priest something else to think about, but she knew making a fuss right now would likely only cement his view about women.

She was also aware of self-doubts creeping into her mind. *Was I wrong to come here and bring all this trouble for Aunt Rose? Am I kidding myself that I can keep my baby and raise him in the face of all this prejudice? Can I really stand up to the kind of criticism and disapproval I'm bringing on myself?*

She thought of Jack and all he'd put up with. *He had much worse than this. It's not as if I'm being physically beaten. Am I being arrogant and self-righteous ... all the things I accused Jack of being? I expected so much of him, yet I'm not sure I can be at all gracious through this.*

She held her feet fast to the floorboards and leaned into the wall. As she did it creaked and she had the horrible sense that her presence had been detected.

As boldly as she could manage, she straightened herself up and entered the parlour.

'Would it be all right if I make myself a cup of tea in the kitchen, Aunt Rose? I don't want to interrupt you.'

'Of course, Fanny,' Rose said. 'I don't think you've met Father O'Rourke. He's the parish priest here in Maclean.'

'How do you do, Father?' Fanny nodded her head towards him.

The priest stood and straightened his robe, without acknowledging her. 'I'll be going, Mrs Hitchens. I've said what I came to say.' He turned towards Fanny and grimaced. 'Your aunt has shown you a great deal of grace, Miss. I hope you appreciate it.'

'I do,' Fanny answered.

'Then it's to be hoped you'll not take advantage of God's grace as well.' He turned and headed for the front door.

Rose cringed, then dutifully followed him.

Fanny was in the kitchen when her aunt returned. 'He's not

averse to speaking his mind.'

'It's his job, Fanny. He's concerned with the spiritual welfare of his parishioners. Everyone has their opinion of what I should have done and what you should be doing.'

'And their opinion is all the same, I presume. You should have put me out. I should have gone to a convent and stayed hidden until my baby was born, then let the nuns adopt it out to someone I don't know and will never have any contact with. Isn't that how it's supposed to work? '

'No need to be sassy, Fanny. Everyone wants what's best.'

Fanny slumped, mixed feelings washing over her. 'I'm sorry. I'm just not sure who all this is supposed to be best for.'

'For all concerned. Your determination to do things your own way will do you no good in the long run, and it won't be a good situation for the baby ... if you keep it, that is.'

'*If* I keep it?'

'I did think you might reconsider as time went on. I'd have helped you find the best way to do it.'

Fanny sighed. 'You've been very kind, Aunt Rose. I don't want you to think I'm not grateful. But this is my decision and I've never said anything but that I'll keep my baby. I couldn't do anything else. I feel that I already know the child.'

She patted her stomach. 'Look, it's almost time for him to be here. I haven't been able to forget about him for a day. Just because no one talks about him doesn't mean he's not making his presence felt every day. He's as lively as a cricket and when I sing to him at night before we sleep, I feel him roll around as if he's enjoying it. Not that I can sing, mind.'

She chuckled. 'I do love him already, Aunt Rose. I'm getting excited about being able to hold him in my arms and look into his eyes. Surely you can understand that?'

There, I've said it. Her baby's life was as real as any of Aunt Rose's children; a life that was already part of her own. If she was gloating then so be it. She couldn't hide her joy any longer and if it was to be laced with hardship and criticism from others, then so be that as well.

141

Rose sank into a kitchen chair and dragged her hands through her hair. She looked weary and lined. Fanny felt sorry for her and patted her shoulders.

'I'm sorry, Aunt Rose. I know I've asked too much of you. I've tried to be helpful and do my share around here. I didn't want to impose, or cause trouble for you, but I think it's time I left.'

Rose looked up at her, her face creasing into a frown. 'Where would you go at this stage? I could still find out about the convent, you know.'

'I have no intention of going to a convent, Aunt Rose. I'll go home. Mum and Dad want me to. We'll work out what to tell the rest of the family, I'm sure.'

'If you're thinking of going home before the baby arrives, then you'd best get about it soon.' Rose looked relieved. 'You can't be travelling at the last minute. You could bring a worse disaster on yourself and the child.'

'This is not a disaster, Aunt Rose. My baby is something beautiful coming out of a bad thing. I know he'll be a blessing.'

'You keep calling the baby *he*. What makes you think it will be a boy?'

'I'm not sure. It's something I've felt recently. Time will tell.'

'Not much time, as I said.'

'Then I'll pack tonight. I was annoyed by the priest's attitude, but perhaps he's done me a favour and made me realise I don't belong here. I belong at home.'

Chapter Fourteen

Grafton, July, 1892

Marlena looked up as her nephew's head appeared at the kitchen door.

'Jim, you're back? Is Jack with you?'

Jim nodded and grinned. 'He's champing at the bit to get onto a horse again. We're feeling lucky this year.'

'And why would that be?' Marlena felt an uneasy twinge in her stomach.

Jim stepped inside the kitchen and let the swinging door close behind him.

'Aunty Giese, what is it? You don't sound like yourself at all. Is something wrong with Uncle Hans?'

'Uncle Hans is fine.'

'Then what is it? You seem angry. Have I done something to upset you?'

'I don't know, Jim. Have you?' She brushed her hands down her apron and moved away from the bench where she was rolling dough.

'What on earth are you talking about, Aunty? We've just arrived from Murrayville. I haven't had time to get into trouble. Has Ma been in? Is she upset?'

'I haven't seen your mother. I've no doubt she's been upset numerous times in the past year. She has plenty to be upset about. I believe it's more your responsibility to find out how she is than mine.'

'I'll try and see her this week, I promise,' Jim said, his eyes dropping. 'I'm sure Fanny will be on to me to do so, as she was last year.' He looked up, his face brighter. 'Will she be in today?'

'Fanny? No, she'll not be in today. She's not here anymore.'

'Not here?' He was clearly shocked. 'She doesn't work here anymore?'

'She doesn't live here anymore.' Marlena narrowed her eyes as she watched him. 'She may have gone back to her parents' home in Brushgrove. I don't know where she is.'

'I don't understand.' Jim shook his head. 'She hasn't answered my letters this time. I thought it was because the mail wasn't getting through to Murrayville. Maybe she didn't get my letters. Why did she leave? Was she sick?'

'In a manner of speaking.'

'Please, Aunty, tell me what's going on. You're acting as if it's my fault that she's gone away. What kind is sickness did she have?'

'First you tell me what was going on last year, Jim. What happened between you and Fanny?' Marlena pushed her fists into her waist and glared at him.

'Nothing happened, except that we were getting to know each other. In September we talked a bit and I thought she liked me well enough. Jack was often harsh with her, but that's his way.'

'So nothing more than that happened between you and her, or between Jack and her?'

Jim walked closer to her and put a hand on each shoulder. For a moment she thought he was going to shake her. His face glared frustration. 'Please tell me what's going on,' he pleaded. 'You have me worried.'

'This is something I need to say to Jack and you together. I need to see for myself if I can trust you to tell me the truth.' Marlena pushed his hands from her shoulders and pulled at her apron. 'Is Jack in the dining room?'

Jim nodded. 'He's talking to some men.'

'Then get him and both of you come back out here,' she demanded.

Jim opened his mouth as if to speak again, then took a deep breath, turned towards the door and pushed his way through it.

Before Marlena could take a few deep breaths, Jim was back in the kitchen with Jack on his heels.

'What's this about?' Jack asked. 'Jim's got himself in a knot about something and we haven't been here five minutes.'

'You might at least say hello.' She frowned at Jack and raised her eyebrows.

'I'd have come to say hello soon enough. Don't I always?' He stood tall and folded his arms. 'Now, why's Jim in such a flap?'

'Fanny's gone,' Jim said.

'Gone?' Jack sounded stunned.

'She's not dead, if that's what you're thinking,' Marlena said. 'At least, I don't think she is.'

Both boys stood silently. Jim looked overwhelmed. Marlena thought he was about to explode.

'All right,' she said, 'I'm going to tell you what I know about Fanny, and I want you both to be honest with me about what you know. If not, I'll wring both your necks.'

'You're frightening me.' Jim almost choked on his words.

Marlena took another deep breath. 'In September, Fanny was attacked out the back here – '

'Attacked!' the boys chorused.

'It was the night before you were all leaving after the spring races. I know there was a lot of drinking going on and I'm sure you two were imbibing as much as any of the boys. I went upstairs early, unfortunately, and I left Fanny to clear up. I thought her brother was going to walk her home, but someone got to her first.'

'Got to her?' Jack growled.

'Thomas – that's Fanny's brother – thought she'd already gone when he left and when he got home and she wasn't there he came back and found her barely conscious out by the stables.' Marlena shook her head. 'She couldn't remember much of what had happened. Whoever it was had long gone and Thomas took her home.'

'Was she badly hurt?' The colour had drained from Jim's face. 'Did she know who it was?' His questions fired out. His fists were clenched by his side.

'It was dark,' she continued. 'Fanny didn't see his face. He spoke to her but she didn't recognise the voice. She said it was slurred, like most of the men's voices in here by that time, I imagine.'

'How badly was she hurt?' Jack's tone was deep with smouldering rage.

Marlena considered her next words. 'The man used chloroform to knock her out.'

'For God's sake, Aunty.' Jack's voice boomed out. 'Tell us how badly she was hurt.'

'She was … interfered with.' Her words came slowly. Her eyes never left the boys' faces.

Jim gasped and reeled back. For a moment he was speechless, then his eyes flew open. 'You think it was one of us?' he said incredulously. 'How could you think such a thing? I'll kill whoever it was when I get hold of him. I'd never touch Fanny like that. Never!' He shouted the last.

'Keep your hair on, Jim,' Jack said. 'I'm sure Aunty Giese's not implying that.' He looked back to her and raised one eyebrow into a question. 'You wouldn't think that, would you?'

'I'm not sure what to think,' she replied, trying to quell her suspicions.

'How could you think that?' Jim pleaded. He looked like he was about to throw up.

'All I know is that you were taken with Fanny, Jim. And when a man's got a few drinks in him, he's not likely to be thinking straight.'

'You think I'm capable of using chloroform on a woman to have my way with her?' Jim's voice was filled with outrage.

'I don't want to think so.' Marlena sighed. 'I've tried to convince myself that you couldn't do such a thing, but I needed to ask you directly.'

Jack stood silently throughout this last exchange, his face like thunder, his eyes blazing. 'She must be in a bad way, not to have come back,' he eventually said.

'She came back within a couple of days,' Marlena said, 'but after a few weeks it was pretty clear she couldn't stay.'

146

Neither boy spoke for moments. The silence was deafening.

'I'm sorry to have to tell you this,' she said. 'Fanny was shocked by the realisation she was to have a child. She went home, and I've had one letter since, saying that she was safe and well. She may have had the baby by now. I hope to God she's home with her mother.'

'Someone must know who did this,' Jack hissed. 'Most of the men come here in groups, or at least in twos and threes. Someone must have an idea who disappeared that night long enough to get chloroform and attack Fanny.' He thumped his fist onto the bench. 'Do you think it was a local? Surely you'd guess if one of them was slinking around here like the animal he is.'

'I've kept my eyes and ears open,' she said. 'Everyone who's a regular in here has been concerned about Fanny. None of them have been acting suspiciously.'

'You mean they know what happened?' Jim's eyes flew open.

Marlena shook her head. 'Only that she wasn't well and went home. They ask about her all the time and they're all hoping she'll come back. I've told them I've heard she's doing better, but that she's not indicated she'll be back.'

'Then more likely it was one of the men who comes in for the races,' Jim said. 'What about that fool who had a go at her at the dance in July, Jack? He was mighty annoyed when you threw him out.'

Jack scowled. 'I don't remember him being around in September, not drinking in the hotel anyway. But we'll be here all week. If we ask the right questions we might get some idea. I'd be surprised if one of this swine's friends didn't know something.'

'They're not likely to tell us anything though, are they? They all protect one another.' Jim's shoulders slumped.

'That's why we'll have to ask the right questions.'

Jack's expression reminded Marlena of earlier times when he'd stood up to his step-father. Hateful defiance was etched into his face. A shudder ran up her spine. She knew Jack would defy any odds to protect those he thought could not stand up for themselves, and she feared what might be ahead. She wondered if she'd done the right thing in telling the boys, but knew she'd have needed a good reason why Fanny wasn't here, even if she'd kept the truth from them.

'You think she's already had the baby?' Jim asked, drawing her attention from Jack's face.

She nodded. 'My guess is it would have been born towards the end of last month, so the baby would only be a few weeks old at most. I'd like to think she'd let me know, but she might be still weak.'

'Or worse,' Jack mumbled.

Jim turned on him and Jack held up a hand as if to ward off an attack.

'I'm thinking she's not much more than a skinny kid herself. I don't know about these things, but I imagine it wouldn't be easy for her to give birth.'

'She's always had plenty of stamina,' Marlena said, patting Jim's arm. 'We've got to believe she's managed all right.'

Jim sagged as he let out his breath. 'How can we find out how she is? I have to know.'

'Give her time to get settled with the baby, Jim,' she said. 'If I don't hear soon I'll see if I can contact her sister.'

'That's it.' Jim's eyes lit up. 'I know where she lives. I took Fanny home one night. Her name's Lizzie and I remember the house. She'll know, surely.'

'Hold on, Jim,' Marlena warned. 'You can't go bolting over there. You're a stranger to the girl. She'll be protective of Fanny, no doubt. I suspect they've had some hard decisions to make about who to tell and what to do about the baby. She might even have decided to give the child up for adoption.'

'I doubt that,' Jack drawled. 'No one would take a child away from Fanny. She'll want to manage herself.'

'I didn't realise you'd given much thought to Fanny, Jack,' Marlena said. 'It was Jim who seemed to be with her all the time.'

'Well, I agree with Jack,' Jim said. 'Fanny wouldn't give up a child. She'd be fiercely protective of it, I imagine.'

'You're probably right, and all the more reason why we should give her time to let me know about the baby if she wants to,' she said. 'She might prefer that no one around here knows anything about the child. I only told you two because – '

'Because you thought we might be responsible.' Jack sneered. 'It's pretty disappointing that you would think so badly of us.'

'I'm sorry, Jack. I thought Fanny might have been protecting you both. She kept insisting it wasn't either of you. I wanted to believe her but I was pretty het up myself.'

'Was there some reason she was sure it wasn't one of us?' Jack asked. 'Did she say anything else about the man?'

'Nothing, except that when I asked her if it was Jim – because he'd been with her a lot – she said definitely not, that it wasn't his voice.'

'So there was something about the voice,' Jack said. 'Come on, Jim. Let's get out amongst the men. I can hear it's getting crowded in the dining room. We'll find out who it was, I promise.'

***

By the fourth night of the week Jack and Jim had spoken to most of the men who frequented the hotel. Most were only interested in boasting of their wins at the races or commiserating with those who'd lost. Jack could barely contain the seething that had stirred in his gut all week. The thought of Fanny's attack, of her suffering, was driving him crazy. He could barely listen as men discussed horses and the weather and the sad state of the country's financial crisis. He forced himself to pay attention to their faces, their gestures, their mood, searching for signs that might reveal a guilty party.

''Tis more than the average man can understand,' said one man in a small group of Irish jockeys, referring to the downturn in the country's economic standing.

'Sure, 'tis companies and rich men involved in wild speculation and dishonest management,' said another, flinging his arms about and knocking a glass of beer to the floor. 'What's so hard to understand about that?' he went on, oblivious to the mess he'd made. 'The banks have sought credit from London to back up borrowers for too long and too much, and now the so-called *mother country* has withdrawn her support, so she has. Nothing surprising about that at all, now is there?'

'I still don't understand,' said the first man.

'That's because you've the brain of a pea,' said a third.

As fists began to fly Jack rose from his seat in the corner and approached the table.

'That's enough, Paddy,' he said. 'You blokes have had enough to drink. Time to go outside and cool off.'

'Now, don't be like that, Jack.' Paddy swung around, almost knocking another drink across the table. 'You'll not be taking the side of the English, will yer?'

'I'm not taking anyone's side, Paddy. I don't want to see anyone hurt. A bit of fresh air's all I'm suggesting.'

'And about time, I'd say,' came a voice from another table. 'A civilised man should be able to have a drink in peace, don't you agree, Clarence?' He leaned over and tapped another man at his table on the shoulder. 'We thought they had this kind of rabble locked up over here, didn't we, old chap?'

'Considering the mother country sent most of them out here for thieving on the streets, it's a bit of a lark for them to be criticising the banks, I'd say.'

'Right on, Gerald,' a third man raised his glass.

There was raucous laughter amongst this group as they chinked their glasses together and continued drinking.

Jack grabbed Paddy's arm as he reared up. He was a thin, wiry man with a wild, unkempt beard and piercing blue eyes. He spun around and glared at the men on the table nearby as he pushed back his chair.

'Now, Paddy. It'll do you no good to get in a fight with those blokes,' Jack said. 'They're twice your size and they have half the belly full you have.'

'They're Brits,' he spat. 'Talkin' all posh. Look at their tweeds. Think they own the place, so they do. They come in 'ere

150

an' take over like they're better than the rest of us. They need a good thrashin' is what they need.'

'Is everything all right, Jack?' Jim came up behind him.

'Will be, if we can get Paddy to go outside for a bit and sober up.' Jack put his arm around the Irishman's shoulders and urged him to turn away from the group of men he was glaring at, who were sniggering into their drinks.

'I'll take him out.' Jim linked his arm into Paddy's and pulled him away. 'Come on, mate. Let's get a little fresh air, eh?'

Paddy stumbled as he straightened himself up. He huffed loudly, shook his head and snarled at the group, but allowed Jim to lead him away.

Jack was about to head back to his own table when one of the Brits spoke. 'Hard to say what's worse. Having to put up with the Irish or the Kanakas. Fortunately we're only in this part of the country for a short while, eh, Archie? I'll be glad to head back to the city, where it's more civilised.'

Jack took a deep breath and stood still for a moment, his back to the group. He debated with himself about the wisdom of speaking to them, knowing they had their horses stabled behind the hotel and they had rooms upstairs. They were obviously wealthy horsemen and Jack had seen them on the race track, intent on winning and pushing their horses hard all week. They were the kind of men Jack preferred to avoid. But their attitude annoyed him and now he decided he couldn't ignore their comments. He turned and made his way closer to their table.

'You'll not win any friends around here with that kind of talk.'

'Is that so?' one said smugly. 'The man's going to tell us what we can talk about now.' There was a consensual chuckle around the table.

'Are you going to escort us from the hotel too?' said another.

'I'm merely suggesting you be careful who you stir up,' Jack said. 'All kinds of people come in here and that's the way the Gieses like it. They're not people to discriminate.'

'So you speak for the Germans as well as the Irish and Kanakas, do you?' The man sneered. 'Quite the politician, aren't you?'

'I'm not speaking for anyone in particular.' Jack moved closer to the table. 'But I don't like to hear anyone put down for the sport of it. It can only start trouble.'

'And we wouldn't want any trouble, would we, chaps? What say, Clarence? How about we have a little wager on a race tomorrow with this one? I've seen him on the track.' The man looked up at Jack. 'You ride that black stallion, don't you?'

Jack nodded. 'Anyone can put a wager on a horse and rider. Suit yourselves if that's what you want to do.'

'No, I mean a substantial wager,' the man said. 'Just between us. What about the horse? One of us beats you and we win the horse.'

'Sorry.' Jack shook his head. 'The horse is not mine to gamble.'

'You hear that, Archie? He doesn't own the horse. Then we should find out who does, eh? Perhaps the owner would like a real rider on him.'

'That's not going to happen.' Jack was determined to control his temper, but these men were pushing him and he knew it would be better if he backed away before things got out of hand.

'So who does the horse belong to then?' Archie pressed.

Jack sighed, wanting to end the conversation. 'He belongs to Hans Giese, the owner of the hotel.'

'Is that so? How convenient,' Clarence said. 'We're his guests. He's always been most accommodating, and he gets a handsome payment to be so. Surely we're entitled to taste all of his services … as usual?'

The laughter was raucous again, and Jack noticed the men winking and rolling their eyes at one another in a lascivious manner that made his blood run cold.

'I gather you've stayed here before?' He constrained his heightened anger.

'We were up last year,' one of the men answered. 'We were testing out some of our horses, getting them ready for the real races in the city. We've brought up a few more this year. It's a practice run, you might say. We're not in the habit of slumming it, though, if that's what you mean.'

Jack was determined not to rise to the bait. 'I hope you did better at the *real races,* than you've done here, then.'

'Ooh, the man's having a go at you, Clarence.' Archie chuckled. 'I reckon this one would give you a run for your money.'

'I'm not interested in having a go at you,' Jack said. 'I'll see you tomorrow on the track. That's the place for pitting ourselves and our horses against one another.'

Jack turned and walked away, his stomach churning and his teeth gritted. He needed to get away from these men and calm down. They had the kind of arrogance that always aroused his anger and he knew it was dangerous for him to continue talking with them.

CHAPTER FIFTEEN

Jack approached his uncle at the stables early the next morning. 'Uncle Hans, I wanted to ask you about the men who own these horses.'

'They're from Sydney,' Hans answered, not looking up as he turned straw over on the floor with a pitch fork. 'They're a fussy lot, think they're entitled. Rich boys, no doubt.'

'So I gathered. Do you know anything else about them?'

'What do you mean?' Hans paused, fork raised in the air. Sweat poured from his forehead despite the chill in the air.

'I talked to them in the hotel last night. I didn't like their attitude. They seem the type who would take advantage wherever they could.'

'Very likely,' Hans said. 'I don't much like they're attitude either, but I'm willing to stable their horses and give them a room for a week. They pay well, and they're gone all day. Did they bother you in some way?'

Jack sighed. 'They were spoiling for a fight with some of the Irish fellows and I stepped in. I almost wished I hadn't. It only took a few minutes and I felt like belting them myself.'

'You'd best avoid them, Jack. No sense in getting into a fight with men like that. I reckon they're used to saying and doing what they want, with rich parents to back them up. Stay out of their way.'

'I'll try.' Jack patted his uncle on the shoulder and headed to Lightning's stable. 'Jim will be over soon. Tell him I've gone out for an early ride, will you?'

'Sure, Jack. You keep your energy for riding, eh?'

'You gave those Brits a thrashing today,' Jim said that night as Jack settled at their corner table in the hotel. 'I thought that dark-haired one with the moustache was going to explode when he came in second to you in the last race. I reckon he'd given it everything he had. He was sure he was going to beat you. I could tell by the look on his face.'

Jack shook his head. 'He pushed his horse till it nearly expired, I know that.'

'Speak of the devil.' Jim looked over Jack's shoulder and rolled his eyes.

Jack turned and saw the group of men walk in. They almost settled near the bar but then one of them looked up at Jack, nudged the one beside him and they all headed for a table close by.

'No doubt about that horse, Jack,' Clarence said. 'I reckon Hans Giese could get a pretty price for that stallion.'

'I doubt Uncle Hans is interested in selling,' Jim said.

'Uncle Hans?' Archie sneered. 'Did you hear that, Gerald? The horse's owner is his uncle.' He jabbed at his friend's elbow.

'You didn't tell us Hans Giese was your uncle, Jack,' Clarence said.

'You didn't ask.' Jack raised his eyebrows in Jim's direction.

'So you have special privileges too?' Clarence said.

'No one has special privileges around here,' Jack answered. 'I told you, the Gieses don't discriminate.'

'So you did.' Clarence nodded, a sly grin spreading across his face. 'Given that there's a black man sitting in the other corner, I'll have to assume you're right. So, is he a Kanaka?'

'You mean Bulla?' Jim said. 'No, he's not a Kanaka, and that's not what we call the Islanders around here. It's considered derogatory. Bulla is an Aborigine. He's one of the roustabouts who come in for the races after a stock drive. Darn good horsemen they are, too.'

'Is that so? And what are the Kanakas good for?' Gerald screwed up his nose.

Jim glanced at Jack as if seeking permission to speak but Jack remained silent. He was busy with his own thoughts.

'The South Sea Islanders are mostly from the Torres Strait,' Jim said. 'They've been brought here as seasonal workers on the cane fields for the last ten years or so. Most are good workers, trying to take a bit of money home to their families. Some of the schooner owners have made a racket of it, though. They trade muskets, powder and tobacco for young Islanders who are pretty much forced to come. There's been some restriction put on it by the government over the years, 'cause some of the Islanders were worked too hard and some even died.'

'I heard that the Queensland government is lifting those restrictions,' Gerald said. 'They've decided too many cane farmers will face ruin for want of labourers. There's always got to be the working class, you see.'

'As long as the abuse of workers is dealt with,' Jack said, tuning in. The man's arrogance was really annoying him.

'Money will always rule, Jack.' Clarence leaned across from his table and patted Jack on the back as if to put him in his place.

Jack smarted. 'We like to believe that in this country fairness will rule.'

'Dream on, Jack. Dream on.' Archie huffed.

'Where's that waitress?' Gerald's eyes went to the kitchen door. 'She's not a patch on that cute little one they had here last year.'

Jack's breath caught in his throat. Before he could speak Jim blurted out, 'You mean Fanny?'

'Yes, I believe that was her name,' Gerald drawled. 'Archie had a bit of a thing for her, didn't you, old boy?'

'I might have had,' Archie whined, 'if Clarence hadn't been such a spoilsport.'

'You knew Fanny?' Jim's voice sounded strangled.

'I wouldn't say I *knew* her, no.' Archie chuckled. 'Not as I'd have liked to.'

Jack's chair flew back as he stood. In an instant he had moved the couple of feet that took him to Archie's chair and pulled the man to his feet by the back of his shirt.

'Now, look here, old man.' Archie could barely speak for the pressure of his shirt on his throat.

'Jack, no!' Jim called.

Jack spun Archie around to face him and was glaring into his eyes, his nose almost touching the other man's. 'You watch how you speak about a young lady,' he hissed. 'If you so much as laid a finger on that girl, you'll have me to deal with.'

'Now, Jack.' Clarence stood and pulled on Jack's shoulder. 'I can assure you Archie never touched that girl. I made sure of that myself. Now how about you sit down and take a breath?'

Jack pushed Archie back into his seat and turned to face Clarence. His face was so close to the Brit's that he could feel the man's breath on his face.

'You fellows are as bad as each other,' he growled. 'Don't try and kid me that you'd keep any of them under control. You all do what you want, to whoever you want. I'm warning you. If I find out any of you hurt Fanny, or anyone else around here that you consider beneath yourself, I'll –'

'You'll what, old man?' Clarence stood to his full height and raised his chin. 'Don't threaten me, Jack. It wouldn't be a good idea.'

'Jack!' The sound of his name being called from the other side of the room made Jack glance sideways. As he did Clarence pushed him hard, causing him to almost lose his balance.

'Jack!' His uncle yelled again from behind the bar. 'Can I see you out back?'

Jack let out his breath and straightened himself up. He glared again at Clarence and then at the other men around the table before he turned and headed to the back door.

'What do you think you're doing?' Hans said, his face fierce. 'I told you to stay away from those men. I won't have brawling in my hotel, you know that. I don't want to have to throw you out.'

'You might consider throwing them out.' Jack's chest was heaving as he tried to calm himself.

'I don't care what they said, Jack. I saw you make the first move and I won't have it. Now you get yourself outside and cool off and don't come back inside until you can control yourself.'

'I'm going, Uncle Hans. I'm sorry to make a disturbance.' Jack was annoyed with himself. He hated to lose control. 'I'd appreciate you telling Jim I'll be back at the tent. I don't think it's a good idea for him to stay in there. He won't like what they're saying, either.'

'Well, he's a grown man, and less likely to fight than you are, so I'm sure he can make up his own mind if he wants to leave.' Hans threw his hands in the air when Jack continued to fume. 'All right, I'll call him out, and the two of you can have an early night. And for goodness' sake stay away from those men. They'll only be here till tomorrow. They're not staying for the end of the week celebrations. They're only interested in the racing.'

'I hope so, Uncle Hans. By God, I hope so.'

***

'I don't think this is a good idea.' Jack followed Jim to the front door of the house.

'We don't even know if Fanny's alive or dead,' Jim said. 'I'm not leaving till I find out if she's all right.'

'What makes you think she'd be with her sister? She's probably well away from here.'

'Maybe, and if she's not here then I'll look somewhere else.'

Jim knocked on the door and shoved his hands into his pocket while he waited for an answer.

The girl who opened the door looked a little older than Fanny, but it was easy to see they were related.

'Yes?' she said, peering at them without venturing out of her hallway.

'We're friends of Fanny,' Jim said. 'We've come to see if she's all right.'

'Why?' Lizzie sounded suspicious.

'We've been at the hotel … for the races,' Jim went on. 'We're used to seeing her there and we were told she wasn't well.'

'She's not here,' Lizzie said. 'She doesn't stay here anymore.'

Jim swallowed and turned to look briefly at Jack, who stood behind him, determined to stay out of the conversation. He had not approved of Jim coming to Fanny's sister's home but was equally uncomfortable with him coming alone. He'd warned Jim not to let on that he knew what had happened to Fanny.

'Could you tell us where we might find her, or contact her,' Jim continued after a minute.

'No, I can't.' Lizzie squinted into the sunshine behind them. She looked about to say something else when a baby's cry came from the house. 'I have to go,' she said, starting to close the door.

'Whose baby is that?' Jim peered over Lizzie's shoulder.

'What do you mean?' Lizzie appeared shocked. 'It's my baby of course. Whose baby do you think it would be?' She frowned and looked more closely at Jim.

'I wondered if it might have been –'

Jack poked Jim in the ribs hard.

'Who are you?' Lizzie's tone was hostile.

'I'm Jim, and this is my brother, Jack.'

'How did you know where I live?' Lizzie glanced over her shoulder as the child's soft cry continued.

'I brought Fanny home one night,' Jim said. 'She wasn't well and Aunty Giese –'

'You're those German boys, aren't you?' Lizzie's hands went to her hips and she moved towards them, causing Jim to move back onto the porch. 'How dare you come here after what you did? I told Fanny she couldn't trust you lot.'

'We didn't do it,' Jim pleaded. 'Honestly, it wasn't us. We're concerned about Fanny and want to see if she's all right.'

'You get out of here or I'll call for the police,' Lizzie yelled. 'You ought to be locked up. Get out of here!' Her voice rose until it was almost a scream.

Jim held up his hands as if to placate the young woman, but she stepped further onto the porch and looked about the street as though she was searching for help.

'Come on, Jim,' Jack said. 'Let's go.' He pulled at Jim's arm and all but dragged him from the porch.

'Fanny might have been in there,' Jim said as they hurried

159

down the street. 'That might have been her baby.'

'And it might not have been. And what were you intending, anyway? To barge in there and drag Fanny out? I thought we agreed not to mention that we knew what happened to her.'

'I wasn't going to, but Lizzie said it first.'

'Great, Jim. That's great. Now she'll know that we know. She's obviously got it in for Germans. If she complains to Aunty Giese about us knowing there's a baby, we'll be in trouble there as well.'

'We still don't know if there is a baby. Lizzie didn't even say whether Fanny's all right. Not even that she's alive.' Jim moaned

'No, so we're no better off. In fact, considerably worse off.'

'All right, Jack, you were right. It wasn't a good idea. But when we leave tomorrow I'm going to Brushgrove. I can't go back to Murrayville without knowing.'

'We agreed to go straight to Mororo when we leave here, to help Gramps out, remember?' Jack's mind was racing with questions about Fanny, but it was hard to think when Jim was running off at the mouth.

'I know Gramps is not well, and I want to help him, Jack. But on the way I have to see if I can find Fanny's parents. Where else could she be? I have to see if she's all right.'

Jack sighed. 'I don't know what we can do about her one way or the other, Jim. It's pretty clear we're first in line for suspicion in everyone's minds. Her parents will probably think one of us is responsible, too. What then?'

'If she'd have me, I'd marry her.' Jim strode down the road.

'What!' Jack stopped in his tracks.

Jim slowed his stride and looked back. 'I said I'd marry her. It's what I wanted anyway. If she's got a baby, then all the more reason to look after her.'

'If you start saying that, people will be sure you're the father of her child.' Jack's words were measured, although his stomach had started to churn. 'You have to think what it would mean if you start saying that.'

'I would mean every word, Jack. I'd marry her today if I could

160

find her. I don't care what people think about the baby.'

'It's more than the baby, Jim. She could have you charged with assault. Where would that get you?'

'Fanny wouldn't do that.' Jim was adamant.

'You don't know that. You haven't seen her since all this happened. She didn't answer any of your letters. How do you know she doesn't want someone charged with what happened to her? It would only be natural.'

'Aunty Giese said she swore it wasn't me. She knows I wouldn't do that. She knows I care about her.'

'She wouldn't admit anything to Aunty Giese, even if she did know. She's too independent, and she'd know how Aunty Giese would go off if it was one of us.'

Jack walked on, trying to control his emotions. He'd felt on a knife's edge all week, thinking about Fanny, wondering if she was safe, furious about what had happened and determined to bring the perpetrator to justice. He wanted to fix it all, set Fanny's world back the way it should have stayed. *Truth is, I'm afraid to think what I really want.*

'You were out late that night, Jim,' he said a few minutes later. 'I remember you didn't come back to the tent for ages. You said the next day that you went down by the river to think.'

'What are you saying?' Jim grabbed his arm.

'I know you'd had a fair bit to drink and I know you were mooning over Fanny. You didn't go looking for her, did you?'

Jim pulled Jack up and glared into his face. 'You think I did it?' He raised a fist as if to punch Jack in the face.

Jack pushed his fist away. 'Keep your shirt on. No, I don't think you did it, but it's easy to see how other people would think so. And saying you were sitting by the river half the night is hardly a good alibi.'

Jim's shoulders slumped and his arms dropped to his side as they walked on. 'I could never hurt her.'

'All I'm saying is that if Fanny was to accuse you, or if her parents believed it was you, you've little defense. So if you go there and start spouting that you'll marry her, you could find yourself in the lockup. You talk without thinking, Jim, and it worries me.'

'All right, Jack. I'll be careful what I say when I go to Brushgrove, but I am going there before I go to Gramps's.'

'He's the only grandparent we have left, Jim. In fact, he's the only family we've got.' Jack felt his heart sink at the thought.

'That's not so, Jack. We've got Bob. He's our brother and we haven't even talked to him about all this. Maybe he saw something that night, someone suspicious hanging around. He lives over the hotel after all, and he's usually up late.'

'I'll talk to him before we leave. I didn't want to go against Aunty Giese and let on what happened to Fanny. You know how easily these things get around.'

'Bob wouldn't say anything. He hardly talks to anyone. He's worse than you about keeping everything private.'

'Well, there's good sense in that when you've got things that people will use against you,' Jack warned.

Jim sighed and stared ahead. They were almost back to the hotel. 'Besides, Bob isn't our only family,' he said. 'There's Ma.'

Jack was silent. He didn't know what he could say about his mother that hadn't already been said.

'We ought to visit her,' Jim went on. 'Even if you don't blame her for what happened in the past, I'm sure she thinks we do, because we never go to see her. We go and visit her father. We help him out, but we do nothing for her. We don't even know how she is. It's not fair. She's our mother.'

'Fanny really got to you with all her talk of making up with Ma, didn't she?'

'I've thought about it a lot, yeah. You get upset when men like those Brits look down on people. You always stand up for someone who's being hurt. Yet you don't want to have anything to do with Ma. You can't say that's even-handed.'

'I know what Fred Clifford is capable of doing to Ma if he thinks she's taking our side, Jim. I saw too much.'

162

'I understand that, but maybe some time when he's away we could go.'

As they approached the door of the hotel Jack nodded. 'I'll think about it,' he said. 'Right now, we need to decide what's most important. Gramps is pretty sick. He wouldn't have sent word and asked us to go to Mororo if he wasn't. And you're busting to go to Brushgrove and find Fanny. We can't wander around the countryside without working for too much longer. What do you want to do?'

'I want to go to Brushgrove first. I have to, Jack.'

CHAPTER SIXTEEN

Woodford Island, July, 1892

Fanny cradled her baby close to her chest. When his breathing slowed to the peaceful rhythm of sleep she'd watched so often the past few weeks, she wriggled down in the bed and let him slide to her side. She stroked his plump red cheek and slid her finger through a tuft of dark hair on the crown of his head. *It's hard to believe he's really mine.*

'Is he asleep?' Granny poked her head in the door. Her graying hair curled around her face, which was lined and pale, though her eyes glowed with youthful joy.

Fanny nodded and patted the bed beside her. 'Come in, Granny. You won't wake him. He's full as a tick and contented.'

A smile spread across Granny's face as she tiptoed to the side of the bed and settled herself beside Fanny. 'He's so beautiful.'

'I know,' Fanny said. 'I can hardly believe he's here.'

'Yes, the first one is a wonder. It took me months to accept that Lotte was truly mine.'

'You were very young when you had her, weren't you?' Fanny ventured.

Granny nodded. 'Far too young in most people's estimation, but that didn't mean I loved her any less.'

'Was it hard … with you being …? Fanny struggled to find the right words.

'It was difficult.' Granny sighed. 'But I had people who loved

164

me and were ready to support me, no matter what I decided.' She grinned. 'No doubt, someone has told you that I had Lotte out of wedlock. I don't mind. It's a long time ago, and it worked out so wonderfully that I hardly think of it as a difficult time at all now.'

Granny's eyes glazed over for a moment and the golden light that had been shining from them moments ago, faded to pale dusky brown. 'Your grandfather and I learned a great deal through that experience – about ourselves, about life, and about God. It often takes something like this for us to know what God is like, Fanny, especially to understand His love.'

'He will love my baby, won't He, even though it's not the best way for him to have come into the world?'

'Of course He will, darling girl. I asked the same question when Lotte was born, although I was more afraid God might not love me.'

'I've wondered about that too. The priest at Maclean definitely gave me the impression that God would not be pleased with me.'

'The priest is a man, no matter his title or role, Fanny. He sees things from his own perspective, not necessarily God's.'

'He does work for God, though, so he should know what God thinks.'

'I thought you went to the Anglican church while you were at Rose's house?'

'I did, and the minister didn't once say anything mean to me. I sensed he felt sorry for me, and that he wouldn't allow anyone to be cruel to me directly, but he didn't go out of his way to let me know he cared either.'

'Some people don't know how to handle these things, love. That's why it's best you're back with family who love you and want the best for you and the baby.'

'I'm so thankful that I ran into you when I got off the ferry.'

Granny chuckled. 'So am I, dear. I thought you were about to have the baby on the wharf.'

Fanny glanced at the baby and felt her heart melt. 'I wasn't sure how you and Grandfather – especially Grandfather – would be with me,' she said.

'Then it's for the best that you stayed here with us and had the baby. You can see how smitten your grandfather is, and I must say it's been a good test of his new heart.'

'His new heart?' Fanny was surprised at Granny's words.

'He wasn't always so able to love unconditionally before focusing on the wrongs and rights of a situation.'

'So what does he think is the right and wrong of this situation?' Fanny was still wary about what her family expected of her.

'He thinks it's your decision, love, which it most certainly is, and he'll support you whatever you decide.'

'But I've already decided. I've never thought about giving my baby up. I love him too much.'

'Then you'll do what's best for him, I'm sure.'

Fanny's heart lurched. 'Do you think it matters if a baby doesn't have his real father?'

'It matters that a child has people around him who love him, Fanny. If his real father is not capable of loving him, then he doesn't belong in the child's life. That's what I think.'

Fanny sighed. 'Thank you, Granny.'

'Now, you rest. Betsy and Francis will be here soon to visit again. It's hard for them to stay away, bless them.'

'They want me to go home soon, and I will, but I feel safe here right now. It's so quiet and peaceful, and I know you understand how I feel.'

'I do indeed, darling girl, and you can stay as long as you want.'

Fanny turned to the baby and felt the soft brush of his breath on her cheek. His eyelids fluttered, then settled again into stillness. He was placid by nature, Fanny could already tell. He was calm when he fed and rarely cried unless he was hungry or needed changing. Her heart overflowed with love and tenderness. She would protect him with her life.

She thought about what Granny had said. *If his father is not capable of loving him, then he doesn't belong in the baby's life.* So she would raise her little boy herself. No one could love him as she did.

'Have you decided on his name, Fanny?' Betsy held the baby in her arms and rocked lightly on her feet.

'Not yet, Mum. I've been thinking about it, though. Don't worry, you'll be the first to know.'

'I don't mind what you call him, love. He's precious.' Betsy sighed. 'Almost makes me wish I had another.'

'I think ten's sufficient.' Francis tapped her on the bottom.

'Will you mind if this one's around the house for a while, Dad?' Fanny asked.

'Of course I won't mind, love.' Francis was quick to answer. 'Does that mean you're coming home soon?'

'Soon, Dad. I promise.'

'Give the girl time to recover, dear,' Betsy said. 'It takes a bit out of a woman, this child-bearing, you know.'

'I didn't notice it taking much out of you,' Francis joked. 'And Fanny seems to be blooming.'

'Well and good, but it will still take her a few weeks to get her strength back.'

'Does Thomas know?' Fanny asked.

Betsy shook her head. 'Your brother hasn't been home for a few months and we wanted to tell him in person. We did as you asked and told him you were away working in a domestic situation. He'll be home for the spring races in September. That's only eight weeks away. Time enough, I think.'

'I'd like to tell him myself,' Fanny said. 'After all, he was there for me when it all happened. I owe him an explanation.'

'Whatever you like, love,' Francis assured her. 'We've told the girls, of course, and they're excited about having another baby around. We've not said anything to the little ones. I think they'll accept it quite naturally.'

'Aren't the girls shocked?'

'It did take a bit of explaining.' Betsy's eyes were glassy. 'We wanted them to understand that this has been a dreadful ordeal for you on the one hand but that the baby is a blessing.'

'Mary Anne and Eliza seemed more relieved that you aren't dying of some dreadful disease, than worried about you having a baby,' Frances added.

Betsy nodded. 'Yes, I think your sisters were worried that you'd gone off to some sanitarium for the terminally ill.'

'I'm sorry to have worried them so. And Lizzie?' Fanny asked.

'We've not told her,' Betsy said. 'We thought it best to wait and see if you'd like to do that. She's likely to be upset at first.'

'She thinks you're still suffering over being attacked,' Francis said. 'She's pretty angry about that from the tone of her letters. But she's not long had her own baby, so she has enough to think about.'

'I'm sorry I haven't been in touch with her,' Fanny said. 'Is her baby all right?'

'She's beautiful.' Betsy rolled her eyes and grinned. 'We went when Annie was born, two months ago. It was a difficult birth and Lizzie was still weak. She asked how you were and we said you were at Aunt Rose's, helping out with her children for a few months.'

Fanny sighed. 'She was so distressed when it happened. I'll go and see her and apologise.'

'I'm sure that's not necessary, love.' Francis took hold of Fanny's hand and gave it a gentle squeeze. 'The apology, that is. When you're able to travel in and see her I'm sure she'll love the visit.'

Speaking of visitors,' Betsy started, glancing at Francis.

Fanny noticed some kind of signal between her parents that she couldn't decipher. 'What about visitors?'

'We had a visitor yesterday,' Betsy said.

'Why are you looking so strangely at each other? Who was the visitor?' Fanny pulled herself up in the bed.

'Don't upset yourself.' Francis patted her hand. 'We didn't tell him anything.'

Fanny's heart leapt.

'It was your friend from the hotel in Grafton,' Betsy continued. 'He was worried about you when you weren't at work. His aunt told him you were unwell, and he – '

'You mean Jim?' Fanny felt faint. 'Does he know what happened?'

'He didn't say much.' Francis shook his head. 'We told him that you were with family and that you were fine. We didn't mention the baby. I'm not sure if he knows more than that you came home unwell. He didn't say.'

'He was on his own?'

'Yes.'

'I don't know what Mrs Giese would have told him.' Fanny sank back down in the bed. 'She was suspicious that it might have been one of the boys, but I assured her it wasn't. I hope she only said I was sick.'

'He seemed a nice young man,' Francis said.

'He is.' Fanny nodded. 'But I'd rather he didn't know about the baby just yet.'

Betsy passed the baby to Francis and sat on the side of the bed. 'If it was this boy, he seemed –'

'Why does everyone keep thinking it was Jim?' Fanny cut in. 'I've said it wasn't over and over. You don't think because he's German –'

'Of course your mother doesn't think that,' Francis said. 'It's just that he appeared to be very taken with you and it seemed to me he'd want to do the right thing, if it was him.'

'Well, I'm telling you, it wasn't him.' Fanny huffed.

'And not his brother either?' Francis ventured.

At this Fanny pulled herself up and folded her arms. 'I don't know what I have to do to convince everyone that those boys had nothing to do with this. People are prejudice because they're German – which they're not anyway. They're as Australian as we are. People are so unfair to hold their heritage against them.'

'You know we wouldn't do that, no matter where they came from. In fact we didn't even think about Jim being German.' Francis squeezed Fanny's arm. 'Please don't upset yourself.'

'Have you had any other … trouble?' Fanny asked. She was

pleased to move away from the subject of Jim and Jack, and she was concerned about what might be happening to her parents. She watched them as they prepared to answer her.

'A couple at church have tried to commiserate with us … about our trouble,' Betsy said, disdain in her voice. 'But we set them straight. We've decided that we'll show nothing but joy about the new arrival in our family and if they have any criticism we'll ignore it.'

'Truth is many people around here are willing to take others as they find them, love.' Francis brushed Fanny's cheek. 'I reckon there's been plenty to test this community's tolerance and acceptance over the years, with so many different nationalities settling here, and with the Islanders working the fields, and the Aborigines about. There's been plenty of clashes over different beliefs and traditions, and plenty of opportunity for the pious to look down on those they disapprove of.'

He sat on the side of the bed and adjusted the baby in his arms, rocking until the tiny snuffles quieted. 'It seems to me that hard times bring out the worst and the best of people. The ground shifts a bit under us when we're confronted with differences, or with things we didn't expect or invite. When push comes to shove we've all made our mistakes and had our tragedies, and in the end we've had to sort out our differences and pull together. When there are floods and fires around here, or any other disaster, no one checks the colour or background of the bloke next to him. They simply get on with helping out, shoulder to shoulder.'

'You can see your father's given this a lot of thought, Fanny.' Betsy rubbed Francis's back. 'We've talked about it and we both feel the same.' Her eyes filled with tears and Fanny could see her father's emotions were also close to the surface.

Fanny nodded, her own eyes filling. She could not find words to express her gratitude and love for her parents.

Francis swallowed and his voice was soft when he spoke again. 'We have plenty of people around us who are solid and loyal. No one that matters is going to give this little one a hard time.'

Betsy nodded. 'I think Fanny's had enough for now, Francis. She's looking tired.'

Fanny relaxed into her pillows and smiled gratefully at her mother. 'I would like to rest for a bit. I'll take the baby now, Dad. He'll be awake soon for a feed, so I'd best get ready.' She held out her arms and her father laid the baby in them.

'I'm sorry if we upset you, love,' he said. 'We won't talk about this again, eh?'

'Thanks, Dad. I know our baby will have all the people he needs to love him.'

'I've no doubt about that, sweetheart.' He kissed the top of her head. 'We'll see you later.'

When her parents had gone, Fanny lay back and gazed out the window. She tried to relax, but her mind soon went to Jim.

Does he know about the baby? What did Mrs Giese tell him? And where is Jack? Does he care at all about me? She closed her eyes and took another deep breath. *I must stay calm and think only about my baby's welfare. He's all that matters now.*

CHAPTER SEVENTEEN

Mororo, Northern Arm, Clarence River

Jack squatted by the river and looked out over the darkening landscape. The mist was gathering over the water. The sky was overcast with thick grey clouds, hastening the evening darkness. His mood was glum and he knew he'd worried Gramps with his sullenness. He needed to pull himself together for the old man's sake, but his heart was heavy, his mind confused.

He rose and headed back to his grandfather's hut. Jim was due the following morning. Then there might be news of Fanny, but for now he determined to put aside his concerns and do whatever he could to help Gramps. The old man was in his seventies and clearly frail and tired. There were fences to mend and clearing of the old canes. The hut was in need of repairs, and if Gramps was to survive the winter he'd need plenty of wood cut.

Jack's best childhood memories were his visits to his grandparent's farm in Mororo. He'd been too young to remember living in Iluka when his father was alive. Once his mother married Fred Clifford there were no good memories at all, except for once a year – usually when his mother was having another baby – when she would bring Bob, Jim and himself, as well as whatever little ones she already had, to Mororo. It was the only time Jack could remember seeing his mother happy.

She would spend a few weeks being fussed over by Grandma, while the boys spent their time following Gramps around the farm, helping with whatever jobs he'd allow them to do. Memories flooded into Jack's mind; feeding scraps from Grandma's wonderful cooking to squawking chooks and grunting pigs, watching chickens hatch and piglets suckle, standing at a safe distance to see the cane cutters swing their scythes and throw bundles of cane onto trucks.

Jack had dreamed of coming back when he grew up, to help Gramps on the farm. There'd never been anything he wanted more, at least not until now.

***

Jack was standing by the fire, warming his hands when the knock on the door came the next morning. Gramps was closer and hurried to open it.

'Hello, Gramps.' Jim pulled his grandfather into a bear hug. 'How are you?'

'As good as you, lad, I'd say.' Gramps stood back and cast his eyes over Jim's frame. 'Thin as a whip, you are, and wet as a shag.'

'I had to hitch a ride out from Iluka and it took three different carts to get me far enough to walk the rest. It's been raining cats and dogs most of the way, and mighty cold to boot. I'll be fine when I clean up.'

'You best get over by the fire with your brother,' Gramps said. 'He's been out in it too.' When Jim had pulled off his sodden boots, Gramps took his coat from his back. 'Jack's cut enough wood to last three years and that's longer than I'll last.'

'Now, Gramps, none of that,' Jim chided. 'You'll get over this bout of sickness soon enough. You're as strong as an ox.'

'No, lad, not any more. The old body's giving up on me. I could be pushing up daisies before year's end.'

Jack stood to the side when Jim joined him by the fire. 'Glad you're here,' he said, as his brother sighed and rubbed his hands together.

'Me too,' Jim said. 'It's always good to get back here, eh?'

Jack nodded and watched Gramps sink into his rickety chair.

He breathed in deeply and let the smells of the room wrap around him, as warm as the flames from the fire.

The old leather-back sofa, where Grandma had always sat to do her mending, still had pride of place in the room. The cushions she had embroidered were wrinkled and sagging but they still had the scent of lavender, which mixed oddly with the smell of leather. Gramps's pipes were in a mug on the sideboard and the strong odour of tobacco also permeated the room. Even the musty dampness, which seemed to leach its way through the boarded walls and floor, had a homey feel that Jack welcomed.

'No more talk of the end, Gramps,' Jack said. 'You'll likely outlive the lot of us.'

Gramps shook his head. 'Now you're here, Jim, maybe you'll tell me what's going on. I could see Jack had a bee in his bonnet when he arrived, and by the look of you, I'd say it's not the rain that's making that face of yours glum. What's really up? I can't get a thing out of Jack.' He screwed his nose up at Jack, then winked at Jim. 'So why did he come on ahead of you? What was so important you had to stay back for?'

'Whoa there, Gramps. Give me time to warm up.' Jim chuckled. 'There was a friend I wanted to look up, that's all. Jack was in a hurry to get here and see how you were, so he came on ahead. Nothing for you to worry about.'

'You can't fool me, lad. I'm not silly. I've seen you two often enough when you've been ready to skin something alive. Is it your mother? Is that no-good husband of hers giving her a hard time again?'

Jim seemed to be waiting for Jack to answer, but Jack remained quiet. He didn't want to talk about his mother.

'We don't know, Gramps,' Jim eventually answered. 'We didn't get to see Ma this trip. Jack asked around and Fred was in town so we didn't go near her place.'

'Poor Janie.' Gramps shook his head and began to stoke his pipe. 'She sure did get herself into hot water with that bloke.' His eyes filled and he took a deep breath. His chest shuddered as he let out air.

Jack wished he could think of something helpful to say, but

174

his mind was blank. He was about to change the subject when Gramps began again.

'She was a bright young thing, always smiling as a child. She loved to run around the paddocks with the sheep down on the Monaro. It was a good life, shepherding. Perhaps I should have stuck with it instead of coming up here.'

'The chance to own your own land was mighty strong, I guess,' Jack said, steering the conversation away from his mother.

Gramps nodded. 'It's what enticed us to migrate in the first place, the promise of land. It was a powerful draw card for a small town Englishman. I thought coming up here would be the best chance for the children to have a good future.' He tapped his pipe on the arm of his chair and shook his head. 'Didn't work out that way for poor Janie.'

'You did what you thought was best, Gramps.' Jim moved to a chair beside Gramps and patted his arm.

'I did.' The old man's lip trembled as he brought his pipe to his mouth. 'She writes me letters, but she don't say much about *him*. She tells me how the children are doing, so I have to believe they're all right. Florrie, the eldest, is sixteen now, she says. A young woman. I guess she'll be getting married before too long.'

'I imagine Florrie will get away as soon as she can, one way or another,' Jim said. He turned and faced the fire, holding out his hands to soak up the warmth.

'The little one's only seven, just started school,' Gramps continued.

Jim nodded. 'Yeah, Daisy was a baby when Jack and I left.'

'You ought to visit more.' The old man's voice cracked a little. 'Your mother's not a bad woman. She was headstrong, and it got her into trouble more than once, but she's paid for it over and over. I wish she'd come up and see me. She hasn't been since your grandmother passed four years ago. I miss her, but there's no way I can make the trip down to Grafton, what with the farm and these blasted turns of mine.'

'I'll make sure next time I'm in Grafton I go see her, Gramps.

175

I promise.' Jim glanced at Jack and his eyes narrowed, as if to make a point.

'When she married your father, she was so happy.' Gramps seemed to be talking to himself. 'Who'd have thought August would die on her so young? And old man Schmidt didn't help. She wanted to be here with us, but he wouldn't hear of you boys leaving Grafton. She didn't have the strength to stand up to him.'

'Yeah, I remember how Grandfather Schmidt was,' Jim said, clearly uncomfortable.

'I reckon she married Fred to spite him, you know. She tried to separate herself from the German community but the old man kept turning up. It was like he was inspecting Janie to see if she was doing things like he thought she should.'

He sucked on his pipe and blew smoke into the air. 'Marrying Fred Clifford was certainly the wrong thing to do, and it wasn't only Philip Schmidt who thought that. If I'd met Fred before your mother married him, I reckon I'd have known right off he was no good for her.'

'Or us,' Jack said under his breath.

'I'm sorry it worked out so bad for you boys. I swear to God if I'd known earlier what he was doing to you, I'd have gone down there and taken him to task.' Gramps laid his head back in the chair.'She never said how bad it was, and you boys didn't let on anything in the early days either.'

'She told us not to,' Jim said. 'She thought Fred would be worse if anyone knew he was beating us.' His words faded away.

'When Bob came up here he told me what had been happening to you boys. I wanted to go down there and kill that man with my bare hands. He convinced me it would be worse for Janie if I tried to interfere. I didn't know what to do for her.'

Jack watched Gramps's eyes fill and his mouth tremble. 'Don't upset yourself, Gramps,' he said. 'Ma made her decision and we all had to accept it. She's got five kids to Fred now. She's not likely to leave him, is she?'

'Seems not,' Gramps said. 'If I thought I could do anything I

176

would, you know that, don't you?'

'Sure we do, and so would we, Gramps,' Jim said. 'Honest, I'll go and see her next time I'm down there and make sure she's all right.'

Gramps nodded and sniffed back tears.

Jack felt helpless to ease his grandfather's mind about the situation. He felt helpless about Fanny too, and his chest ached as his thoughts returned to her. *Did Jim find her? Does she blame us for what had happened to her?* He needed to get Jim alone and find out what he knew.

He watched Jim later as they ate their evening meal. He could see that his brother was no less worried than when he'd headed for Brushgrove, and so assumed there'd been no good news about Fanny, perhaps no news at all.

'These rabbits make a mean meal, Gramps.' Jim smeared a thick slice of bread across his plate and mopped up the last of the gravy.

Gramps nodded, his mouth bulging. 'I can't cook 'em like your grandma used to do, but it's not bad. Fills a hole.' He chewed slowly, glancing from one of the boys to the other. 'So, are you going to tell me what's going on with you two or not?'

There was silence while Jim upended his mug of tea and drank it. Jack had no intentions of worrying his grandfather with talk of Fanny. He tried to catch Jim's eye before he started talking, but failed.

'There's a friend of ours from Grafton in a bit of trouble, is all. We'd like to help but it's hard to know how.' Jim mopped his plate with a chunk of bread.

'I see,' Gramps said. 'In financial trouble is he? Lot of that around. We get swaggies coming through here all the time now. Men roaming the country on foot, everything they own on their backs, and trying to get a bit of work here and there, or a free feed. I've had a few come in here. I give 'em a meal and send 'em on their way. I've not a penny to be paying 'em for any work. Can't see how you two would have anything to spare either. You can't get blood out of a stone, boys.'

'We know that, Gramps,' Jim said. 'But it's not a financial problem.'

177

Before Jim could continue Jack leaned across the table. 'You need to be careful, Gramps, with those swaggies coming in here. If you bring them in for a meal, they'll know you live alone. You don't know what they might do.'

Gramps waved his hand around above the table. 'It's not much of a risk. They soon see I've nothing worth stealing.'

'Not only that, Gramps,' Jack went on. 'One of them could decide this would be good shelter for a bit, and they'd only have to knock you on the head once. You'd be a goner.'

'I suppose,' Gramps said. 'But you can pick up at the door when a bloke's genuine. If they seem a bit suspicious, I send 'em on their way before they have a chance to jump me. I always have the shotgun handy behind the door.'

'Still, I don't like you being here alone, Gramps. Anyone can see it's all getting a bit much for you.'

'I won't deny it, Jack, but apart from when the seasonal workers are here to cut the bit of cane I've still got, I can't afford to have anyone else working with me.'

'What about James?' Jim said. 'Isn't he interested in taking over the property?'

'Nah.' Gramps shook his head and raked his fingers through his grey-streaked beard. 'I'm afraid my son doesn't care for life on the land. He prefers to work in town. He has his family out at Casino now. I get the occasional letter, but there's no chance he'll come back and work the farm.'

'I'm sorry about that,' Jim said. 'It must be disappointing to work a place all these years, then see it go downhill.'

'Actually, I'm glad you raised that.' Gramps sat back and poked at his pipe. 'I've been wondering if you two might be ready to settle down.'

'What do you mean, settle down?' Jack asked.

'I mean you're not boys any longer. What are you, Jack, twenty-three? I'm surprised you haven't found yourself a nice girl and started a family of your own.' He sucked back tobacco juice and blew into the air.

Jack sank his teeth into his bottom lip and took a deep breath. 'Not too many girls wandering around in the bush where Jim and I work, Gramps.'

'Precisely.' Gramps tapped the table as if he'd scored a point. 'What about when you go to Grafton for the races? See any nice girls there?'

Jim cleared his throat and glared at Jack.

Jack had no idea what his brother was trying to convey. He shook his head and half-grinned at his grandfather. 'Too busy with horses that week, Gramps,' he said.

'Well, I reckon it's time you thought about your future,' the old man went on, more seriously. 'I've been hoping you'd consider coming up here before too long and taking over this place.'

'Take over this place?' Jack was taken aback by his grandfather's idea.

'Yeah, maybe both of you,' Gramps continued. 'Like I said, my James is not interested. The girls' husbands have work in Maclean. You two are my oldest grandsons, apart from your brother, Bob, of course, but he's interested in the hotel business. It's you two who I'd like to have this place.'

Jim sat silently, a stunned look on his face.

'I don't know what to say,' Jack said. 'We thought we'd be woodcutting for a bit yet. I haven't thought about what I'd do next.'

'Well, it's time you did.' Gramps rested his elbows on the table and leaned across at the boys. 'You're right that this is getting too much for me. You can see how run down everything is. A lot of work's needed, and you'd still have to do some woodcutting in the off season for a while, but I reckon you could build this place up again. It'd be a real shame to see it go begging.'

Jack shook his head. He'd wanted to come and help his grandfather get things back in shape but he hadn't considered he'd ever have the chance to make a life of farming. He couldn't deny the excitement the idea gave him deep down, but it scared him too.

'Jim might be better suited to this kind of thing, Gramps,' he said when Jim still seemed too stunned to respond. 'Especially the finding a nice girl and settling down part.' He sat back and folded his arm. 'That's not where I'm headed.'

'Every man thinks that until the right girl comes along and changes his mind.' Gramps chuckled. 'It'll happen, you mark my words.'

Jack's stomach lurched but he ignored it and turned to Jim. 'What do you reckon?' He prodded his brother.

'I don't know,' Jim said. 'I'd like to think I'd … find a girl and have a family. But …' He seemed lost for words.

'Well, it's something to think about, boys,' Gramps said. 'I hope you'll consider it, if not right away, then soon. I'm not sure how much longer I've got.' He pushed back from the table and raised himself awkwardly from his chair. 'As you can see, these old legs aren't enjoying the workout I'm giving them.'

He tapped his pipe into a dish, emptying tobacco ash. 'I'm off to bed now, so I'll leave you to it. Throw the dishes in that bowl over there. We'll clean up in the morning.'

He hobbled towards his bedroom. 'Plenty of water in the kettle for another cuppa if you want,' he said over his shoulder before disappearing from the room.

Jack sat quietly for a moment. Something pushed at the back of his mind but he refused to entertain it.

'What do you reckon about that, Jack?' Jim said.

'I'm not sure. I'll think about it later. First tell me what happened when you went to Brushgrove. It's obviously stuck in your craw.'

'Fanny wasn't there. Not at her parents' home. They said she'd been staying with an aunt and helping out with the children. They didn't seem upset or anything, so I didn't know what to think.'

Jack took a deep breath. 'That could mean she didn't have the baby. Maybe she lost it.' The thought made him surprisingly sad. 'Maybe her parents made her give it up for adoption.'

'I can't imagine that.' Jim shook his head.

'You don't know her parents.' Jack felt annoyed and didn't understand why.

'They seemed caring, and besides, I'm sure Fanny would do what she wanted.'

'I agree, but if she has a baby with her, she's not going to be up to looking after someone else's children, is she? She's tough, but not that tough.'

Jim slumped into his chair and sighed. 'They didn't let on anything. I had a feeling they were protecting her, but I'm not good at picking up on what's going on behind the scenes. That's why I would have preferred you to be with me.'

Jack sat back and pushed his hands through his hair. 'Well, I had to get up here to Gramps. You can see how weak he is, and given what he's said, I reckon he's worse than he lets on.'

Jim stared at the table in front of him for a few moments. 'You know, I'd like nothing better than to come up here and work this place, Jack, if I had Fanny with me.'

Jim's words caused Jack's breath to catch in his throat. He could have guessed as much, but hearing it out loud was painful in a way Jack could not fathom.

'You don't even know where she is,' he said. 'So you can hardly start making plans around her.'

Jim looked bereft and Jack wondered how deeply Fanny was going to affect his brother. He was beginning to wish they'd never met her, and yet he couldn't deny his own concern for her and the rage that twisted his gut when he thought about what had happened to her.

**

'I've decided to call him Percy, Mum.' Fanny looked down at her baby. 'It's been a month. I can't have him nameless as well as …' She was about to say 'fatherless', but thought better of it. She was happy to be settled back into her parent's home, but she preferred to avoid any mention of her baby's father. Her sisters were too prone to speculate about who might be a prospective husband for her and father for her baby.

Betsy turned from the table where she was folding the washing.

'Percy?' she said, a frown spreading across her face. 'Where has that come from?'

'Mostly from my cousin, Percy,' Fanny answered. 'Of all of Aunt Rose's children, Percy was the one who was the kindest to me.'

'My sister wasn't kind to you?' Betsy sounded shocked.

'Yes, actually, I've used the wrong word, Mum. They were all kind to me, but Percy seemed to understand more than anyone else what I was going through. That sounds strange, considering he's only ten years old, but he stood up for me. He was brave in the face of criticism at his school. I'm not sure what it was exactly, but I felt safe with him.'

'I'm sorry you had a difficult time at Rose's, love.' Betsy patted down a pile of folded nappies, came and stood behind Fanny, and massaged her neck and shoulders.

'It was my decision, Mum, and I'm not sorry. I felt better for saving you from some of what happened over there. I know there's still some criticism but at least there's no question now in anyone's mind that I'm keeping my baby.'

'Yes, dear, we all accept that. None of us could bear to be without the little darling. So you'll call him Percy? That's lovely, and I'm sure Rose will be chuffed.'

'Percival Hilton,' Fanny said. 'That's what I've decided.'

'Percival Hilton,' Betsy repeated. 'That is a mouthful, and a very English one.'

Fanny sensed her mother's intrigue. 'You don't think I'm being silly, do you?'

'No, love, I don't. If you're trying to distance yourself from any speculation about a German father, then I think it's a bit of an overreaction, but it's your choice, and you aren't likely to be swayed from it. You're a strong girl, Fanny, and just as well. I'm proud of you.' She squeezed Fanny's shoulders.

Fanny took a deep breath and allowed her mother's hands to relax her. She felt relieved to have made this decision and confident it was the right one. If there was ever going to be a fuss made of Percy's origin, she didn't want more prejudice aimed at him by people who believed he had German heritage. It would be hard enough for him to live with the fact that he'd been born out of wedlock. But that was something for the future and she was determined to live one step at a time.

'How about we go outside and sit in the sunshine for a bit before Percy wakes up?' she suggested.

'All right, dear. And we'll plan for his christening, eh? Thomas will be here in about four weeks. Perhaps that will be a good time.'

Fanny nodded. 'Yes, I'll be glad to see my brother. I need to help him understand all this. I think that's another thing I'll need some heavenly guidance for.'

CHAPTER EIGHTEEN

Brushgrove, September, 1892

Fanny watched Thomas's face crumble with shock as she told him
the truth of what had happened that night behind The European. By
the time she'd finished her brother's eyes were blazing with anger.

'You've kept this from me all this time!' He turned to his
parents. 'The scoundrel got away with this and you've done
nothing to find him?' He spat the last words as his head spun back
to Fanny. 'And you! How could you sneak off and have a baby
without telling me? You know how worried I was about you.' He
threw his arms in the air, his face twisting as he struggled to find
words. 'I can't believe any of this.'

Springing from his chair, he strode to the window where
Percy's cradle was catching the morning sun through the curtains.
He looked down on the sleeping child and shook his head.

'I'm sorry,' Fanny said. 'I know this is a terrible shock, but I
don't want to find the man. I want to forget about him and raise my
son in peace. Please try and understand.'

'Raise him in peace!' Thomas spluttered as he returned to the
chair in front of Fanny. 'How can you do that when everyone will
be talking about him … calling him a –'

'That's enough, Thomas,' his father cut in. 'We've been all
through this. Fanny has made up her mind. She'll not be swayed
and we must all accept her decision.' Francis rose and gripped his
son's shoulders. 'I know it's not easy to take in. It's been hard for

us all, but there's an innocent child here, and we've to love and care for him and Fanny. That's what's important now.'

'Well, you've had time to take it in. I haven't.' Thomas pursed his lips and looked into Fanny's eyes, as if searching for more answers.'

'Please let it go, Thomas,' she said. 'For me, please.'

He dropped his head into his hands. 'What does Lizzie think about all this?'

Fanny looked away, finding her brother's piercing gaze uncomfortable. 'Lizzie doesn't know yet. She thinks I've been helping Aunt Rose with her children – which I was for a while – but I haven't told her about Percy. I wanted to wait until you were here. I was hoping you'd come with me to see her. She's not long had her own baby and I didn't want to upset her.'

Thomas slapped his hands onto his knees and rolled his eyes. 'Good grief. You know she'll be upset, no matter when you tell her, and all the more for having been kept in the dark for so long.'

'I've tried to do what's best for everyone concerned, Thomas.' Tears welled in Fanny's eyes and she looked away.

'No more, Thomas.' Betsy stood behind Fanny, rubbing her shoulders. 'Upsetting Fanny will be no good for her or for Percy. Why don't you take a little time to think about all this? I'm sure when you do you'll want to support your sister.'

Thomas gazed up at his mother and nodded. He took a deep breath and patted Fanny's knee. 'I'm sorry, Sis. I know this has been a terrible ordeal for you. I'm in shock. I do need some time to get my thoughts together. Tomorrow I'll take you into Grafton to see Lizzie.'

***

If Thomas had found Fanny's story hard to hear, it was nothing compared to Lizzie's reaction. Fanny could feel her sister's horror growing with each word. Eventually she stopped and waited for the eruption she could see coming.

'You've lost your mind.' Lizzie was pacing backward and forward, two of her young children scuttling out of her way, and almost being trodden on in the process. 'You think you can

185

suddenly produce a child, then go about your life as if nothing's happened, while everyone's pointing the finger and talking about you. You'll be disgraced from one end of town to the other. And more so if you've the daft idea that you can raise him on your own. It's absurd! Poor Mum and Dad. How are they coping with this?'

'Mum and Dad are fine, Lizzie,' Thomas interjected. 'They're concern is for Fanny's wellbeing, and for the boy. They adore him, that's clear.'

His tone was calm and reassuring and Fanny was grateful that he seemed to have come to terms with her decision over night. It didn't seem that Lizzie was going to be so easily convinced.

'Good grief, Fanny. You sound like one of those suffragettes everyone's talking about.' Lizzie resumed her tirade. 'Women who think they can be like men, marching around with placards, singing songs about being independent, supporting themselves … making a living.' She rolled her eyes. 'I can't imagine what Alf will say.'

With her hands planted on her hips she stood over Fanny. 'You should have given the baby up. It could have been adopted into a real family, who could raise it properly.'

'He, Lizzie. My son is not an it.'

'Well, that's how he'll be thought of. He's an illegitimate child. How could you think to keep him? You're always taking a stand about something, but this is too much.' She paced around the room again. 'And why on earth would you want a child from that … situation? It doesn't bear thinking about. He'll be discriminated against, spurned …'

'Perhaps by you.' Fanny rose from her chair and faced her sister. 'Perhaps you and Alf will spurn my son, but I will love him and protect him, from you and anyone else who chooses to be so narrow-minded. Now, it's time I left. I love you, Lizzie, and I hope you'll change your opinion when you've had time to think. But for now, I'm not prepared to hear any more of what you've got to say.'

She turned to her brother, whose face had drained of colour. 'Please take me home, Thomas. Percy will be awake and looking for a feed.'

186

'You might have brought him to show me.' Lizzie's tone was a little softer.

'I'd like you to see him, Lizzie, but not until you can love him.'

As Fanny was gathering her jacket and bag from the table, Lizzie came up behind her and touched her arm. 'It would be different if you were going to marry the father. People would understand if it had been ... someone you cared for.'

'Well, it wasn't, and the father will have nothing to do with Percy's life.' Fanny turned on her sister. She sensed what was coming next.

'Was it one of those German boys?' Lizzie almost whispered, as if she thought a soft voice might draw the truth from Fanny.

'I refuse to have this discussion with you again, Lizzie. I told you before they were not involved.'

'It's what everyone will think,' Lizzie's voice was pleading. 'That will be even worse for the child. Don't you think another family could –'

'Goodbye, Lizzie. I hope next time I see you, you've changed your ideas. Otherwise, I'm not sure I can come back.'

Fanny wept most of the way home. She sat close to Thomas on the buggy and kept her head down, but as they approached the farm, she looked up at him.

'I won't change my mind, Thomas. With or without Lizzie's approval – or anyone else's – I will raise Percy myself.'

'I accept that, Sis,' he said as he slowed the horse. 'I only want what's best for you. I still think some justice is lacking, but I will support you, whatever you decide.'

***

Marlena's heart fluttered with joy as she fussed over Percy. It was October and she had barely contained her concern for Fanny over the past few months. Now she felt she might burst with the excitement of having the girl in front of her, and with this beautiful baby.

'He's adorable.' She cuddled the infant and looked down into his tiny face. 'Of course you couldn't give him up. A child needs his mother's love. He belongs with you.'

'I'm so glad you agree with me, Mrs Giese,' Fanny said. 'But I have a favour to ask of you.'

'What is it, *liebling*? I'll do anything to help.'

'You're very kind, but I may be asking too much.' Fanny paused, as if unsure whether to continue.

Marlena nodded, encouraging Fanny to go on.

'I'm determined to care for Percy myself. I'd like to get work, and I'm not sure there are many people in town who'd give work to an unwed mother. '

'Are you saying you'd like your job back … here with us?' Marlena's heart began to flutter.

'I know it's a lot to ask.'

'Of course you can come back. I've missed you terribly. You make two of most girls we've had working here.' Marlena moved closer to Fanny and hugged her, still holding Percy on her ample hip. She felt like … dare she even think it? *This must be how a grandmother feels.*

'Thank you so much, Mrs Giese.' Fanny sighed.

'There's one condition,' Marlena said, feeling a smile stretch across her face.

Fanny looked down at the baby. 'If it's about Percy …'

'We've rooms upstairs,' Marlena rushed on. 'You'll both be comfortable, and I can help you look after him. It would be a pleasure, an absolute delight.' She chuckled and her belly rolled up and down. 'Look, he's smiling at me.' Her eyes were drawn again to the baby's face.

'That would be wonderful,' Fanny said, 'but what's the condition, Mrs Giese?'

'That you call me Lena from now on. You're like family to me, *liebling*, and now that you'll be living here, with this darling boy …' Her eyes filled and she sniffed back tears.

Fanny's eyes also filled with tears and she seemed unable to speak. They stood for moments looking down at Percy and smiling in the exaggerated way that mothers and grandmothers do, drawing a wide grin from Percy whose eyes moved from one face to the other, clearly amused.

'He's a happy boy,' Fanny eventually said. 'And he doesn't make much noise. He's not a crier.'

'Because he's contented, *liebling*. Anyone can see that.' Marlena began to hum and caress Percy's forehead. She felt lost in happiness.

'Mrs … uh, Lena, I must ask you something else,' Fanny said after a few moments.

'Anything, *liebling*.' Marlena couldn't drag her eyes from Percy.

'Do you still wonder if Percy's father might have been …?' Fanny stopped half way through her sentence. She seemed to regret asking.

'You mean do I think Jim attacked you?' Marlena looked up. 'No, I don't. I was silly to suspect my nephews. They're good boys. I know they'd not intentionally hurt anyone. They've been through too much themselves. They're both distressed about the situation.'

'You mean you told them I was having a baby?'

Marlena drew in her breath. 'I'm sorry, *liebling*. It did all come out. I wasn't sure then if you'd had the baby, or if … well, things happen, and I didn't know if you'd gone full term, or – '

'It's all right,' Fanny said. 'They'd have found out sooner or later. Jim went to my parents' home after Percy was born, but I was with my grandparents, and Mum and Dad didn't say anything about me having a baby. I wondered if Jim thought I'd been ill.'

'They were both worried about you, *liebling*.'

'So were they not here this month for the races?' Fanny asked.

'No, they were worried about their grandfather in Mororo. I suspect they've gone to help out with his farm. I doubt they'll be back until July now.'

'I see.' Fanny seemed disappointed.

Marlena watched her face drop and her eyes glaze over. 'Fanny?' She caught Fanny's attention and reached for her hand. 'If you're worried what they'll think of you, don't. They're not ones to hold with discrimination. They've had more than their share of that.'

189

'Yes, I know they have.' Fanny sighed. 'And their mother? How is she?'

'I don't know,' Marlena said sadly. 'I learned a long time ago not to interfere in Jane's life. She knows I'm here if she wants my help.'

'You're the kindest woman I know. Do you think Mr Giese will mind me coming back?'

'He'll be as delighted as me, I assure you.' Marlena turned back to Percy, who was gurgling in her arms. 'You've made me very happy, and Hans will be just as pleased. In fact I can hear him outside now. Can I show him this precious bundle?'

'Of course.' Fanny beamed.

***

Fanny took a deep breath as Marlena disappeared through the door with her son. She felt safe, regardless of the hotel being the place she'd been attacked. How she would feel when all the jockeys came in for the races next July, she wasn't sure, but she'd deal with that when the time came. She had work, and a place to live, people who cared about her and would not stand for any prejudice against her in their hotel.

She could still go home once a week, and hopefully any talk about her amongst their neighbours would die down. Her young sisters, although they'd been understanding, would not have to face so many questions. She'd not seen Lizzie again since her visit, but she would give her time, and pray that her heart would soften.

She held her breath as she moved towards the spot she'd been attacked. The smell of straw and horse manure made her head spin for a moment, but she took a deep breath and focussed on the sight of the older couple clucking over her son.

'He loves the horses.' Marlena chuckled as she held Percy close to a stallion's head.

The horse was straining against the gate and sniffing at the child. Percy was straining equally hard in Hans's arms, reaching out towards the huge nostrils and smiling as if his face would split.

'Well, I'll be,' Hans said as Fanny approached. 'Will you look

190

at this? A jockey in the making, I think.'

Fanny smiled, even though a shudder ran up her back. She moved close and stroked the horse's nose. 'A love of horses runs in the family,' she said. 'In fact in most families around here, don't you think?'

***

The next few months passed peacefully for Fanny. The regulars at The European were pleased to see her back and asked few questions. She guessed most did not even realise she had a child. There were always plenty of willing hands to mind Percy when she was working. He rarely cried or made a fuss, and constantly made Marlena and Hans laugh at his antics. Even Bob seemed to take more trips upstairs than necessary, and was often found making faces and gurgling noises at the child.

Fanny went home to Brushgrove on Sundays. There was great excitement as one of her sisters, Mary Ann, planned her wedding for March of the following year. Her youngest sister, Alice, was only two years older than Percy, and the two little ones were like siblings. Fanny was fascinated with watching her son grow; delighted by each change in his expression as he began to form words, by each new achievement as he pushed his limbs this way and that and began to move about.

'It's almost too easy,' she said one Sunday afternoon after Christmas, as she watched Percy crawl across the floor with Alice toddling after him, screeching with giggles.

'How's that, dear?' Betsy looked up from her mending.

'Even at church people don't glare or say mean things. Are they ignoring the fact that I have a child, or do they think Percy's yours?'

Betsy smiled. 'I suspect most are being gracious because they know we all have our struggles. Some will prefer to think of Percy as mine, because then they don't have to make a judgement at all. People mostly want peace, and if they are not pushed to have an opinion, they'd rather mind their own business.'

'I'm very grateful but there are always those who cannot help

191

but have opinions and make judgements, Mum. I'm sure you've encountered some of those.'

Betsy put her head down for a moment. Her fingers moved deftly through the garment she was stitching. 'A few,' she eventually answered. 'But your father and I dealt with those early, as we told you.'

'Thank you. I love you both so much.' Fanny took a deep breath. 'I wish it was so easy with Lizzie.'

'I'm sure your sister will come around. Have you tried to see her again?'

Fanny shook her head. 'When you said she and Alf weren't coming for Christmas, I figured she was still angry, so I thought it best to wait a bit longer.' She paused and caught her mother's eye. 'Have you seen her lately?'

Betsy nodded. 'I visited before Christmas. I think she's softened a bit, but she was worried that Alf would not approve of her seeing you. She doesn't want to upset him. But give her a bit more time. I'm sure she misses you.'

Fanny's eyes welled. 'I miss her too. I can't believe she's become so … judgemental.

Even before I had Percy she seemed so quick to judge people who are different or who don't behave the way she thinks they should. It makes me sad.'

'She's been influenced by Alf, I'm afraid, love. He's put a lot of ideas into her head. He worries about his reputation and his business. He mixes with people who are picky about the company they keep. But Lizzie loves you. She'll come around.'

Betsy picked up her mending and concentrated on it for a while before she spoke again. 'You know Thomas went to see her?'

'No, I didn't.' Fanny was surprised.

'He didn't say anything to you because he thought it would upset you.'

'Why would that upset me? I don't want this to come between Thomas and Lizzie.'

Betsy sighed and seemed to be tossing up whether to speak or not.

192

'Mum?' Fanny prodded.

'Lizzie told him that the German boys had visited her, looking for you. They apparently acted strangely when they heard her baby crying, but they left before Lizzie could make any sense of what they were saying. She's still thinks it was one of them.'

'Mum, please.'

'I know, dear. You've convinced me that's not true, but Lizzie did put the idea in Thomas's head, I'm afraid. He believes that someone should be called to account for what happened to you.'

Fanny shook her head and pursed her lips. 'I don't know why he can't let it go.'

'He's your brother, dear. I think he blames himself for not protecting you. But don't worry, he'll be up north for a few months. Perhaps he'll put it behind him while he's away.'

'I thought Uncle Bernard didn't need him to work this summer.'

'He doesn't. Bernard's actually taken on some Islanders for his cane cutting. He wants to give them work where they'll be fairly treated. He's angry about the way some farmers still mistreat them.'

Fanny smiled and made a face at Percy as he crawled back towards her. 'I'm glad about that, Mum, but what is Thomas going to do?'

Betsy shrugged. 'He said there's plenty of wood cutting work available.'

Fanny tried not to feel skeptical but she had a nasty feeling her brother was going to try and find Jim and Jack. Her heart sank at the thought. 'So will he be back for Mary Ann's wedding?'

'I'm sure he'll be back for that, dear. He wants to try his hand at different work, that's all.'

'Does he now?' Fanny bit her tongue to avoid saying more and prayed silently that her brother would do nothing rash.

CHAPTER NINETEEN

Grafton, February, 1893

Marlena kneaded her dough this way and that on the bread board. She hardly had to think about making bread, but this morning she was particularly distracted.

'Is everything all right, Lena?' Fanny asked.

Marlena shook her head. 'This rain reminds me of the floods in '90. The water was ankle-deep all through the hotel. It was a dreadful mess to clean up. I'm praying it won't go that high again.'

Fanny nodded. 'I'm worried, too. The river's such a mess that most of the boats have stopped running. My sister, Mary Ann, is getting married next month in Maclean, and if the water doesn't go down a lot of the guests won't be able to get to the wedding.'

'I'll be adding that to my prayers, then. And let's pray that there are no more of those cyclones we had last month. They say the coastal areas were devastated.' She raised her eyes to the ceiling and took a deep breath. 'I'm trusting the boys are all right. They work in some dangerous places when the rain's bad.' Her chest tightened as she pushed away images of Jack and Jim trapped under logs or dragged into the river.

Fanny's face creased into a frown. 'My dad was reading in the papers that it's flooded from Rockhampton all the way down here to Grafton, and out as far as Toowoomba. They say it's the worst flood in white memory. In Brisbane the water's so high that three ships have washed up into the Botanic Gardens. Some are saying Brisbane's a doomed city.'

'And eleven dead already.' Hans's deep voice broke into the room. He had a newspaper spread between his hands. 'I was coming to tell you the news, Lena.' He grimaced. 'It's terrible. I've had some of the boys sandbagging around the entrance, but the water's already up over Pound Street. The bottom end of Prince, Villiers and Queen Streets are well under. There'll be no boats docking for a spell.'

'I'm more concerned about Jack and Jim.' Marlena pushed down hard on her rolling pin. Flour puffed into the air. 'Where did people die?'

'The report didn't say, but I suspect in the Brisbane Valley. That's where the reports are mostly coming from.' He stood behind Marlena and rubbed her shoulders. 'The wood cutters are wise to the dangers of the river, love. I'm sure the boys will be careful.'

Marlena huffed. 'I hope so, Hans. I couldn't bear it –'

'Now, none of that. Let's concentrate on what we need to do here … and trust the boys to God. It's what we've always done.'

He turned to Fanny. 'You'll not be heading home for a bit, lass. Not until this settles. It's too dangerous to travel.'

Fanny nodded. 'I hope Thomas knows that. He's up on the North Arm somewhere, but he'll want to be home for Mary Ann's wedding. I hope he'll be sensible.'

Marlena turned back to her bread and sunk her hands into the dough. *Three boys to pray for. Please God, keep them safe.*

***

Jack and Jim sat in a pub in the small North Arm village of Harwood. They were saturated to the skin, and muddy from head to foot.

'I can't see the river being safe for weeks. We'll have to go back to Mororo on foot, or hitch a ride with someone.' Jim shivered as he lifted his mug of ale to his mouth.

'We'll do a bit more work first,' Jack said. 'There's more rubble in the waters around here than men to drag it out. We can afford a few more days.'

'Crazy, isn't it? We're usually floating logs into the river, and now we're dragging them out. Pity we couldn't round up all the wood that's been washed in, and use it for some good.'

'It'll cause the boats no end of trouble if it's not cleared.'

Jack looked up as a young man approached. He tipped his sodden hat and sat down at the bar near them. 'Mind if I sit with you?'

'Not at all,' Jack said. 'This is my brother, Jim, and I'm Jack. Where are you from?'

'Brushgrove,' the stranger said. 'I came up to North Arm to see if I could get work logging, but I've spent the last month clearing. It seems you've been doing the same.'

Jack watched his brother's eyes fly open.

'Brushgrove, you say?' Jim emptied his mug. 'We know someone who lives there.'

'You'd mean my sister, Fanny, I'm guessing.'

Jack's chest tightened.

Jim leaned towards the man. 'You're Fanny's brother?'

'Thomas.' The man nodded. 'I've been asking around about you. The man at the other end of the bar pointed you out.'

'You've been looking for us?' Jim's forehead creased into tracks of half dry mud.

'I'd like to find out what you know about … what happened to Fanny?'

Jack sensed anger in the young man, who he guessed was not yet twenty years old, and whose life experience probably hadn't prepared him to deal well with anger. Jim was now perched on the edge of his stool as if about to pounce on an unsuspecting rabbit.

'We know very little,' Jack said before Jim could speak. 'Our aunt in Grafton told us that Fanny was attacked behind The European. We were sorry to hear it, but we haven't seen nor heard anything since.'

'Is that so? And you wouldn't have been at The European at the time?'

'Now, look here.' Jim bristled. 'We're sick of folks thinking we were involved in what happened to Fanny. We'd never hurt a hair on her head. She's our friend.'

196

There was a long silence while Thomas and Jim glared at each other, as if both were waiting for the other to say something that might give them reason to throw a punch. Jack had never seen Jim so aggressive.

'There's no reason for any hostility here, Thomas,' Jack said. 'You're obviously upset about what happened to Fanny, and so are we. It was a shock to both of us when we heard. In fact, we've tried to find out who it was ourselves.'

'Oh?' Thomas turned to Jack, his eyes scanning both boys' faces. 'And what did you find out?'

'Nothing,' Jim said. 'If we'd found out who it was, we'd have taken him to task.'

'Whoever it was needs to be horsewhipped, and not only that, he needs to take some responsibility for that boy.' Thomas banged his fists on the bar. 'So if I find out that either of you –'

Jim jumped to his feet and moved in so close to Thomas that Jack thought they were about to butt heads.

'Calm down, both of you.' He pushed them apart. 'We've told you, Thomas, we didn't do it. If you don't believe us, then there's nothing else to be said here. I think you ought to move on. My brother's fond of Fanny. He's as ready as you to fight anyone he thinks would hurt her.'

Thomas shrank back into his seat, his eyes still narrowed and focussed on Jim.

Jim breathed out and repositioned himself on his stool. 'A boy, you say? Fanny had a boy?'

Thomas nodded. 'You didn't know that?'

'I told you we've heard nothing since our aunt told us about the attack,' Jack said. 'So Fanny decided to keep the baby, then?' He could feel his heartbeat thumping against his chest, and was trying to convince himself it was caused by being unjustly accused.

'Of course she decided to keep him. She's as stubborn as a mule.' Thomas's face relaxed almost into a grin. 'She thinks she can raise him alone. I doubt she has any real understanding of what's she'll have to face, but she's not going to change her mind,

197

if I know my sister.'

'Has there been any trouble?' Jim asked. 'Has anyone upset her?'

'Not that I know of, but I only saw her at weekends once she started back at The European. I doubt she'd say anything at home, even if she'd had some trouble in town.'

'She's back working with Aunty Giese?' Jim looked incredulous. 'With the baby?'

Thomas nodded. 'Not right, if you ask me, and I know Mum and Dad don't think it's the best thing for her, but as I said, she's determined.'

Jim's eyes glazed over and Jack could almost read his mind. 'We can't be rushing back there, Jim. We need to get back to Gramps.'

Jim shook his head, clearly in two minds. 'I'd go back and marry Fanny right off, if she'd have me. She needs someone to look after her and that boy. It's not right for her to be on her own.'

'You'd marry her?' Thomas looked shocked. 'You know how that'd look?'

'I don't care how it'd look,' Jim snarled.

'Don't you two start again,' Jack said. 'No one's going down river any time soon, anyway.'

'I'm supposed to be back in Maclean in a few weeks for my sister's wedding – one of my other sisters,' Thomas added when Jim's eyebrows rose sharply. 'I'm hoping I can make my way back overland.'

'You can't go far up here without having to make a river crossing, lad. Don't take too many risks. I doubt your family needs another tragedy.' Jack patted Thomas on the back.

'My family doesn't think of this as a tragedy.' Thomas shrugged. 'They see Percy as more of a blessing than a tragedy.'

'Percy,' Jim repeated softly.

Thomas nodded. 'One of our cousin's name ... but I suspect Fanny also chose it because it sounds British.'

'British?' Jack snapped. 'Why British?'

Thomas shrugged. 'She's avoiding anything that sounds German. I thought she seemed a bit too insistent on not blaming you. That's why I wanted to find you for myself.' He paused and looked into both their faces, holding up his hands. 'I believe you,' he said. 'I'm sorry for coming across hostile. I needed to be sure.'

Jack wasn't going to say any more out loud, but this news had made him suspect that one of the mouthy British group from Sydney was the most likely culprit. He didn't want Thomas or Jim confronting that lot, but he meant to follow it up himself as soon as he could get back to Grafton. At least now he felt reassured that Fanny was in good hands. He couldn't deny the desire to see that for himself but first he had to go to Mororo and take care of Gramps.

***

By the end of June they were able to travel on the river so Jack and Jim headed down to Grafton in time for the July races, leaving Gramps with a stack of wood for the winter and a larder full of salted beef and canned vegetables.

Jack avoided going into The European the first few days. He focussed on enjoying riding, and had more than a few wins, but as the days passed he became restless and irritable.He knew he was putting off seeing Fanny. He couldn't even articulate to himself why the thought of seeing her agitated him so much. He'd tried to convince himself that knowing she was safe with his aunt and uncle was sufficient, and even though other emotions gnawed at him, he pushed them aside. The longer the week went on, the less able he felt to come face to face with her.

Late one afternoon he found his brother sitting on a log beside the river. He strode up behind him and tapped him on the shoulder. 'I thought you were going to get the fire started,' he said, kicking at the cold embers in their camp fire.

Jim looked up and shrugged. 'Sorry. I've been sitting here thinking and time got away.' He began to pile small sticks on the fire. 'What have you been doing?'

'Helping Uncle Hans groom the horses.'

'Did you ask him about those Brits? I reckon we need to check them out.'

'Uncle Hans says they haven't come as far as he knows.' Jack kept his voice calm. He'd avoided fueling Jim's suspicions with his own. 'Some people are still mopping up here after the floods. A couple of the hotels near the river have been closed for months and he's not sure they'll recover their losses. Some of the usual riders haven't come into town.'

'Yeah, it's bad around the river edge. It was hard to find a campsite without a heap of rubble to clear.'

Jack could hear the soft lapping of the water against the river bank. It was still much higher than they were used to and the murky brown colouring made it look ominous. 'Uncle Hans said we should have stayed at the hotel.'

Jim rolled his eyes. 'It was you who didn't want to. It's freezing down here. I'd have gone there happily.' He lit a taper and blew on the sparking embers. 'Did he mention Fanny?'

'He's noticed you moping around her these past few days, if that's what you mean.'

'I haven't been moping, but I haven't ignored her like you have.'

Jack picked up the axe to split some logs and swung it over his shoulder. He felt the churning in his stomach that came each time there was a discussion about Fanny. He was annoyed with himself that she affected him so. Perhaps he was a little annoyed with Jim for pursuing her too, but he couldn't entertain that idea for long.

'You went to see her yesterday, didn't you?' he said, twisting the axe in his hands.

'Yeah, but it did no good.' Jim stoked the sticks in the fire. 'I asked her again about marrying me but she says it wouldn't be right. She says people would think I was Percy's father. I told her I don't care if they do, but then she admitted that it's more than that.'

Jack swung the axe high and brought it down on the log with such force that it split completely in half. He glanced at Jim, but didn't speak.

'She won't spell it out, but I don't think she cares enough for me to marry me.' Jim looked dejected. He spat to the side of the fire.

'Do you think there's someone else?' Jack positioned himself behind another log and swung the axe up again.

'Maybe,' Jim murmured. 'I can't understand why she'd want to stay on her own. The boy's a year old now.' He chuckled despite his solemn mood. 'Aunty Giese sure is enjoying having him around, but I'd have thought Fanny would be happy to have a man look after her so she can concentrate on being a mother.'

'Fanny doesn't seem the type who wants to be looked after, Jim.'

Jim sank onto the grass and rested his elbows on his knees. 'You haven't spoken to her all week. You don't think badly of her, do you?'

'Is that what she thinks?' Jack threw a piece of wood onto the fire.

'She asked me why you were staying away from the hotel, that's all. Truth be known, I can't tell what's she's thinking.'

'Never easy to know what a woman's thinking.' Jack pulled open their bag and found some cans of beef. He sat down next to Jim and handed him one.

'I want her to be happy, Jack. Is that so wrong? She deserves to be happy, I reckon. Don't you?'

Jack shrugged. 'Everyone deserves to be happy, I guess, but it doesn't always happen that way. She seems contented enough with her situation from what you say. Maybe you have to accept that.'

Jack didn't know what else to say. Being happy wasn't something he thought about too much. Being safe, and keeping his brother safe, was what had occupied his mind for most of his life. If he thought about being happy, it was usually in relation to Jim.

Perhaps it was time he let his brother stand on his own two feet. Jim seemed to be straining at the bit, wanting to make his own decisions, determined to look after himself in future, and to look after Fanny and Percy as well. The thought caused the stirring in Jack's gut that had become all too familiar lately.

'I'd like to head back up to Mororo after tomorrow's race,' he said after a few minutes of silence while they opened their beef and ate from the cans. 'Gramps will be suffering with the cold, despite all that wood for the fire. Probably finding it hard to get out of bed. I want to make sure he's all right.'

Jim nodded. 'I guess he needs more looking after than Fanny

right now. I'm not so sure about Ma, though.'

'Ma? What do you mean?'

'I've been to see her,' Jim said. 'I decided it was time.'

'And how was she?' Jack kept his eyes on the fire.

'She's worried. Fred's been out west for weeks and she hasn't heard from him. He was supposed to be back by now.'

'Reason to be glad, I'd say.'

'She relies on him, Jack. She said he doesn't treat his own like he did us. She needs a man around to help her. She's not strong.'

'So, you'd like to stay and look after her, too, I suppose.'

'You don't think I can?' Jim arched up and kicked at the fire.

'I didn't say that. I thought you liked the idea of working Gramps's land. He'll want to know if one of us is willing to do it. You have to make up your mind what you want soon.'

'You know what I want.' Jim tossed his empty can in the fire and threw his hands in the air.

Jack grabbed Jim's knee and squeezed it. 'You decide, Jim. I'm all right with whatever you decide.' He hoped his brother would hear acceptance in his voice.

Jim sighed. 'I'm not sure what to do, but I guess I'll go with you to Gramps. Fred may turn up soon, and I don't want to be around Ma when he does. I'm going to get some sleep.' He pulled himself up from the log and headed into their tent.

***

Fanny knocked on Lizzie's door. It was time she faced her sister and tried to make up. It was making her heart heavy to think about their estrangement. She'd found herself being a little short with customers in the hotel and she was pretty sure it was worrying about her sister that was eating at her.

Of course, it hadn't helped her mood that she'd had to turn Jim away. She didn't want to hurt him, but she could not marry him. He was not the man for her and it would be cruel to let him think he was. It had been difficult to refuse him, but he was gone now and still her mood had not lifted.

She had to admit she was also miffed that Jack had avoided her all week. Jim had insisted that he did not think badly of her, that he respected her decision to raise Percy herself. Fanny wished Jack had made his feelings known to her himself. *But then, Jack hardly ever makes his feelings known, so I don't know why I'm surprised.* Thinking about Jack hurt her head, and she was glad he was gone, too.

'Fanny!' When the door opened Lizzie stood in the hall with one daughter on her hip and another gripping her skirt. She was largely pregnant, but seemed to be blooming with it.

Fanny saw her eyes fill with tears. 'Hello, Lizzie. I'm sorry if it's a bad time.'

'No, it's not a bad time,' Lizzie insisted, standing aside and ushering Fanny into the hall. 'Please come in. It's cold out this morning. You should be more rugged up.'

'I'm fine.' Fanny smiled at the familiar mothering from her sister. 'The walk did me good. Mrs Giese insisted I take a break before the lunch crowd. I think she wanted to play with Percy, but I wanted to visit you, so I'm grateful.'

Fanny followed Lizzie into her parlour and waited until she'd put Annie down on the floor and awkwardly lowered herself into a chair. Her other two children were playing with a tea set in the corner of the room.

'Please, sit, Fanny. I'm glad you came. I've been thinking about you so much. Mum told me you were working back at The European, and though I can't imagine how you're managing that, I've been thinking I'd go and see you soon.' She sniffed back tears. 'I've missed you so. I'm sorry we fought. I don't want us to be ...' Her words faded away and she dropped her face into her hands.

'Neither do I, Lizzie. That's why I've come. We're sisters and I love you, and even if we have different ideas about things, we can still accept each other, can't we?'

Lizzie took a deep breath and nodded as she wiped her eyes.

'Will Alf mind that I've come?' Fanny asked.

'I don't think so.' Lizzie sniffled. 'He knows I've been

203

miserable about our fight, and when I told him I wanted to see you, he said all the talk seems to have died down, so it might be all right. Although he wouldn't be keen for me to go to the hotel, so I'm glad you came here.'

'Me too. Now, how about I get us a cup of tea? You look about ready to have that baby. You'll certainly have your hands full. And look at Annie. How she's grown. She's toddling about like Percy.'

'I wish you'd brought him with you, Fanny. I only got a peek at him at Mary Ann's wedding when Mum was wheeling him about. I didn't think it was the right time to be trying to make up with you.'

'It was a lovely wedding, wasn't it? Despite the weather. I think Mary Ann was disappointed it was so miserable getting in and out of the church. Poor dear, after all her planning.'

'Yes, it was a shame, but still, she's married now and happy. Pregnant already, I suppose Mum's told you?'

Fanny nodded. 'Yes, and now Eliza's planning her wedding for next year. Mum will soon have so many grandchildren, she'll forget who belongs to whom.' She laughed and chucked Annie under the chin. The infant leaned into her mother's knee and grinned.

'I'm sure Mum would be happiest to hear *you* planning a wedding,' Lizzie said, playing with her daughter's ringlets and not looking up at Fanny.

Fanny took a breath. She was determined not to get into an argument with Lizzie, now that they were making up, but she knew she'd have to be careful.

'I'll bring Percy next time,' she said. 'If you're sure …'

'Of course I'm sure. In fact, I was wondering if you might leave him with me some of the time while you're working. I hate to think of a little one running around a hotel –'

'Percy's not running around the hotel,' Fanny cut in. 'When he's not with me, he's with Mrs or Mr Giese. They adore him. I'm sure Mr Giese will have him riding a horse before he's two.'

Lizzie gasped. 'Well, that's not …' She drew in a breath as if deciding she'd best not say what she was thinking. 'Anyway, I thought it would be nice for him to be here playing with my lot.'

'I think that'd be grand. I'd love Percy to get to know his cousins. Are you sure Alf won't mind?'

'He'd hardly notice an extra one. He's out early and gone all day.'

'Then perhaps next week I'll bring Percy to have a play and see how they get on.'

CHAPTER TWENTY

Grafton, September 1893

Marlena spoke without looking up from the chopping board where she was deftly turning odd shaped parsnips and carrots into neat chunks for her soup. 'Thank goodness we've had a good crop of vegetables this winter. It looks like it's going to be a full house for the spring races.'

'You'd best make another batch of pies, too.' Fanny grinned. 'You know how the jockeys love your pies.'

Marlena chuckled. 'I know my nephews love them, and I think they'll be here by tomorrow. Hans has the stallion ready for Jack. He loves to ride that horse, and no doubt he'll be champing at the bit to beat those Brits again.'

'The ones from Sydney?' Fanny's eyes flew open.

Marlena noticed the frightened expression on Fanny's face. She answered slowly. 'Yes, they're bringing three or four horses they want stabled.'

As Marlena watched, Fanny almost put the end of her knife through her finger. She jerked her hand away, then put her head down and went on chopping the parsnips.

Marlena's mind churned with speculation but she sensed it would be no good asking questions of Fanny.

'Careful there, *liebling*, you need all those fingers for Percy. Darling boy, I miss him around here through the day. By the time you bring him back from your sister's in the afternoons, he's off to bed.'

'He misses you too.' Fanny smiled and the fear on her face dissolved. 'But he's enjoying playing with his cousins. He needs to run around a lot more now. He's grown so fast, I can't believe it.'

Marlena poured stock into a large saucepan and positioned it above the burner on the stove. 'You've been a wonderful mother, Fanny. And you've handled the critics well.'

'I think it's you who's handled them, Lena. I know you've told a couple of people not to come back. I'm sorry you've had to do that for me.' Fanny paused her slicing and looked up. Tears were welling in the corners of her eyes.

Marlena patted her hand. 'I wouldn't have it any other way. Hans and I have never put up with any kind of prejudice, and we're not going to start now. We know what it is to be looked down on.'

'Thank you.' Fanny sniffed and seemed too overcome with emotion to go on.

'Besides,' Marlena continued, her heart swelling. 'You may end up really being family … if our Jim has his way.' She raised her eyebrows. 'Are you any more inclined to accept him? He's a good lad, you know. He'd treat you well, and he'd love Percy. And you'd be safe from any trouble.'

Marlena's stomach churned at the thought of Fanny having to face her attacker. In all the time she'd been back at work there'd never been a hint of trouble, but Marlena knew there was always the risk. If Fanny felt threatened and was to move away, it would break her heart. She could think of nothing she'd like better than to have Fanny as part of her family. It was how she thought of her, anyway. She knew before Fanny spoke that it was not going to be Jim who would bring her into the family, but she didn't dare voice her deeper hopes.

Fanny's face fell. 'I'm sorry, Lena, but I'm not looking to marry anyone. I hope Jim will be more accepting of that this time. I don't want to hurt his feelings again.'

'If I know Jim, he'll still be hoping, but you know your own mind, *liebling*, and it's your decision.' Marlena winked and tipped a pile of carrots into the soup pot. 'You'll have to be prepared to let him down again, I suspect, but he's had to accept disappointment before this. He'll manage. And one day there'll be someone for you. I'm sure of it.'

It was soon apparent to Fanny that it wasn't going to be Jim she would need to fend off.

'Come on, sweetie, give us a smile.' The man the others in the British group called Ronald had approached her numerous times, flirting confidently. She'd put him off as politely as she could, but she was getting annoyed. He wasn't at all familiar to her and she was sure he hadn't been with the group the last time they'd been at the hotel.

She was relieved that the one called Archie, whom she suspected had been her attacker, was not with them. For the most part the group had gathered in the back corner of the dining room and kept to themselves, making it easy for her to avoid them.

'May will be out with your meals in a minute,' she said, as the man followed her towards the kitchen door. 'We're busy, as you can see, and I've no time for nonsense.' She cast him a withering glance over her shoulder.

'You break a man's heart, my dear. Surely you've time for a sweet dalliance after work. You'll not be disappointed, I assure you.' He caught up with her and touched her elbow.

'That'll be enough from you.' Jack's deep voice came from behind the man and at the sound Fanny's heart beat rapidly.

'Get in line, lad.' Ronald's retort sounded as if he was speaking to a servant.

Fanny knew there would be trouble. She reached the kitchen door and pushed through, precariously balancing the plates she was carrying.

'What is it?' May's eyes flew open when Fanny almost dropped the plates onto the bench. 'You look all undone.'

'It's one of those Brits.' Fanny took a deep breath. 'He's being a nuisance, but I think Jack is about to make it worse. He won't take being spoken to like that.'

'Like what?'

'You know how those Brits talk down to everyone.'

'Yeah, I've noticed they think they're above the rest of us.

Think they're gentry, they do.'

'Perhaps they are.' Fanny scraped the plates into the pile of scraps. 'But I think that one's chosen the wrong person to offend. Mind you, Jack did interfere.'

'Interfere?'

'He was trying to protect me, I suppose, but he probably shouldn't have.'

A grin spread across May's face. 'You ought to be grateful when a man's protecting you. It's nice to think there are some good ones around.'

Fanny was thinking about how to respond when the noise coming from the dining room indicated that tensions had risen. She sighed and put down the plate she was scraping, hoping that Jack would keep his irritation under control.

He'd hardly spoken to her since he'd arrived three days ago. Jim had caught her attention on numerous occasions and smiled at her with an expression of pleading, obviously hoping she'd changed her mind about marrying him. She'd been friendly, but made sure she didn't give him any mixed messages. As usual, she'd been unsure whether to approach Jack, and uncertain what she would say to him if she did. But now there was a fight going on in the dining room and she had little doubt Jack was involved. *I'm sure he'll think this is my fault.*

She didn't want to draw attention to herself, but had to see if he was all right. She pushed the kitchen door open a little. Hans and Jack's brother, Bob, were breaking up what looked like a free for all. *Why men respond to the sight of two men fighting by throwing punches at whoever they can find is beyond me.* It seemed they all had pent up energy that they leapt to expend at the slightest opportunity.

'Out, all of you,' Hans yelled when the men staggered back from a couple sprawled on the floor.

Bob was holding Ronald from behind, while the Brit continued to thrash his arms about. Jack stood to one side, rubbing one fist into the other hand, as if he'd thrown a heavy punch. His eyes were blazing as he stared at the man in his brother's grip.

'You speak like that again and we'll continue this outside,' he hissed.

'I said out,' Hans repeated, glaring at Jack. 'And don't come back tonight unless you're able to control yourselves.'

'I'll handle this one.' One of the Brits came from the back of the dining room, and took hold of Ronald's arm. 'My apologies, sir. He's a bit of a hothead.'

As the man spoke, Fanny's head swam. Her throat went dry and when she tried to swallow, she almost threw up. *That's the voice. That's him!* She backed away from the doorway and almost fell over the bench. *But he had seemed a gentleman! He'd tried to be helpful. I thought it was the other one.* She gripped the bench and pushed herself upright.

'What's the matter, love?' May came to her side and took her arm. 'It's over now. Mr Giese's sorted it.'

'It's just that I find it so … distasteful, seeing men carry on like that.' Fanny struggled for words. Her chest felt like it would explode.

'Not surprising, if you ask me. They're all the same when it comes to it, even the ones that seem good.' May huffed as she went back to serving soup into bowls. 'Blimey, now these are nearly cold. I'll have to put this back in the pot and start again.'

'Perhaps you'd best see if whoever ordered it is still there. I think a few will be out on their ear, if I know Mr Giese.' Fanny took a firm hold on her emotions.

May nodded and peered through the door. 'Yeah, the Brits are gone. Guess they won't be wanting their soup after all.'

'Would you please go and see if anyone's still waiting, May? We may be done for lunch.'

Fanny waited until May left the kitchen, then sank onto a stool. She felt so nauseous she was sure she couldn't even look at food. It was hard to think straight, or even to breathe properly. When the door opened again she expected May to reappear, but when she looked up, it was Jack's face in front of her. She gasped in shock.

'Now, you'll apologise.' Hans followed Jack into the kitchen. His face was red with anger. 'No doubt you've embarrassed Fanny. I'm sure she doesn't appreciate you causing all that fuss on her behalf.'

Fanny couldn't speak. Her throat was so dry she could hardly swallow.

Jack stared at her for what seemed like minutes before he spoke. 'I'm sorry if I embarrassed you.' His voice was rigid and cold. 'I couldn't abide the man's tongue.'

'Regardless of what he said, you need to control yourself,' Hans said. 'Nothing good is achieved by fist fights.'

'I had no intention of fighting him.' Jack sounded remorseful as he turned to his uncle. 'He started throwing punches. I was telling him to mind his tongue, that's all. I fended him off when he started –'

'That's enough,' Hans snapped. 'It's over now, and it better not happen again. A man like that's not going to put up with you telling him how to talk.'

'A man like me can't stand by and listen to that about ...' Jack's words faded away and he turned back to Fanny. 'I'm sorry. I thought he was bothering you. I didn't mean to start a fight.'

Fanny was still having trouble finding her voice. Her heart was thumping in her chest and she didn't know if it was from what had happened or her proximity to Jack. Her thoughts were all a jumble, her feelings a fluttering mess.

'I think we've been to this place before,' she said, searching for words. 'I don't need you jumping to my rescue.' She immediately regretted what had come out of her mouth. It wasn't how she felt at all, but she couldn't come to terms with what had become patently obvious to her in the past few minutes.

'Right, then.' Jack snorted, clearly rebuffed. 'I'll be off. Jim's still down at the track. He'll be wondering where I've got to.' He spun on his heel and left by the back door.

'I think he's sorry.' Hans moved closer to Fanny and rubbed her arm. 'He's clumsy, but I'm sure he thought he was doing right by you. He can't abide seeing anyone harassed or hurt.'

'I know,' Fanny mumbled. 'I shouldn't have been so hard on him. I don't know why I always end up on the wrong footing with

211

him.' Tears filled her eyes and she rubbed them with her sleeve.

'Perhaps you'd both best think about that some more,' Hans said, wrapping his arm around her shoulder. 'Now, how about you leave the rest of this to May, and get ready to pick up Percy? It's all but done in the dining room for a while. The rest of them will be rushing back to the track to see if there's going to be more of a scuffle.'

'You don't think Jack will fight again, do you?'

'I think he'll do all he can to avoid it, but if those fellows push him hard enough, I'm not sure what he'll do. Don't you worry. He can take care of himself. You get to that little man of yours.'

Fanny nodded gratefully. She needed to get away and think. She needed to hug her darling boy, hold his little face in her hands, kiss that sweet button nose and see his beaming smile. How she loved the way his face lit up when she approached, the way he snuggled into her arms and pushed his lips into her neck. The smell of him, his cute attempts to talk, she loved it all. She loved him with all her heart. Being reminded of how and from whom he came, would not change her adoration of him, nor her protection of him. *I'll never let anyone hurt him, no matter what I have to do.*

***

As Jack strode back into the race track he heard a group of men talking about the rage they'd seen in him in the pub and laughing about the clumsy Brit who'd taken him on. He shook his head and hurried on. *They're like old women gossiping*. He fumed as he passed them, looking for Jim.

He was sure now that one of those Brits had attacked Fanny. He gritted his teeth as he remembered the disgusting slurs they'd made, suggesting that she had made herself available last year and was obviously playing hard to get now for a lark.

He'd felt such rage erupt in his chest. But he hadn't thrown the first punch. In fact he hadn't punched the man at all, as much as he'd wanted to. *I'd have killed him for sure, if I'd started.* It had taken all his self-control to merely protect himself from the punches that were thrown at him. He was disappointed Uncle

Hans didn't take his side more, but once there were five or six men, all throwing punches, he knew it would be hard to see who was at fault. Even his brother, Bob, had taken him to task. He was fed up with getting himself into trouble with everyone.

He was trying to do the right thing by Fanny. *And that's what seems to get me into the most trouble.* For a moment he wished again that he'd never met her. But immediately the thought formed, he knew it was not true. He wished he didn't have such mixed feelings about her. She was obviously annoyed with him again. *It seems I can never do the right thing by her, so why do I even try?*

'There you are.' Jim's voice interrupted his thoughts. 'What happened at the pub? Everyone's talking about it.'

'Are they, now?' Jack scowled. 'It was a scuffle. No big deal. One of the Brits was mouthing off, is all.'

'Mouthing off about what?'

'About Fanny.' It was out before Jack could bite his tongue. *It won't help to tell Jim. Although he'll likely hear it from someone else anyway.*

'What about Fanny?' Jim demanded.

'You know what they're like, prancing around like aristocrats. One of them was annoying her and I told him to quit. He didn't like it. He started throwing punches. Forget it, Jim. Let's not make more of it than it was.' Jack picked up Lightning's towel and started to drag it down the animal's rump.

'I've brushed him down,' Jim said, his eyes still wide. 'Now, tell me about Fanny. Is she all right?'

'She's fine. I apologised for embarrassing her and I think she's gone back to her sister's.' He patted the horse's neck and raked his fingers through the mane.

'I don't know why you always manage to upset her. That's sure not going to help me.'

'I said I'm sorry.' Jack gritted his teeth. The last thing he needed was an argument with his brother.

'Not that she's going to change her mind, anyway.' Jim slumped against the fence.

'About marrying you?' Jack said absentmindedly. His thoughts

213

had gone back to the British group. *Which one was it? The one who'd been annoying her today seemed to have just met her. Maybe it was the one who hadn't come this year, the one they'd called Archie. Perhaps too ashamed to show his face. Probably afraid Fanny would recognise him. And if she did, what would she want done about it?*

'Hey, are you listening to me?' Jim nudged him.

'Sorry, I was thinking about something else.'

Jim huffed. 'Are you going to stay here this afternoon?'

Jack nodded. 'I've got another race.'

'I thought I'd go and see Ma.'

Jack stopped brushing the horse and looked up. 'Do you know if Fred's around?'

'I haven't heard anything since we were here before when she was worried Fred hadn't come back from Moree.'

'Well, be careful.'

Jim arched up. 'I can take care of myself.'

'All right.' Jack shrugged. 'I'd come with you if you wanted. We could go tomorrow afternoon, after the last races.'

'No, I'll go alone. I think you'd make Fred madder, if he is there. I don't think he'd take to me now.'

'Maybe.' Jack dropped the towel and lifted the feed bucket close to the horse's nose. 'You want any more, fella?' he said, then turned back to Jim. 'I agree. It's probably best you go alone. You're older now, and so is Fred. I'm sure you can handle yourself.' He grinned. 'Tell Ma hello from me. I'll visit soon.'

***

When Jim arrived back at their campsite that night Jack could see he was in a state. He immediately feared the worst. 'What did he say?' He held out a water bag to Jim and led him to a log by the fire.

'He's dead.' Jim flopped onto the log and took a long drink.

'What?' Jack sat down beside him.

'Ma's beside herself. He's been out at Moree all this time. She got word a couple of months ago that he was sick and needed to rest

214

up for a while. Then she got a note three weeks ago to say he'd died.'

Jack's mind reeled. He felt an enormous sense of relief, then a rush of guilt. His mother must have cared for Fred or she wouldn't have put up with so much. Even if she'd been scared of him, it seemed she wanted him around. Jack couldn't feel any grief himself over the loss of the man, but he didn't want his mother to be sad. She'd suffered enough.

'What's she going to do?'

'She doesn't know what to do. It seems he's been buried out there with some of the other family. She didn't get to say goodbye, and now she can't even see herself getting out to see his grave.'

Jack sighed. 'I meant, what's she going to do for the future? Can she stay in the house?'

'The letter said she can stay there for as long as she needs to. None of his family wants her cottage. They have a huge farm. And they know she still has little ones.'

'Generous of them.' Jack sniffed. 'They ought to be helping her more than that. They've plenty of money, from what I've heard.'

'Well it doesn't seem they're going to do any more. I told her I'd stay.'

Jack turned to him. 'You mean permanently?'

'I have to, Jack. She needs someone. Gramps can't help. She hardly sees her brother and sisters, and they have their own families. She's in a real state. Florrie's eighteen now and got herself a domestic job down south somewhere. Clarrie's sixteen. He's started work in the saw mill, so he's bringing in a bit, but with the others being so young, Ma needs help. I said I'd get some work around here. Maybe the mill, or one of the pubs.'

Jack was having trouble gathering his thoughts. 'I'm sure Ma will appreciate that, Jim. I'll go and see her tomorrow, but then I have to go back to Gramps. He's expecting us … one of us, at least.'

'Yeah, I understand. I think Ma will too, but she'll be real glad to see you before you go, I reckon. She asked me about you.'

'It'll work out, Jim.' Jack tapped his brother's shoulder. 'It'll be different now, with Fred gone. I suppose she'll miss him,

215

though God knows, I find that hard to understand. But she'll do her grieving and you'll be a comfort to her.'

The relief flooding Jack was almost tangible. It was like a great ball of dread in his stomach had shriveled up. The sense of threat he'd carried since he was a small child lifted from his shoulders. It left him feeling free in a way he couldn't describe, but he liked the feeling of it.

He was glad for Jim, too. It would be a good thing for his brother to have someone to look after. He'd been itching to do that for a while, it seemed. Another thought crossed Jack's mind before he could stop it. *Maybe now Jim will get over his infatuation with Fanny.*

Putting paid to his wondering Jim sat up and smiled weakly. 'Maybe if I'm around Fanny will give me another chance. She'll see I can settle down to family life. What do you think, Jack?'

'It's up to you, Jim … and Fanny. I've no idea what she wants.' Jack drew in a breath and felt his chest knotting again. 'It would be a lot for you, taking care of Ma and her little ones as well as taking on Fanny and a baby.'

'Percy would be no trouble. He'd probably like having big brothers and sisters.'

'Perhaps.' Jack swallowed hard. 'And do you imagine you'd all live in the one house together?'

'Maybe I could add on a room or two. I'd have to find out if Fred's family is going to take it back eventually. Maybe Fred's left orders for it to go to Clarrie when he's of age.'

Jack shrugged. 'Hard to say.'

'Maybe by then I could rent us another place.' Jim's mind seemed to be brimming with ideas, and with hope.

Jack tried to be glad for him, but he felt the need to end the conversation. 'We've got nothing left here to eat, Jim, so we'd best get cleaned up and head over to the pub for a meal.'

'You won't start up again with those Brits, will you?'

Jack shook his head. *Maybe there's no point in worrying about them at all now.*

Chapter Twenty-One

Lawrence, January, 1894

Fanny sat by her sister's bed, holding her hand. There was barely a movement in Mary Ann's chest under the sheet. *Surely she's not going to die?*

'I'm here, Mary Ann. Please hold on. Your baby needs you.' She was unsure whether Mary Ann could hear her at all.

Fanny had been at Lawrence for three weeks now. When Ed had sent word that he had to be away for a few weeks and Mary Ann was unwell with her pregnancy, Fanny had offered to come and stay with her. The baby shouldn't have been born for another week yet, and Ed was due back before that. He'd be shocked to find he'd missed the birth, and more so to see what a terrible state his wife was in. The midwife said she was lucky to survive. The baby had been so weak that the midwife had found another nursing mother who was willing to feed the poor little mite until Mary Ann was strong enough.

Now Fanny was beginning to wonder if her sister was going to recover at all. She'd been hardly conscious since the birth three days ago, and Fanny felt out of her depth caring for her. The midwife had sent word to Betsy, and Fanny was praying her mother would arrive soon to help. It was difficult to leave Mary Ann's side, even to prepare food. When she did, Mary Ann would only take a spoonful of broth, and then it seemed her temperature rose again. Fanny had to get cold compresses and mop her forehead until she settled into an easier pattern of breathing.

Percy couldn't understand the gravity of the situation, of course. He was fretting for his cousins and wanted to go outside and play, but Fanny was afraid to go out for long. Not only because she couldn't leave Mary Ann, but also because another trauma, which had started two days earlier with a banging on the door, had left her wary.

She'd settled Percy into bed and had been about to feed Mary Ann. She'd rushed to the door, hopeful it was her mother, or perhaps Ed back home. Instead she'd been faced with a disheveled man, who'd smelled dreadful and was demanding food. His clothes were ragged and on his back was a large pack, which Fanny suspected contained all the man owned. She'd heard about swaggies who roamed the countryside, out of work and looking for handouts wherever people were kind enough to help them. She pitied the man, but another person to care for was more than she could cope with.

After giving him a plate of stew, she'd told him she had a sick sister to care for and asked him to move on. But he'd insisted he had nowhere to go and wanted her to give him shelter for the night. It wasn't as if it was cold out. The summer air was balmy and the nights had been clear of rain. Fanny said it wouldn't be appropriate for him to stay and pleaded with him to go. She'd been relieved when he picked up his swag reluctantly and left.

She'd sat with Mary Ann all that night, catching a little sleep in her chair, but the smell and look of the man kept invading her mind. She pitied him, but was frightened by the thought that Ed and Mary Ann's home was isolated. There were no close neighbours, and she wondered if she'd made it too obvious that she had no real protection should he decide to come back.

Sure enough, the following night the banging had come again. She'd passed him some bread and closed the door. 'I'm sorry,' she'd called. 'I can't help you more than that. My sister is unwell and it's all I can do to care for her. You need to move along.'

She'd heard him rustling about outside the house and was sure he'd gone to the back to see if the other door was open. Panicking, she'd pushed a table against the back door and piled boxes against the front door. She'd felt foolish, but protecting her sister and her son was paramount, and she would not take any risks.

It had been a long night, with little sleep again. The following morning she'd been reluctant to open the doors, but Percy had been so anxious to go out and play that she'd relented, and after having searched the surrounds she'd sat in the sun for half an hour and watched him chase butterflies and do somersaults on the grass at the back of the house. She could see that the vegetable garden needed attention, but apart from feeding the chickens and throwing a few scraps to the three pigs in their pen, Fanny hadn't had time to think about doing anything but caring for her son and her sister.

By the end of the third day Mary Ann roused a little. Colour began to return to her cheeks, and she was murmuring about wanting her baby. When the wet nurse came that evening and presented little Maude to Mary Ann, her eyes lit up, and Fanny gave thanks to God that all was going to be well, then burst into tears. She wasn't sure if they were tears of relief or exhaustion.

'I'm sorry to put you through all this,' Mary Ann said the next day, as Fanny helped her feed the baby.

'It's you who's gone through the worst,' Fanny said. 'I'm glad I could be here for you. Not that I could have saved you. It's only by God's grace that you and little Maude are here.'

Betsy arrived the next day. 'My poor girls,' she said as she came through the door and dropped a basket on the table. 'I had to collect your Grandma to mind my little ones, and Alice put on a great turn when I was leaving. I think I've spoiled your youngest sister, girls.'

'She's not four yet, Mum,' Mary Ann said weakly. 'Of course she'll not want to be without you. I can't imagine letting this one out of my sight until she's at least ten years old.' She looked down on the baby, asleep in her arms, and sighed contentedly. 'I can't imagine how you leave Percy and go to work, Fanny.'

'I'm with him every day.' Fanny smarted. 'I'm there when he wakes and when he goes to sleep every night. He has a lovely time playing with Lizzie's children when I'm at work for a few hours through the day. It does him no harm at all, I'm sure. He's surrounded by people who love him.'

'Let me have a cuddle of my new granddaughter,' Betsy said,

as if to distract Fanny from her defense. She reached for the baby. 'I won't wake her.'

Fanny smiled her thanks to her mother and crept out of the room. She'd done what she could do for her sister and was anxious to get back to Grafton, but she wouldn't go until Ed arrived home. She couldn't leave her mother to deal with the swaggie if he came back.

She did hope that once back in Grafton she could escape the thoughts she'd had these past few days, about how difficult it could be for a woman alone, trying to protect her family. However, Lizzie would be no help in that regard. Though Fanny was glad to have reconciled with her sister, and they'd been getting along well, Lizzie was still apt to remind her that it was not natural for a mother to be raising a child on her own, especially in a hotel, and that she should be looking for a suitable husband and father.

Fanny was tired of these nudges from her sisters. *None of them can imagine a woman being happy unless she's a wife.* But she was also more than a little aggravated that her experience here with Mary Ann seemed to have validated their concerns.

***

As she travelled home, Fanny thought again about Jim. He'd come into the pub regularly throughout November and December, updating her about the progress his mother was making, about how happy he was to be on good terms with her again, and how right Fanny had been to stress the importance of forgiveness and reconciliation. Fanny was pleased about that and let him know she was proud of him, and happy for his mother.

However, Jim had also hinted at the possibility that she might reconsider his proposal, now that he was in a better position to look after her and Percy with his regular job at the sawmill. The pleading expression on his face left her feeling guilty and sad for him. Still, her heart was not in the idea, no matter how much her head told her it was worth considering.

The worst part was that every time she thought about the future, the same face invaded her mind. Though why her heart was drawn to Jack she still couldn't understand. There was no indication he was interested in her. *And why would he be? A defiled woman, raising a child on her own, shunning society's expectations.* As much as she tried not to be influenced by other people's opinions about her situation, it was hard not to feel unworthy.

Although she'd been able to shield Percy from any exposure to prejudice so far, she knew there were people in Grafton who whispered behind her back and pointed their fingers at her from across the street. *I've made a scandal of myself, even though few people have been mean to my face. And there may well be harder times ahead, for me and for Percy, God help us both.*

She couldn't blame Jack for avoiding her. He'd had enough to contend with in his life. Still, she looked forward to seeing him in July, and hoped this time they could at least remain on friendly terms. *It seems it's all I can hope for.*

***

Jack arrived in Grafton in the middle of a huge storm. The rain had battered the river boat for the best part of the trip from Mororo. However, the weather could not be blamed for his unease. It was the storm in his mind that was rattling him.

It had been hard to leave Gramps. Bright's disease, the doctor had said. It would continue to cause bad turns, shortness of breath, swollen limbs – and eventually his heart would give out. It was only a matter of time. Jack hated to think about it. He'd promised he'd return to Mororo as soon as he could, and this time for good. He'd promised to work Gramps's land, to make it his own.

'You've given me peace of mind, my boy,' Gramps had said. His face had softened and his breathing slowed and Jack had been frightened that he was going to die right then.

'Please hold on, Gramps,' he'd said. 'There are people in Grafton I have to see, one of them being Ma. If there's any way I can bring her to visit you, I'll do it, so you have to hold on.'

'You're a good boy, Jack.' Gramps had smiled from ear to ear, though it was almost lost in the creases of his face and his unruly beard. 'I'll understand if Janie can't make it, but tell her I'd love to see her before I go, eh?'

Jack was determined not to disappoint Gramps, but he had no idea if his mother would agree to the trip. Then there was Fanny. Thoughts of her invaded his mind like the persistent birds pecking at Gramps's vegetables; thoughts he could make no sense of, and which he chased away just as he had the flapping intruders in Gramps's garden. But he knew he had to face them soon.

***

'I'll have no argument from you this time, Jack,' his aunt said the minute he knocked on the back door. 'You'll take a room upstairs. This weather's not fit for man or beast.'

'Thanks,' Jack said, shaking his sodden coat behind him. 'I'm not here to argue.'

'I'm not sure there'll be much riding this year, either,' she said. 'The grounds are so wet, most won't risk their horses going down in the mud.'

'We'll see.' He dragged off his boots and left them with his coat inside the door. Riding wasn't uppermost in his mind. 'I've things to see to. That's why I'm a bit early. Anyone else here?'

'Not yet. A few have booked in, but it remains to be seen whether they cancel.' She pulled a mug from the shelf. 'There's hot tea in the pot, and I'll get you some fresh bread and soup. Then you can tell me what's going on. You have that look about you I used to see when you were young. You've plans for something, I can tell.'

'Maybe.' Jack shrugged. When his aunt stood solid in front of him with her arms on her hips, he grinned. 'I mean to see if I can get Ma to go visit Gramps. He's … he's dying. Not right away, I hope, but he's going downhill fast, and I know it'd mean a lot to him to see her again.'

She nodded. 'I imagine you're right. She seems a lot better these days. Having Jim with her has made a difference. I visited last week. I even got a smile out of her.'

'Sounds promising. I've no doubt life's better for her without

222

Fred.' Jack sat at the bench and rubbed his hands together before starting on the bread and soup. 'This is great, Aunty, as usual.'

'You always felt better after fresh bread and tea,' she said.

Jack swallowed a mouthful of hot soup. 'So how is everyone here?'

'Fine, love.' She smiled and ruffled his hair. 'If you mean me and your uncle.'

'And Jim? Is he managing all right?'

She shrugged. 'Sometimes it's hard to tell. He comes in here a bit … I think to see Fanny. He says he's happy, but he still seems lost.'

Jack raised his eyebrows into a question.

'She hasn't changed her mind,' she said, reading him easily.

He waited, hoping for more. He broke a lump of bread into pieces and dipped it in his soup.

'She's been a little restless herself, has Fanny. Especially this last week or so. I think she's worried about who might come in for the races.' His aunt's face creased.

'Oh?' Jack's heart began to thump. He took a long drink of tea and kept his eyes averted, though he could tell she was watching him.

'It's those Brits she's worried about, isn't it?' she said.

'How would I know what she's worried about?' He continued to eat.

'Percy's two years old now. He's cute as a button, and he has the round face and fine features of an Englishman. I doubt anyone could see any German in him. No square chin and high cheekbones like you.'

Jack almost dropped his spoon. 'Like me?'

She moved closer and rubbed his shoulder. 'Don't get yourself in a knot. I'm merely saying that if others are still trying to guess about his father, then those with half a brain will know it's an Englishman.'

She took his plate and spooned in more soup until he held up his hand. 'Not that it should keep a good man of any background from courting Fanny. She's as dear a girl as you'd find, and a wonderful mother.'

'You said she's not changed her mind about Jim, so it seems she's not interested in a man, regardless of his background.' Jack kept his eyes on the soup plate. He knew if he said another word he'd choke on it.

His aunt held onto his plate firmly. She didn't speak until Jack finally looked up at her. 'You want something, lad, you need to ask for it.' They stared at each other for a long moment before she pushed the plate back in front of him. 'You're a stubborn man, Jack. Always were. Asking for what you need is not so hard, you know. Didn't I teach you that when you were a boy?'

Jack swallowed loudly. 'You always knew what I needed.' He wrapped his hands around the soup plate.

'Well, you're not a boy any longer. What you need now is as plain to me as the nose on your face, but you'll have to admit it to yourself and go after it.'

'What if it hurts someone else?' His voice was almost a whisper and he spooned soup into his mouth before he could say any more.

'You can't always stop others from getting hurt, *liebling*.' She moved close to him and touched his cheek. 'I know you hate being compared with your grandfather, but let me tell you, it isn't only your stubbornness that makes you like him. He was a good man underneath the hard exterior. He wanted nothing more than for his family to be safe and happy, to have a good life. He did everything in his power to make it happen. He refused to let go of what he believed in strongly but central to those beliefs was that he was responsible for his family's wellbeing. It crushed him when he thought they were suffering. What Papa wasn't good at was asking for what he wanted for himself. So he died heartbroken.'

When she stopped speaking, Jack looked up. There were tears in her eyes and her bottom lip was trembling.

'I've been praying for something good for you since you were three years old, Jack. Don't throw it away when it's staring you in the face.' Her voice cracked and she turned back to the stove. She pulled a handkerchief from her pocket and with her back to him she blew her nose loudly.

'There are some things in this life that we don't get even when we do ask.' She continued without turning around. 'We have to learn to live without those, but we must have the courage to receive what is there for us.'

As she turned back to him, Jack nodded. He knew his aunt had grieved deeply over not having any children of her own. He hoped she knew how much he appreciated her love and care for him and his brothers. She'd been like a mother to him, and he'd not told her enough how much she meant to him.

'You know …' he started.

'Of course I do.' She seemed to read his mind again. 'But I'm not finished what I was saying.' She took a deep breath and fixed her eyes on him. 'There are things God brings to us that are good for us, whether we acknowledge the need of them or not, and if we refuse to take hold of them, well, that's plain stupid.'

She planted her hands on her hips. 'You have to stop running from your past, Jack. If you don't accept where you've come from and let it go, you're never going to figure out where you're headed in the future.'

There was a long silence while his aunt cleared cooking utensils from the bench.

'Gramps wants me to take over his land,' he said, sitting back on his stool. 'I've said I will.'

'Well, that's a good thing.' Her eyes lit up for a moment before her forehead creased. 'You'll still come down for the races, won't you?'

He nodded. 'Depending on what needs doing on the land.'

'Good,' she said. 'That's a good thing. The land, I mean, as well as coming for the races. Papa would be pleased.'

'Why would that please him?'

'Because he wanted his grandchildren to inherit land. He promised himself, and us, that we would have a good life here. One we couldn't have had in Germany. He believed we would truly belong here if we had land of our own.' She wiped her eyes with her apron. 'Your father tried hard to live up to Papa's hopes for him, but …'

'He died,' Jack said. The loss still tore at his heart.

'They would both rest in peace knowing you had inherited Jane's father's land. You would make them both proud, Jack.'

He nodded, unable to find words. Perhaps it would make a difference to how he felt about his past, if he could accept things as his aunt did, if he had her faith. He rubbed his fingers across his forehead, wrestling with all she'd said.

When he looked up she was at the stove with her back to him. She bent down with a soft grunt and pulled the oven door open. The smell of freshly baked bread wafted over him as she rose and laid a tray of crisp, browned loaves on the bench.

'Perfect,' he said with a grin. 'As usual.'

'Nothing's perfect, love.' She crinkled up her nose. 'But I think you've taken a step in the right direction, Jack. You will stay upstairs won't you? I'm worried about those Brits being here, and I reckon Fanny is too.'

'Are they booked in?' Jack dropped his spoon.

She nodded. 'Due tomorrow. Hans is ready for them.'

Jack frowned. 'I'll not cause any trouble, if that's what you're thinking.' He pushed back from the bench.

'I've sent Fanny home for a few days, just in case. Her sister, Eliza, is getting married next week, and I'm sure the family will appreciate her help.'

Jack looked away. He knew his disappointment was showing on his face. He coughed and covered his mouth, arguing with himself internally. 'I think I'll head straight over to Ma's while there's a break in the weather,' he said, distracting himself.

'All right.' His aunt nodded, a sly grin on her face. 'The wedding's here in town on Saturday, so I reckon we'll see Fanny before the end of the week. Try and be pleasant to her, will you?'

'I'm always pleasant.' Jack smiled and planted a kiss on her cheek. Then he drew her into his arms and hugged her tightly. He could feel shock ripple through her and realised he couldn't remember when he'd last hugged her. Or any other woman either. He sensed the shuddering of her body as she clung to him and he knew she was weeping.

'I'm sorry, Aunty. I should have told you before … how much you've meant to me … and my brothers.' His words faded as he lost control of his emotions and tears rolled down his cheeks.

'Oh, *liebling*, my dear boy, you've meant every bit as much to me. You'll be fine now.' She looked up at him, her eyes red and puffy, but a broad smile on her face. 'God bless you, you'll be just fine now.'

As she slipped from his arms she slapped him lightly on the back. 'Say hello to your mother for me, too.'

***

Jack was surprised at the noise coming from his mother's house. His heart had started beating loudly at the sound of it initially, until he realised it was more laughter than yelling.

'Jack!' Her face broke into a wide smile when she opened the door. He couldn't remember seeing her so happy, and wondered if it was because she no longer had to worry about Fred, or whether Jim was bringing her such joy.

'Hello, Ma.' They stood a moment looking at each other, until she moved towards him and wrapped her arms around his shoulders. She held him for a long time and when she pushed back there were tears in her eyes. *That's the second hug from a woman in one day. Something must be changing.*

'It's good to see you,' she said. 'I can't believe I have both my boys home.'

'I'm only here for a visit, Ma. I need to talk to you about Gramps.'

She stood back and ushered him into the small parlour, which seemed to be crammed with people.

Jim looked up from the young boy whose bootlaces he was untying. 'Jack, what a surprise. Did you just arrive in town?'

As Jack nodded a girl pushed herself up from the floor, where she'd been crouched with another two children. Jack didn't recognise her. She looked about eighteen – fine featured, dark hair

227

pulled back from blue eyes.

'Hello,' she said brightly. 'I'm Ester.'

'Hello.' Jack nodded in her direction.

'Ester lives a few streets away,' his mother said. 'She and Jim walk the young ones to school most days.' She grinned and Jack again marveled at the difference in his mother's face. She looked younger than the last time he'd seen her. He felt glad for her. It had been a long time coming.

'I'll be going then, Mrs Clifford,' Ester said. She turned to Jim and her face lit up with a smile that Jack thought held more than friendship. 'Nice to meet you, Jack,' she said, turning to him. 'Jim's told me a lot about you.' Looking down at the children around her she took hold of two hands. 'Come on, you two. Say goodbye to Lance and Daisy. We'll see them tomorrow, eh?' Her eyes then turned back to Jim as if she was waiting for him to speak.

'I'll walk you out, Ester,' he said. The two left the room in a flurry of children's giggling and waving.

'She's taken with him.' His mother watched them leave, then turned to Jack.

'It seems so,' Jack said. 'And is he taken with her, too?'

'He seems undecided. She's young, only eighteen, but she's grown up for her age. She has seven younger brothers and sisters. Like a mother to them, really. Her ma passed a year or so ago. She was my friend. I miss her, but Ester comes a lot now, especially since Jim's been here. Her brothers and sisters and my young ones are about the same age. She and Jim are great with them.'

'I see.' Jack felt a surge of emotion he couldn't name. *It's because Ma is happy. And if Jim's happy too, all the better*.

'Now, what's this about Pa?' She asked as she sank into a chair. 'He hasn't had another one of those turns, has he? Last time he wrote he was a bit vague, but I reckon he's not well.'

'He's not well at all, Ma.' Jack sat opposite her. He explained Gramps's problems as gently as he could before suggesting a trip to Mororo. 'I'd arrange it all. The children could go too. Gramps would love to see you all.'

His mother took a while to take in all he'd said. Her happy face had crumbled as he'd talked and he was sorry to have taken her smile away.

'It would only be the three younger ones,' she eventually said, her frown still ageing her face. 'Florrie's in service now, and Clarrie has his job at the sawmill, but I suppose … I've been thinking I'd love to see Pa. Do you think I could manage it?'

'I'm sure you could, Ma. I'll fix it, right?'

She nodded, then looked him up and down, shaking her head and smiling. She seemed lost for words.

'You look … happy,' he said, after a few minutes.

Her eyes filled and she wiped them on her sleeve. 'I'm fine, Jack. And all the more for seeing you. You're so grown up.' She held out her hands and he stood and pulled her into his arms.

'I'm getting there, Ma.'

CHAPTER TWENTY-TWO

Grafton, July, 1894

Jack sat opposite his brother in the dining room of the hotel. They'd been eating in silence for a few minutes before Jim spoke.

'Thanks for coming to see Ma. She was beside herself when you came back to have dinner with us last night. She fussed all afternoon about what to cook, then worried that she'd overcooked the meat. And I've never seen her go to so much trouble with an apple pie.' He chuckled. 'She's excited about going to see Gramps, too.'

Jack nodded. 'I think she'll be worried when she sees him, but I hope it will be good for them both. We'll head off first thing Monday. Are you still right to come up the following Sunday and bring her home?'

'Yes, I'd like to go for longer, but with my job at the sawmill I can't take time off.'

'You've done well, Jim, settling down to a regular job. Can you see yourself being happy here for the future?'

Jim took a while to answer. He fidgeted in his chair and seemed uncomfortable.

'I think so. I'm not sure ...' His words faded away as he put his head down and began to eat.

'Not sure of what?' Jack prodded.

'Well, there's a girl.' He took a few more mouthfuls.

'Ester?' Jack asked.

'How did you know?' Jim looked up and Jack could see that

his face was flushed.

'I met her at Ma's earlier in the week, remember? Ma said she was sweet on you.'

'Oh, yeah. I forgot you saw her. She's a nice girl, Jack, and she needs ...'

'Needs looking after?' Jack finished for him.

'Her mother's passed and there's little ones ... brothers and sisters, I mean.'

'Do you love her?'

'I think I could. It's hard for me to compare her with Fanny, though.'

'Then don't.' Jack knew he'd spoken too quickly. 'I mean it'll do you no good to be comparing every girl with Fanny. She's different ...' He ran out of words.

Jack had spent so much time trying to avoid thinking about Fanny that any attempt to describe her made his mind go blank. He'd seen her arrive at the hotel the day before, pushing a perambulator along the footpath. He hadn't been able to take his eyes off her until she turned into the lane beside the hotel and headed for the back door.

Her smile had captivated him; a smile he'd rarely noticed, and certainly not one that had been aimed at him. She'd been too preoccupied with chatting to her son to even see him, and for that he was glad, for he was sure he'd not have been able to think of a thing to say, and sure she'd have taken that the wrong way.

'Jack? Are you listening to me?' Jim sounded as if he'd been trying to get his attention for minutes.

Jack shook his head, chasing away thoughts of Fanny. Before he could answer, Jim looked past him and his face fell. 'Here's trouble.' He nodded towards the front door.

Jack turned and followed his brother's gaze. He watched as the British jockeys filed into the dining room and sat at a table by the front window. His stomach began to knot up. He stared at each of them, wondering which might be Fanny's attacker, and feeling bile rise in the back of his throat.

'Best ignored,' he said, turning back to Jim, although his words belied his thoughts.

'Give over, Ronald.' The voice of one of them carried across the room. 'She's not here.'

'I reckon they're looking for Fanny,' Jim said. 'They're always going on about her.'

'I know,' Jack hissed. 'Well, she's not here. Aunty Giese said she'd keep her away while they're around.'

'Do you think it was one of them?' Jim's frown deepened.

Jack shrugged, unwilling to say too much in case Jim did something that would cause a ruckus in the hotel. 'Perhaps we'd best leave well enough alone, Jim. Let Fanny live in peace, eh?'

'It's not like you to let a wrong go unrighted, Jack.' Jim leaned across the table. 'Have you spoken to Fanny this week?'

'No, she's just arrived back from Brushgrove. She's been helping her sister get ready for a wedding, from what Aunty Giese said.'

'Well, if those fellows bother her again, I won't be sitting by and doing nothing.' He clamped his hands around his mug and lifted it to his mouth.

'Fanny doesn't want any trouble, Jim. We have to respect that.'

As Jack spoke he saw Jim's eyes widen, as if he was trying to send him a message.

'Did you say Fanny's in trouble?' The voice came from behind him.

Before Jack could respond the chair beside him was dragged out and one of the Brits dropped onto it. 'Fanny's the cute girl who was serving here last year, isn't she?'

'If you're waiting for dinner, I'm sure one of the girls will be out to serve you any minute now,' Jack said, controlling his rising anger.

'It's not so much dinner I'm interested in as the girl,' the man continued, his face breaking into a sly grin. 'I think you intervened last time I tried to get to know her better.'

'Fanny won't be interested in getting to know you better,' Jim spat, half rising from his chair and glowering at the Brit. 'She's a decent girl.'

'Is that so? But not always as choosy as you suggest.' The man glared back at Jim confidently.

'Come on, Ronald,' one of his friends approached. 'I've told you to give it a rest. Perhaps the girl's not working here now.'

Jack looked up into the face of the man and noted he was the one they'd called Clarence last September. He seemed slightly older than the others, perhaps his own age, and he'd made some attempt to take charge of Ronald, if Jack remembered rightly.

'Maybe you should take your friend somewhere else to eat,' Jack ventured. 'It might avoid trouble.'

'Is that right?' Clarence cast Jack a scathing sneer, clearly not as keen to avoid trouble as Jack had hoped. 'Perhaps you should take your own advice. Just because you're good on that stallion doesn't give you the right to dictate where we eat.'

Jack held up his hands. 'I'm trying to keep the peace.' He turned to Jim. 'Why don't we go out back – '

He was going to suggest that he and Jim get something to eat in the kitchen, but Jim pushed back his chair and held up his fist to the Brit. 'Now, you look here. You blokes make a nuisance of yourselves every time you come in here. And you've taken far too much interest in Fanny for my liking. She's too good for the likes of any of you, no matter how grand you think you are.'

'Do you usually speak for her?' Ronald said, his tone condescending. 'Is she unable to speak for herself, then?'

'She's got more to do than waste her time speaking to you at all.'

Jack stood and attempted to intervene. He could see Jim was beginning to lose control of himself. 'Jim, I think we should –'

'She's got a child to look after for a start.' The words had erupted from Jim before Jack could pull him away.

'Jim!' Jack raised his voice. 'I said we'd best go.'

'A child?' Clarence's shock was obvious. The colour drained from his face.

'She's married?' Ronald pushed himself to his feet. 'Hey, Archie,' he yelled across the room, 'You didn't say she was married.'

'I had no idea she was,' Archie called, spinning around in his

233

chair.

Three or four other men in the dining room stopped their chatter and turned towards Ronald.

'If you mean Fanny,' one called. 'She isn't. She's one of these modern lasses who's doing it all alone.'

'You shut your mouth.' Jim started towards the man's table.

Jack grabbed his arm. 'I said, we're leaving,' he hissed into Jim's ear.

'How old is the child?' Clarence caught Jim's shoulder and spun him around.

'Fanny and her boy are none of your business.' Jim shoved Clarence and pulled himself free of the man's grasp.

As he did Jack took a firmer hold on Jim's arm and dragged him towards the kitchen. Almost throwing him through the door, he snarled at him. 'What are you thinking? How many times have I told you to keep your mouth shut?'

'What in the name of heaven …' Their aunt stood up from where she'd been crouched behind the bench. 'If I hadn't already dropped this knife on the floor, I'd have thrown it at you two. Crashing in here like a couple of drunk sailors. What's going on?'

'Sorry, Aunty.' Jack took a deep breath to calm himself. 'Those Brits are in the dining room and ready to make trouble again, no small thanks to Jim's mouth.'

Jim headed for the wash bowl and sluiced his face with water. 'They'd rile anyone, the way they talk about Fanny. They disgust me. They deserve a good thrashing.'

'Maybe, but it won't be happening in this establishment, my boy. Now, you two sit over there out of the way and I'll get you something to eat in a minute. Hans is about to open the bar, so he'll deal with anyone out there who's making a fuss.'

She clapped her hands at them, and pointed to the stool at the end of the bench. 'And if either of you says one word of this to Fanny, I'll wring your necks.'

***

234

The following morning Jack was again on the stool at the end of his aunt's kitchen bench. He was drinking strong coffee, poking at the pile of scrambled eggs and bacon in front of him, and nursing a headache. He'd hardly slept a wink all night, and was finding it hard to think.

'You'll not be leaving here to ride a horse all day without you eat every bit of that,' his aunt said, thrashing at a bowl of beaten egg.

'Are you sure you don't have a horse in that bowl,' he said, wincing at the sound.

'It'll be you I'll be beating if you don't come to your senses soon, my lad.'

'It's Jim you should be beating, Aunty. He's the one with the big mouth.'

'Yes, and lecturing him won't stop that, will it?'

The conversation was interrupted at that moment as Fanny pushed through the kitchen door, and beamed a smile at his aunt.

'Good morning, Lena – oh, Jack, I didn't know you were here.'

The flush that rose on Fanny's face only made her more beautiful. Jack stared at her for a moment, noticing her blue-green eyes, her wheat coloured hair, the daintiness of her, the prettiness of her skirt and jacket. It was as if he was seeing her for the first time, and he realised he'd been wishing all night that he could meet her all over again, that he could go back three years and see her coming to serve him pie in the dining room, just as he was seeing her now.

'Jack, you're scaring Percy with that glum face.' His aunt moved to Fanny's side, and crouched beside the child, who'd hidden his face in his mother's skirt. She lifted him into her arms and cuddled him close to her chest.

'My beautiful boy,' she crooned as he buried his cheek into her neck. 'Percy, this is Jack. He's looking a bit sad this morning, but I bet you could make him smile if you could say his name.' She gently turned Percy's face towards Jack. 'Can you say Jack?'

The boy looked at Jack and a shy smile spread across his face. 'Jack,' he said, then giggled as he pushed his nose back into Aunty Giese's chest.

Jack couldn't help but smile; at the boy, at his aunt's antics, at the beauty of Fanny. He wasn't sure which had lifted his spirits most, but he was grateful for the relief from the darkness in which he'd woken.

'So, Jack,' Fanny said. 'Is there a reason for your sadness? Have you had no luck at the races?' Her tone held no jibe which might once have prompted a smart answer from him.

'I've had my share of wins,' he said evenly, although his heart had started to beat erratically. 'I'm a bit under the weather this morning, is all. I didn't sleep very well.'

'I'm sorry to hear that,' she said. 'I hope you feel better soon.'

She turned to his aunt. 'I'll be going, Lena. I'll take Percy to Lizzie's and I'll be back as soon as I can to help you with the vegetables for lunch.'

'No rush, *liebling*.' His aunt handed Percy to Fanny, kissing him on the cheek as he leaned into his mother's shoulder.

Jack watched Fanny disappear out the back door, then dropped his head into his hands. *I might as well be a stranger to her.* He looked up to find his aunt staring at him.

She shook her head. 'You'll have to do better than that, Jack.'

'I've got a headache, Aunty. I can't think straight, so I've no chance of working out what's going on in your mind.' He pushed away his breakfast plate and strode from the kitchen.

***

When Fanny arrived back at her sister's that afternoon to pick up Percy, Lizzie seemed on edge.

'Lizzie, what is it? Has Percy been misbehaving?'

'Of course not,' Lizzie assured her. 'He's as good as gold. He's ready for his afternoon sleep now, though. Poor little thing.'

'What do you mean, *poor little thing*?' Fanny picked Percy up and brushed wisps of hair from his forehead.

Mimicking her actions he pushed a curl of her hair away from her cheek, laughing as he did. 'Mummy hair,' he said, brushing his tongue past his two newest teeth.

'He seems fine.' Fanny looked at her sister. 'What's wrong,

Lizzie?'

'I worry about him, that's all.' Lizzie sighed. 'It seems so unnatural for him to be living at a hotel. Sleeping above all that carry on … men drinking till all hours, and you coming and going. And no father. You bring him here after Alf's gone to work, and take him back before Alf gets home. The boy doesn't have any idea what a father is. It can't be good for him.'

'Alf has made it clear he thinks of Percy as illegitimate! What good would that possibly do my son? And as for where he lives, it's a loving, accepting home for him and for me. He sees Hans Giese every day and couldn't have a better man to show him what a man should be. Every Sunday we go home to Mum and Dad, where Percy is part of a normal, loving family. I don't know what's got into you today, but whatever it is, I hope you'll recover from it.'

Fanny knew she was being defensive, but the words kept coming. 'I'll not have Percy being pitied. If you can't accept my decisions, I'll not continue to bring him here.' She picked up his carry bag and stuffed it into the back of the perambulator.

'Fanny, please don't be like that.' Lizzie followed her onto the front porch. 'I want the best for you both.'

Fanny lifted Percy into the perambulator and strapped him in. 'Then you'll have to trust me to know what the best is, Lizzie. Can you do that?' Lizzie nodded solemnly as Fanny started down the path. 'Good, then I'll see you tomorrow morning.'

Fanny was still smarting when she lifted her sleeping son from the perambulator and carried him up to her room. She laid him on the small cot beside her bed and kissed his forehead.

'My darling boy,' she whispered. 'I love you so much. I want to do what is best for you. I'm praying every day that God will guide me to do that.'

The next day she was in two minds about taking Percy to her sister's home.

'You know he'd be fine here, Fanny.' Marlena fed Percy his breakfast while Fanny packed a change of clothes for him.

'I know he would. And you wouldn't do a scrap of cooking

for playing with him.' Fanny chuckled. 'I don't want to argue with Lizzie. I know she's taking good care of Percy, but she has such strong opinions about what's good for him. I'm tired of hearing them.'

'You're his mother, love. You must decide what's best.'

Fanny sighed. 'I'll take him over there this morning. Lizzie will think I'm angry if I don't. But I hope she'll think twice before harping at me again.'

CHAPTER TWENTY-THREE

Fanny had a tray of soup bowls in her hands and had started for the dining room, when Lizzie burst through the door of the kitchen. Her face was flushed red, her eyes wide with what seemed to Fanny to be terror.

'Lizzie? What are you doing here? Has something happened to Percy?' Fanny felt rooted to the spot. Her heart started to hammer in her chest.

'Is he here?' Lizzie gasped.

'Here! What are you talking about? I'm not due to pick him up for another hour.'

She laid the tray back on the bench. Her hands were trembling and her legs felt like jelly. 'Lizzie, you're frightening me. Where's Percy?'

'I don't know.' The redness faded from Lizzie's face and she turned pale. 'Someone came for him.' Her voice was almost a whisper. 'The children were in the front yard, playing. I was inside for a little while, seeing to the baby.' Her words came between gasps. She was struggling to breathe. 'When I went out, Percy wasn't there. Tommy said a man came to take Percy home.'

Fanny stared at her sister, trying to comprehend what she was hearing. 'A man? What man? Lizzie, are you saying that Percy's been stolen?' Her head reeled and she was sure she was about to pass out. She clung to the bench to stop herself from falling. 'Dear God, no … no.'

The kitchen door opened and Marlena was suddenly holding her up. 'What's happened, Fanny? I heard you yell. What's going on?'

'It's Percy. He's been taken.' Fanny's words almost choked her.

'Taken!' Marlena turned to Lizzie, her expression demanding an explanation.

'It's my fault.' Lizzie began to sob. 'I should have told you yesterday.' She leaned on the wall and dropped her head into her hands.

'Stop crying at once and tell me exactly what happened, girl.' Fanny had never heard Marlena sound so angry.

Lizzie looked up and wiped her eyes. 'Yesterday a man came to the house.' She sniffed loudly. 'He said he was Percy's father.'

'What?' Fanny's stomach lurched and she almost threw up. She felt Marlena's arms tighten around her.

'Go on, Lizzie,' Marlena demanded.

'He said he thought it would be best for the child to be with him, that his parents had lots of money. They have a big farm and servants, so Percy would be well cared for, and have every opportunity in life, more than he'd ever have here. He wanted to take Percy right then.'

'Dear God,' Fanny gasped. 'It's him.'

'Him?' Marlena turned to her.

'The British jockey. I heard his voice last September. It was him.' She folded herself into Marlena's arms. 'I've kept Percy out of sight all week. How could he even know I have a child?'

Marlena rolled her eyes. 'He must have overheard someone talking about Percy. If he wanted to find out where Percy was during the day, there's a few who'd have told him for a few bob.'

'I'm so sorry, Fanny.' Tears rolled down Lizzie's face. 'I didn't know what to think, but he seemed so sure he was the father. I got angry with him. I told him he was despicable to have done such a thing to you. He said he was sorry, that he'd had too much to drink. He even mentioned about the chloroform, so I knew it must have been him.'

Fanny clenched her hands. Her head was clearing, and her

240

anger was rising. 'I'm going after him.' She pushed back from Marlena and looked around wildly. 'They'd be heading back to Sydney. Did they have a cart, Lizzie?'

Lizzie shook her head. 'I'm not sure … yes, actually, Tommy said the men were in a cart.'

'Then they'd have to stick to the road. Please, Lena, can I borrow a horse?'

Marlena looked startled, then rushed from the kitchen into the dining room.

'You can't be serious,' Lizzie screeched. 'You can't go after them. What do you think you'd do if you caught up with them? It's out of the question.' She threw up her arms. 'I'm so sorry, Fanny. I told him I wouldn't give Percy to him, that he'd have to talk to you. I didn't think for a minute that he'd take him like that.'

'But you did think it might be better for Percy to have such a father, didn't you?' Fanny almost spat the words. 'That's why you were so edgy yesterday, why you urged me to think about what was best for my son?'

'I only wanted – '

Fanny was about to break into Lizzie's explanation when Marlena pushed back through the door with Jack on her heels.

'Jack will go,' she said, taking Fanny's hand. 'And I've told Hans to send for the constable. They'll get a couple of men and follow. I'm sure they'll catch up with the scoundrels.'

'I'm going too.' Fanny said adamantly.

'Don't be silly, Fanny,' Jack said. 'I'll go on horseback. If they've a cart, I'll catch them. You would slow me down.'

She glared at him. 'I said I'm coming. You're not the only one who can ride a horse. This is my son we're talking about. He'll be frantic. I'll not sit here waiting for someone else to rescue him. I'm the one he needs.' She turned to her sister. 'I'll get him back and I'll never let him out of my sight again.'

Lizzie's face dropped. 'Fanny, please be sensible. Let the police handle this. You mustn't – '

'How long?' Jack snapped, bringing Lizzie up short. She stared at him, stunned for a moment before he repeated impatiently, 'How long since they left with Percy?'

'I'm not sure,' she stuttered. 'It took a few minutes for me to understand what the children were saying, then I took them all inside and went to get my neighbour to come and mind them. She was giving hers lunch and she had to pack them up and bring them with her.' Lizzie's eyes darted about the room as if she was searching her memory. 'I almost ran all the way here ... perhaps it's been an hour or a little more ... I was praying all the way that Fanny really had sent someone to get Percy.'

'We're wasting time,' Jack said. 'I'm going to saddle up.'

'If Mr Giese won't loan me a horse, I'll beg in the dining room until I get one.' Fanny stared at Marlena.

Marlena nodded. 'Saddle up two, Jack. There's no use arguing with Fanny. She's as stubborn as you. And she can ride, don't worry. She's exercised Hans's horses in the past. I've seen her.' She grabbed Fanny and hugged her. 'I'll be here praying for you, *liebling*. You'll have your baby back, I'm sure. Hans and the constable will be along behind you. Please take care.' Tears spilled from her eyes.

Fanny nodded. 'Thank you.' She squeezed her hands, then turned and followed Jack out the back door, leaving her sister with her mouth hanging open.

***

Jack rode hard for over an hour. It was not exactly like racing, but his heart beat with the same concentration and determination. Chasing after justice was even more compelling than rising to the challenge of a race. He was looking only forward, thinking only about what was ahead and it drove him with an energy and enthusiasm for life that he longed for. He could also sense fear gnawing at his gut. *What if I can't save Percy? What if I can't take away Fanny's suffering?* He couldn't let those thoughts have any space in his mind.

He was aware of Fanny riding close at his heels. He was impressed with how well she'd kept up with him. As he slowed his horse and pulled up beside a creek he turned back to her, and noted that she looked tired and shaken.

'We need to take a break and let the horses have a drink,' he said, leading the stallion towards the water.

She slid from her saddle and followed suit with the gelding, still catching her breath.

'Where did you learn to ride like that?' he asked, patting his horse's neck.

'I've ridden all my life,' she said, between gasps. 'Though I don't think I've ever ridden like that before.' She looked up at him. 'We rode around the farm, and sometimes to school, depending on which horses were being used for farm work. Only Dad and Thomas ever rode in the races.'

Jack nodded. 'You've done well, then.' He grinned. 'I thought ladies rode side-saddle.'

'Perhaps they do,' she said, her chin jutting out. 'The only lady I ever saw riding side-saddle was our minister's wife, and she told me at a church picnic that it must be an idea thought up by men because it was so uncomfortable and awkward she'd rather walk.'

Jack chuckled. 'I'm sure she wouldn't approve of you riding with that skirt all bunched up around your knees, though.' He felt his cheeks flush as he spoke and hoped he wasn't going to get her back up. *I'm trying to ease her mind of her worry about Percy, but I'll likely get myself into trouble again.* He shook his head and tried to relax.

Predictably, Fanny arced up. 'If you're offended by the sight of my boots and a little woollen stocking, then don't look. It's not like I had time to change.' She stroked her horse's nose as he pulled up from the water and snorted.

'Your hand's trembling.' Jack's attention was drawn to her gloved fingers. Concern for her overtook his frustration at his own bumbling. 'Are you cold?'

'A little, but I'm shaking because … I'm frightened.'

'Of the pace we're riding?'

She sucked in her breath. 'Of not finding Percy.'

Tears welled in her eyes and spilled onto her cheeks, and

his heart went out to her. 'We'll find him.' He moved closer and reached for her hand, but stopped short of touching it.

'What if they didn't come this way? What if they hid somewhere in town, thinking this is what we'd do? They might have even gone north first to fool us.' Fanny gripped the horse's mane. She seemed on the verge of panic.

'Don't worry,' he said. 'That lot are arrogant enough to think they can take what they want and walk away without retribution. They think their money and power will protect them. I'd bet my life on them being ahead of us. We'll catch them, Fanny, I promise.'

She nodded and dropped her head into the horse's neck.

'Please don't cry.' Jack's voice caught in his throat.

'I'm not crying,' she said, looking up. 'I'm praying. I'm thankful you're here, Jack. I appreciate your help, but it's Percy's life we're betting on this chase, and I need to ask God for help.'

Jack nodded, knowing they needed all the help they could get. He waited a moment and then tapped her shoulder. 'If you think God won't mind you praying with your stockings showing, perhaps you could pray while we ride, eh?' He smiled and was relieved when a grin spread across her face. 'Let's go.'

As he helped her climb back onto the horse, he could feel his heart beating strongly, and he knew the time had come to listen to it.

***

Another hour and a half passed as they galloped along the road, Fanny praying earnestly. Surely God would not let her lose her beautiful boy now, not after all she'd gone through to keep him. *Please, don't let him be harmed. Please don't let him be frightened.*

Suddenly Jack put his hand up in front of her and slowed his horse. She pulled up beside him as he pointed ahead.

'Smoke,' he said. 'Looks like someone's lit a fire. It could be them. The light's beginning to fade. They'll be looking to camp overnight. They'll feel they're far enough from Grafton to stop.'

'But that fire doesn't look anywhere near the road,' Fanny said, squinting at the ribbon of smoke rising from the trees.

'They're not so silly that they'd stop in plain view.'

'What will we do?' Fanny's heart began to race.

'We'll move up quietly towards that smoke, and make sure it's them before we do anything.' The confidence in Jack's voice reassured Fanny.

'How many of them do you think there'll be?' Fanny asked. She'd only been thinking about that one man, trying to remember the look of him when he'd followed her into the kitchen, acting so chivalrously. Her stomach turned over and rage gripped her chest. *How dare he steal my son after what he did?* She felt she could tear him limb from limb herself.

'Slowly,' Jack warned as she rode beside him. 'I reckon there'll be four of them. The same ones I saw in the dining room.' He lowered his voice. 'Try to keep the horse at walking pace so we don't make a noise. When we get closer, we'll go on foot.'

She nodded and concentrated on doing as he said. *How foolish I was to think I could have done this alone.*

When Jack indicated, she climbed from her horse and watched him tie both reins to a tree. She lifted her skirts and followed him through the bush until they could hear voices. Then they both huddled behind a large rock and waited.

'I think I can hear three different voices,' Jack whispered.

'I can't hear Percy.' Fanny pushed into the rock and peeped around the side. 'What if it's not them?' *Please God, let Percy be safe.*

As if in answer to her prayer one of the men called. 'I hope you finally got him to sleep, Clarence. I don't think I can bear that whining much longer, let alone a week of it.'

Fanny's eyes flew open and she edged to the top of the rock. Through the trees in front of her she could see Clarence walking away from the cart which was on the far side of the campfire. He headed back towards the other three, who were crouching around the meager flames.

'If you can't stand it, Archie, then you can head off on your own.' Clarence's tone was biting. 'And you can keep going when you get to Sydney. You'll not have a job at the property.'

'All right, old man. Don't get your knickers in a knot. I simply don't understand why you'd want to take on a child. He'll be more trouble than he's worth.'

Fanny gritted her teeth and slid down the rock. Her fists were clenched at her side. 'If he hurts a hair on Percy's head, so help me …'

'Shh,' Jack whispered, patting her arm. 'It'll be dark soon. They'll be swilling whisky soon and getting drowsy.'

'You think we can sneak in and get Percy without them knowing?'

'Perhaps. Or Uncle Hans will get here with help and we'll take the lot of them into custody.'

'You'll have to douse that fire soon, boys.' Clarence's voice came again. 'Can't risk being seen.'

'I doubt they'll come after us,' one droned. 'The silly girl's probably glad to be rid of him. Especially once her sister told her you'd come for him, Clarence. I could see she thought it a jolly good idea for the boy to go to a rich family.'

Fanny jerked back and might have jumped to her feet in rage if Jack hadn't grabbed her arm and held her down. He shook his head at her, but all she could see in his face was compassion. She settled back against the rock and took a deep breath.

'Pass that bottle, Ronald,' came another voice. 'I can't eat another mouthful of that tinned stew. It's disgusting.'

'You sure your father's going to appreciate you doing this, Clarence?'

'He's been at me for years to settle down. He wants a grandson to carry on the family line. I'm not about to settle for one woman for a while yet, but a boy might shut him up.'

'What if he doesn't believe he's yours?'

'I think there's enough resemblance to convince him of that.' Ronald chuckled. 'A handsome lad, really.' The sound of gurgling from a bottle followed.

'Mother will be chuffed, and more than ready to take him in. She's been dying for another child to fuss over.'

'And she's plenty of servants to do the work, eh?' Ronald's

voice was beginning to slur.

Suddenly there was a soft crying sound. Fanny went rigid. The tension in her body was such that her legs would barely move. She wanted to run into the group, screaming her rage. If she could scratch out the eyes of the monster who'd stolen her son, she'd have done it gladly. Mostly, she wanted Percy safe in her arms. Gritting her teeth, she leaned into Jack's shoulder, her hands clenched so tight that she could feel the skin tearing under her fingernails.

'Soon.' Jack put his arm around her shoulder and drew her close. 'Try to stay warm.'

Fanny realised she was shaking. She was cold, but knew her body was reacting more to her anger and fear than the elements. Still, she felt calmer with Jack holding her.

There was another cry from Percy.

'I'll strangle that child myself if you don't do something to shut him up.' This sounded like Archie and his mood was definitely deteriorating.

'Right, that's it.' Jack pushed himself to his knees. 'I'm going in there,' he whispered. 'Once I've got them talking, you sneak around the back and get Percy from the cart. Then run towards the road. Do you think you can do that?'

Fanny stared up at him. The fading light made it difficult to make out his expression. She nodded. 'But you can't take on all four of them.'

'I can keep them occupied long enough for you to get to the road. They won't even know Percy's missing if you're quiet.'

When she hesitated he pulled on her arm. 'Come on, before Clarence heads back to that cart to shut Percy up.'

That did it. Fanny was on her haunches. She peeked around the rock to see the easiest way to the cart.

As soon as she heard Jack's voice break into the clearing, she began to move. Keeping as low as she could she skirted the campfire and made her way to the back of the cart.

She could hear the raised voices of the men, numerous obscenities being shouted at Jack. She felt torn. *What if they attack him? Perhaps she should find a stick and go and help him.* A whimpering sound from the back of the cart refocused her thoughts on Percy. She moved to the far end of the cart where she could just make out what looked like a raised pile of rugs. Reaching in, she pulled the rugs aside and lifted Percy into her arms. He thrashed about for a moment, then, recognising who had him, he buried his face into her shoulder and put his arms around her neck.

'Mummy's got you now. Shh, we must be quiet.'

Dragging one of the rugs from the cart she moved back through the bushes until she was again behind the rock. She held Percy close, wrapped him in the rug and turned her attention to the scuffle in the clearing.

The obvious noises of fighting made her shudder. There were loud grunts and the crunching sound of fists meeting body parts, bodies thumping to the ground. More obscenities. None of the voices sounded like Jack. *Should I do as he said and head for the road? How can I leave him to fend for himself? Eventually those men will overcome him, no matter how hard he fights. Surely Mr Giese can't be far off now. Please God, don't let Jack be badly hurt.* Indecision and fear immobilised her.

248

CHAPTER TWENTY-FOUR

Percy wriggled in Fanny's arms and whimpered. He was shivering. She pulled the rug around him and rocked him gently. 'Mummy's here, shh,' she whispered again. She knew she must follow Jack's instructions. If she was discovered by one of the men when the fighting ended, she'd have no way of saving Percy.

She was pushing herself to her feet when a dark figure appeared in front of her. She fell back in fear, then heaved a sigh of relief as she looked into Hans Giese's face.

'Stay there,' he said as he moved past her.

He was followed by three other men, one carrying a shot gun. A moment later the air rang with the sound of a shot. There was a sudden silence, then the scuffling sound of men dragging themselves to their feet, and muffled cursing.

'About time,' Jack's voice rose above the other noises.

The fighting could only have been going on for five or ten minutes but to Fanny it felt like an hour. She crept from behind the rock and stood behind Hans Giese, trying to assess how badly Jack was hurt. He was brushing down his shirt and rubbing one fist into his other hand gingerly. Two men were kneeling on the ground near the fire, staring into the barrel of the shotgun and holding up their hands. The other two Brits, including Clarence, were standing on the far side of the fire, looking as if they'd not got involved in the fight at all.

Likely assumed two men were sufficient to overcome Jack. Or perhaps they're simply cowards. Fanny glared at Clarence, even though she knew it was too dark for him to see the outrage on her face. However, he could obviously see that she was holding Percy.

'That's my son, girl.' He started to walk towards her but Jack intervened.

'You take another step and I'll flatten you.'

'I have rights,' Clarence hissed. 'You may have the upper hand right now, with your guns and your thug friends, but you'll rue the day, boy.'

'I'm not your boy, and neither is that child.' Jack grabbed the front of his shirt and glared into his face.

'That's enough, Jack,' Hans said, then turned to the men who were still facing the shotgun. 'This is Constable Fredricks, lads. I'd suggest you pack up your things quick smart and get out of here before you're all arrested and hauled back to Grafton.'

'Wait a minute,' Jack said. 'You're not going to let them go! They're criminals.' Dropping his hand from Clarence's shirt he moved close to his uncle. 'They should be gaoled.' He pushed his hair back from his forehead and jammed his fisted hands into his hips.

'Easy, Jack,' the constable said, not taking his eyes from the Brits. 'If we took them back to Grafton, they'd have a fancy lawyer up here in a flash, and there'd be no chance of justice. We have their details at the hotel and I'll make sure a report goes to the Magistrate in Sydney where it will be followed up properly by people who'll have equal power to their family lawyer. It's not like they're going to leave the country.'

'You've got no idea what our family lawyer will make of this.' Clarence sneered. 'Come on, lads,' he said, turning to his friends, 'Let's go.'

'You're not going to give in that easy, are you, old man?' Ronald grumbled, dragging himself from the ground. He couldn't stand without swaying but spat into the fire before holding up his fist to Jack as if he was ready to fight again.

'Make it snappy, men,' the constable warned, raising his rifle to Clarence. 'If you're not out of here in a couple of minutes, I

250

might just accidently shoot one or two of you.'

'You won't be so clever when my father gets word of this.' Clarence turned to Fanny and scowled. 'And you, miss, will be sorry you weren't nicer to me in the first place.'

Fanny had felt rooted to the spot for the last few minutes. Clarence's words jolted her into action and she started towards him, only to be stopped by Hans. Straining against his hand on her arm, she scowled at Clarence.

'May God forgive you for the despicable things you've done,' she said. 'And may He help me to forgive you as well, for I'll not be able to do so in my own strength. If it were up to me you'd be drawn and quartered.'

'Come on, love,' Hans said, easing her back. 'Think of Percy. He's trembling badly. We need to get him warmed up and take him home.'

Hans's words brought Fanny's attention back to Percy, who'd clung to her from the moment she'd taken him from the cart. She kissed his cheek and nodded to Hans. As Clarence and his men gathered their belongings and backed away, Jack moved to Fanny's side and touched the boy's forehead.

'He's cold, and in shock. He's been in the back of that cart for hours without enough cover by the look of him. He may have caught a chill. I'll build up the fire so he can get warm.' He led her to the fire and pulled a log close so she could sit down.

As Fanny sat and settled Percy on her knee, he turned his face to Jack and grinned.

'Jack,' he said, before burying his face back into Fanny's chest.

'He remembers you,' Fanny said, smiling.

'Well, let's hope he's as good at forgetting.' Jack patted Percy's back through the rug. 'We'd not want much of today to stay in his mind.'

***

251

Fanny huddled by the fire, rubbing Percy's back to warm him up. Her heart was still racing. Thoughts of what might have happened to her son were unbearable and she pushed them away. She didn't want to carry rage or thoughts of revenge with her. It would do her no good and certainly wouldn't be good for Percy. She prayed God would help her to forgive the man who had almost ruined her life twice.

She glanced at Jack, realising she understood his struggle much better now. There was so much hurt in his past and he'd battled to overcome it the best way he could. She wished they could support each other through the healing they both needed. He'd been so set on helping her today, so gentle with her and Percy, so understanding. It was a side of him she'd not seen and she wanted to see more of.

Hans brought his cart closer to the clearing and carried two large bags to the campfire. He dropped them on the ground near Fanny and Jack.

'You'll find food in there, no doubt. By the time I got back to The European with the constable this afternoon, Lena had these packed. I'm sure there'll be something for Percy. I've got more blankets, too.'

'I'll have to find something to change him into,' Fanny said. 'He's wet through.' She shook her head. 'I can't imagine how those men thought they'd care for a child all the way to Sydney.'

'They didn't think about anything but themselves,' Jack said. 'I can't believe we let them go. They should be locked up.'

'Now that's something Fanny needs to think through carefully.' Hans crouched by the fire and unwrapped packages of food for the constable and the other two men. 'Constable Fredricks warned me about what might happen, and I think it's best you listen to him.'

Fanny found a change of clothes for Percy in one of the bags. *Thank God for Lena.* She redressed him in front of the fire and gave him one of the fruity scones he so enjoyed in Marlena's kitchen.

'Clarence said he's got rights.' She looked up at the constable. 'He wouldn't be able to take my son from me, would he?' She pulled Percy close to her body. He still felt cold to the touch and his nose had begun to run. 'That man wouldn't know the first thing

252

about looking after a child.'

'That may be so, love.' The constable crouched beside her. 'But you should know that the law would be on his side if this went to court. His family has money. They'll have a big home, servants, and a lot of power. They'll use stories of young girls having babies they can't care for ... dreadful stories of children dying, being badly treated –'

'I've heard those stories.' Fanny shuddered. 'I don't need to be reminded. I'm not destitute or desperate like those girls must be. I have family who love Percy.'

'You're saying Clarence's lawyers could use those cases to take Percy from Fanny?' Jack's voice was cold and hard.

'I'm afraid so, lad.' The constable nodded. 'A magistrate would take the man's side in most cases, especially if he has means. But we can't be sure his family would take this on. We don't know how they'll react to Clarence's claim to Percy, and once the authorities inform the parents about Clarence's attempt to kidnap the boy, and also his attack on Fanny ... well, they may not want all that dragged through the courts.'

Jack kicked out at the rocks around the fire. 'Where's the justice?' he mumbled. 'I should have thrashed him when I had the chance, made him think twice about coming anywhere near the boy again.'

'That's not the way, Jack.' Hans moved behind Fanny and wrapped another blanket around her and Percy.

'Then what is the way with men of means?' Jack spat and pounded one fist into his other hand.

When Percy jumped, he relaxed his hand and rubbed the boy's back. 'Sorry, little one,' he said.

'The way is certainly not to take them on physically.' Hans passed around a basket of scones, then sat opposite Jack. 'Let's hope Clarence's parents have enough integrity to put a stop to his plan, even if they protect him from the law.'

Jack stared into the flames.

'This is a time for using your head, Jack. And you might also consider letting your heart have a say.' Hans's eyes were riveted on Jack across the fire.

Fanny's thoughts were racing. 'I'm scared, Jack. I couldn't bear to lose him.'

'You won't,' Jack said.

Hans rose from the ground and looked to the constable. 'Let's get this stuff packed back in the cart. We'll let these two warm up for a few more minutes and finish off those scones. Then we'd best head back to town. It's getting late, and Lena will have worn her knees out praying.'

'She'll be glad to know her prayers have been answered,' Fanny said.

'It will mean more to her than you can imagine, love.' Hans nodded. 'You can ride back in the cart with Percy. I doubt he'll want to let you out of his sight for a bit.'

'Thank you, Mr Giese. I don't want to let him go either, and I don't think I could manage any more horse riding for a few days.'

Jack chortled and bit into one of his aunt's scones. Fanny could see that he was deep in thought.

'I'll take Percy back to Brushgrove after Eliza's wedding on Saturday,' she said when they were alone. 'Mum and Dad will be worried when they find out what's happened and I'd rather not be in Grafton for a week or so, in case … oh, Jack, I can't believe this has happened.'

'Nothing else is going to happen to Percy, I promise.' He dropped to his haunches beside the fire.

He sounded so confident that Fanny relaxed a little. Her body was tense and she was beginning to ache all over. She stroked Percy's forehead as he gazed into the flames, mesmerised. She could feel him drifting into sleep against her shoulder.

'I'm sorry, Jack.' Fanny struggled to find the words she knew she must say. 'I didn't understand you before, but now …'

'Now that you've something to be angry about?' He sat on the end of the log where she was sitting and stretched out his legs. The flames threw flashes of light across his face, emphasising his rigid jaw.

254

She nodded. 'For a long time I didn't think about him. I didn't want to be angry. I wanted to be happy for Percy. But once I heard his voice again, then seeing his face, I feel such rage inside. If he hadn't taken Percy, if he'd gone back to Sydney and I hadn't seen him again ...'

'Yeah, I used to think that too. If only I didn't think about Fred. I guess Jim told you enough about him that you know what I'm talking about. I used to think if I didn't ever see him, hear his voice, I could forget. But it doesn't work. I know that now.'

'It's hard. I want to forget. I don't want to be angry.'

'I know I'm not one to talk.' He shuffled about on the log. 'God knows I've carried my anger long enough. But I won't be the last one to say this to you. The only way is to let it go. Aunty Giese would call it forgiveness, I guess. I can only think of it as giving up any need for revenge, or even justice.'

'I can see how hard that is to do now.' Fanny's eyes filled with tears. 'I've realised I still have so much to learn.' She could feel the warmth of Jack close to her shoulder and allowed herself to sink into him.

'We'll have to trust Uncle Hans and the constable about some justice being done, I guess. But whether it is or not, you don't want to be carrying the weight of your anger around with you for the rest of your life. It'll hurt you and Percy.'

His voice was thick and she wondered if he was close to tears.

'So how will you let your anger go?' She glanced sideways at him again and saw him swallow and purse his lips.'

'With the help of God, I imagine.' His face relaxed a little. 'And reminders from my aunt, no doubt. I know she's right. It's never done me any good holding onto what can't be changed.'

'She's very wise, isn't she?'

'Sure is.'

They sat in silence for a few moments, the quiet of the bush broken only by the crackling of the fire and the muffled voices of the men as they readied the cart.

'What do you think I should do, Jack?'

'Well, going to Brushgrove's a good start. I'm sure some time with your parents will help. I've promised to take Ma to Mororo, so I'll be away next week, too.'

'I'm glad.' Fanny laid her hand on his arm and squeezed it. 'Your mother must be so happy.' Then, realising she'd taken a liberty with Jack that may have made him uncomfortable, she withdrew her hand and wrapped both arms around Percy.

He glanced sideways at her and grinned.

I still don't know what he's thinking. 'Then what will you do?'

'That depends.'

Fanny waited, her heart thumping in her chest. She wasn't sure how much of it was her fear for Percy and how much was the closeness of Jack.

'Depends on what?'

'Gramps is real sick. I don't know how much longer he's got. I want to be there for him. He wants me to take over the farm. I've been thinking lately that it would be good to have some land of my own, and it seems it's what my grandfather always wanted.'

'Which grandfather?'

There was a long silence. Fanny felt Jack tense beside her for a few minutes before his shoulders dropped.

'Perhaps both,' he eventually said. 'I think both my grandfathers came to Australia looking for the promised land, so I guess they'd both be pleased for me to have this opportunity.'

'I'm sure they would.' Fanny had mixed feelings. Jack seemed to be resolving some long held pain, and for that she was glad. But she also felt a sense of loss and her heart slumped. 'So you'd stay in Mororo?'

'Probably.' He fidgeted on the log and almost caused them both to topple off.

Fanny sighed. 'Sounds like you've as much thinking to do as me. We should get going. Your uncle will be waiting for us.' She felt overwhelmed with all that had happened, and still might happen. She was anxious to get Percy home and safely into his bed. He'd dozed off in her arms but he was clearly unwell and traumatised. She had to focus on what was best for him, not only immediately, but also in the future. As she lifted her weight from the log, Jack spoke again.

'You should marry.'

'What?' She dropped back down, Percy's weight falling back into her lap.

'You should marry,' he repeated. 'You know Jim's been asking you to marry him for ages. If you had a husband and the means to raise Percy in a real family, then Clarence would have much more to fight against. He mightn't even try.'

Fanny's heart thumped. 'I don't love Jim. He's kind and caring, but I couldn't marry him. I'll stay with Mum and Dad if I have to. They're a real family. They'd raise Percy as their own if necessary.'

'I see.' Jack pushed his boots into the dirt in front of him. 'It seems there's someone else for Jim, anyway. There's a girl hanging around Ma's place. She seems to have her heart set on him.'

'I'm pleased to hear that. Jim deserves someone who'll love him.'

'So you'd have to marry someone else.' His words were so soft Fanny hardly heard them.

She pulled herself to her feet. 'Well, I don't see a line up for that role,' she said, knowing her tone was a little sour. 'Men who want a fallen woman with a child are few and far between.'

'You're not a fallen woman.' He stood abruptly and pulled her by the shoulders until she was facing him. 'I'll marry you.'

The shock went straight to Fanny's knees and she almost collapsed. When she was sure she wasn't going to fall over, she looked up into his eyes. It was too dark to be sure but she thought she could see tears welling in the corners.

'You'd do that to save Percy?'

'I'd do it because it's what I want.'

His face was so close to hers that she wondered if he was about to kiss her. She waited. Her heart was banging so loudly in her chest that she was sure he must hear it.

When it seemed presumptuous to wait any longer, she said,

'Really?' She peered into his eyes in the dim light. 'It's not because you feel sorry for me, is it?'

'Who said I feel sorry for you?' A hint of a grin creased his cheeks. 'Will you always be trying to guess what I feel?'

'If you keep your feelings so hidden, what else am I to do?' Fanny sensed they were heading into the sparring that had so often been part of their relationship. She wondered if it always would be so. She waited a moment longer, searching his face, before she adjusted Percy on her hip and kissed his cheek.

'So does that mean you don't want to marry me?'

His words made her heart sink. It *was* what she wanted. Perhaps what she'd hoped for, for longer than she cared to admit. Perhaps they'd both have to get a lot better at expressing their feelings honestly.

'I need to know it's what you really want.' Her voice was almost a whisper.

Jack's eyes held her own like a clamp. 'Aunty Giese said it's time I started asking for what I want … and that's what I've done.'

Fanny couldn't stop a smile spreading across her face, but her mind still raced with questions. 'Do you think people will get the wrong idea if we marry? They'll probably talk about us behind our backs.'

'So?' Jack shrugged. 'I've had plenty of that. I can handle it.' His eyes didn't leave hers. 'I'd never let anyone hurt you. Or Percy.'

'I know that.' She let out a deep breath, her shoulders relaxing. As she leaned into Jack's chest Percy stirred in her arms. 'Hello, little man,' she said. 'We're going home now, and we're never going to let that awful man near you again.'

'So what do you think?'

There was a vulnerability in Jack's eyes that Fanny hadn't seen before. She had to avert her gaze lest she plant a kiss on his mouth. She had no doubt now that there would be a time and place for that.

'I know you don't like the idea of being looked after,' he said when she remained silent.

'Perhaps I do after all … at least a little.' Her heart was now doing somersaults in her chest. 'What do you think, Percy? Jack has a proposal for us to consider. Would you like to live with Jack?'

Percy yawned and turned to Jack, whose face was inches from his own.

'Jack,' he said and wrinkled his nose.

'I think that's a yes,' Fanny said.

Jack grinned and nodded. He brushed his hands together and tapped Percy's nose. 'Right,' he said, as he rewrapped the rug around Percy's shoulders and kicked dirt into the fire to douse the flames.

As he led Fanny towards the cart he seemed to find his voice again. 'Maybe you could come with me to Mororo on Monday. We could get married up there and stay with Gramps. Those Brits wouldn't think to look for you there. Or we could live somewhere close to Gramps so I could still look after him. I could get a job on the ferries or in the timber mill at Harwood. It's not far.'

Fanny squinted into the darkness and tried to concentrate on picking her way through the small shrubs.

'Or if you'd prefer, you could stay at Brushgrove with your parents while I sort out things with Gramps,' Jack went on. 'I know you'd miss your parents. Of course, even if we were at Mororo, we could visit – '

'I've never heard you do so much planning for the future.' Fanny giggled.

'I've spent most of my life looking over my shoulder to make sure no one was sneaking up behind me. I think it's time I looked ahead, don't you? Now, watch out for those sharp twigs. They'll catch your skirt. Perhaps I should carry Percy. I don't want you tripping over with our boy.'

They were both chuckling when Hans's voice came through the darkness. 'How much longer are you two going to be?'

'A very long time, Uncle Hans.' Jack put his arm around Fanny's shoulders and she leaned into him, her heart singing. When he planted a kiss on her forehead, she felt her legs would go from under her.

'And there are three of us now,' Jack continued, 'not two anymore.'